S0-AKL-496

Jane's
Bad Hare Day

WITHDRAWN

Jane's
Bad Hare Day

a novel by

Carol Ann Sima

WITHDRAWN

Dalkey Archive Press

COLORADO COLLEGE LIBRARY
COLORADO SPRINGS
· COLORADO

© 1995 Carol Ann Sima

First edition, 1995

Library of Congress Cataloging-in-Publication Data

Sima, Carol Ann, date
  Jane's bad hare day : a novel / by Carol Ann Sima.
  I. Title.
PS3569.I472353J36   1995   813'.54—dc20   94-25160
ISBN 1-56478-072-4

Partially funded by grants from the National Endowment for the Arts
and the Illinois Arts Council.

NATIONAL
ENDOWMENT
FOR THE
ARTS

Dalkey Archive Press
Campus Box 4241
Normal, IL 61790-4241

Printed on permanent/durable acid-free paper and bound in the
United States of America.

PS
3569
I472353
136
995

This book is dedicated to

Selma and Morris
Hollie and Robin
Diane and Mark

✗

Heartfelt thanks . . .
For putting the spark there: Selma, who understood.
For sustenance of spirit. First in my thoughts: Hollie and Robin.
Artists and writers both.
Whatever sense of belonging I have I owe to Diane. She named
this book. She is indispensable.
For fatherly advice: Morris.
In remembrance: Bubbe and Aunt Beaty.
For the pleasure of their company: Saul (I should follow you
around with paper and pen), Yolanda, Al, Tiffany (rare treasures),
Chris and David (like family), Drew and Lauren (dream kids), Lew
(a hard act to follow), Jane (indefatigable helping hand), Vicki
(clear-headed when I am muddled), Mark (a knight), Arnold (a
lifeline).
For typing day and night: Cathy.
For sheer magic: Susan. My reader. My lifelong friend. It would
take a book, maybe volumes, to do her justice.
For granting this wish: Steve, my editor, in gratitude always.

The past isn't dead, it isn't even past.
—Faulkner

No facts are to me sacred; none are profane; I simply experiment, an endless seeker with no Past at my back.
—Ralph Waldo Emerson

my head's so-so.
unusually so-so.
just so you know.
bordering engine trouble.
So-so days, so-so moods. Everyone plods through. Nobody feels they've been through an ordeal. Moderation's the key. So-so conversations, the principle's the same. Let's say I say in passing, Mondays I'd like it to be Fridays, and I get back, in return, isn't this winter mild, and I toss off, winter Mondays are unfit for human consumption, and tossed my way, winter Fridays are fitter than winter Mondays. What's happening is an exchange of banalities. No ripples. No waves. So-so's have a look and feel. Knowing how ideal so-so's are supposed to sound, qualifies you to red tag unusual so-so's. So when you're bordering engine trouble, every step of the way, you've been fully informed. It helps to keep in mind the differences between fixtures and monuments. The neighborhood newsstand, for example, is not the Statue of Liberty. The Statue of Liberty cannot be found on every corner. The Statue is the rarer of the two. Monuments make impacts fixtures don't. More or less, the more your so-so's resemble the Statue of Liberty, the less innocuous, the more atypical, the less amenable to low profile. The more over the border.

✗

My head's so-so.
Unusually so-so.
So much so, it's monumentally so-so.
Just so you know.
Bordering engine trouble.
(I wouldn't say so if I didn't have a reason to say so.)

✗

So's October. Notoriously so-so. From the word go, October is not the corner newsstand. In October, I do what leaves do. Take the plunge. Dip down. Hit lows. The rituals of fall. I subscribe to three. Beginning with dipping into my savings. In fall, the first to fall is work. October first to October thirty-first, no gainful employment. Substitute teaching suspended. History, on a per diem basis, postponed. Along with part-time research. For an hourly wage, I dig the past up, how things came to be, why they botch. Record-keeping: Any's better than none. Second fall ritual, taking stock. What has and hasn't fallen short. Sorting through. Catching up. Fall on it promptly or risk falling further behind. Fall behind, you may never see the end of it. And depending on how you see ends, ends have a finality beginnings don't. The fall previous to this one, I caught up to (subsequently terminated too) a backlog of odds and ends, starting with socks and bras and bathing suits, ending with socks and bras and bathing suits. Catch-up project of the moment, more the same. Depending on how you see ends, some things never end.

✗

My head's so-so.
Unusually so.
I've already said so.
Monumentally so-so.
Over and above routine dips.
Fall is so very so-so.
Fall's never been this so-so.

✗

Third fall ritual, extensive walking. As leaves fly, so do I. Logging miles. Never knowing what I'll stumble across, what will stumble across me. Walking just so. The New York street walk, slowing to window-shop, quick to duck. Evasive maneuvers. Walk tall, walk invisibly. Adopt a posture. In that I fall somewhere between pragmatic and leafy. Sudden dips, height shifts, ups and downs, rising . . . falling.
My head's so-so.
So too it seems . . . my walk. So-so.

But not unusually so-so.
Nor monumentally so-so.

Isn't the weight of the world frequently said to drop on individual shoulders? Try lap instead. I've been known to walk with knees in the lead. Making the occasional splash, I do not make history. Not if you count the vast number of historical precedents set by shoulders trying to bear up. Then bolo laps, the dip and dive and slip and slide of them follow strict historical formula. And on my say-so, you don't have to take my word on it. But believe this: Whenever there's emotion, you'll find jiggles and wiggles, soaring and flooring, flipping and flopping. We dance out our moods. At rest, who is really still?

✗

So here's how it stands: October first to October thirty-first, the dispersal of leaves, so-so in the head. Fall's the culprit. Spontaneous lap curtsies, spirits sinking. Fall is the winter of my life. Trees shedding, leaves estranged. A downward fall spiral. Fall I fall all over myself. Catch-up season. The historian catching up on personal history. What's fallen by the wayside? What falls under my jurisdiction? My how the chips have fallen. Depending on how well I've caught up, ending with or without an end in sight. Mostly, fall ends no better than it starts. Fall sets me in motion. The flight of leaves. Setting out daily. Never knowing what I'll fall up against, what awaits me.

✗

So-so. More so than usual.
In my place who wouldn't be?
Monumentally, unusually . . . so-so.

✗

Struck soundly on the head, who wouldn't be put out?

✗

The eve (no less) of the fourth anniversary of my monumentally one-sided divorce, I was clobbered on the forehead. Fourth fall anniversary. The eve (no less). Four years, hence. Hammered on the

11

head. Not felled, though it felt split. A monumentally one-sided split. Bordering on trauma. A hefty blow to the head. One day short of the fourth official annual observance of a divorce (the husband insisted, the wife resisted, the husband filed first, the wife filed under duress), what woman wouldn't be unusually out of sorts?

✗

So let the record read:

I got a good look at my assailant. Whoever you are, Jane Samuels can identify you. Bunny ears. Bulky stalks. Enormously rabbity.

✗

Like so.

✗

He didn't have a trace of bunny civility. Not one iota. I will never again look at a rabbit and think cuddly toy. A week ago to the day, eve of the fourth anniversary of my deliverance (every fall since my deliverance from the man who filed. First. "deliverance" falls from my lips, either you fall for it or you don't) a maniacal rabbit kangarooed me. Neanderthal feet in my face. Eyewitnesses described him as walking on his hind legs, taller than a Beatrix Potter hare. Armpit legs. High rib cage, broad chest, manly. Sub-human. A rabbit of indeterminate age. So much legginess—you see this in teenagers all the time—they look older than their years. Speckled Caucasian, dark cinnamon raison dollops. A fur jumpsuit. Though body hair can look furry and fur can look fake, his was natural fiber. The second skin fit. No zippers, seams or buttons. You couldn't tell this baby apart from the real thing. Which probably explains why, on the eve of the fourth anniversary of my deliverance from the man who filed. First. I noticed, I stared, I veered. I didn't crowd him. I did everything but cross the street.

Citing history: My reactions were perfectly in sync. Ten times out of ten, bunnies are associated with Easter bunnies. Even lacking the traditional pink suit, rabbits get away with murder. Nobody assumes the worst.

I learned the hard way.

12

Watch your back.

A rabbit packs a wallop.

The emergency room doctor, inches shorter than the hare, hare tall for a hare, doctor short for a doctor, paw marks on my forehead—in their stocking feet—coming up to his forehead, wrote a detailed report. No fractures, slight swelling. No scarring. Release recommended. New York Hospital didn't keep me for observation. Rightly so. So-so isn't sick. So-so, you don't get, nor do you expect more than a Band-Aid. The bulk of your health—insofar as where so-so draws the line doesn't begin to touch and go.

✗

I have yet to regain full height. The so 'n' so cottontail who clipped me on the cranial didn't maul my feminine mystique. My perennials weren't poached. No paw transgressed my prize marigold. I'm still laying low. In inches, a solid three quarters total. Shaved off, but not in the permanent sense. Like weight, inches fluctuate. Well before the eve of the fourth anniversary of my deliverance from the man who filed. First. I was gaining and losing inches. Often within the same minute. Dating from the very eve of the very first fall anniversary of deliverance from the man who filed. First. A trick knee lap. Out it juts. The tip of a tongue. Open drawer out when it really skids. Out like a candidate's handshake. Out like I'm sitting this dance out. Out like I'm out of commission. It's the latter set, of course, that distinguishes me most from my fellow pedestrians, all of them walking upright while I crimp.

Origami infolds.

In those instances, laps half my age think my walk is a walk on the wild side. And halved again, they think a stride with a lap is comic. My own generation doesn't know what to think. Woman's trouble, gall bladder, hangover. Walking as if I'm buckled up for safety cuts me off at the waist. My hem sweeps the sidewalk; my arches fall in disrepute; ten-year-olds dwarf me.

Citing history: So the argument went, still goes: If the weight of the universe can fall on shoulders, surely elbows, chins, laps, just about any place can take a beating.

Citing personal history: This thing with my lap isn't an unhinging. Come fall, my lap doesn't fall apart. My lap merely indexes emotion. Barometric readings. Long after arms have been relieved of packages, arms still ache. Why not laps? Moods swing. Hot and cold, severely so-so to barely so-so. Why not laps?

So you heard it here first.
The lap wasn't built that can't fall into pitfalls.
So there . . .
Cite history, you cite human behavior.
So to speak.

✗

Not housebroken, nor housebound.
My lap's mobile.
My lap gets around.

✗

The Hardware Store on Third is where I go when I'm short on wares. The place comes on referral. Word of mouth. Screws as dependent on public relations as gynecologists. What the Hardware Store on Third has going for it are fewer sharp edges. Less exposed wiring. Wider aisles. A lap like mine (barometric, leafy, possibly hyperbole) needs what any toddler needs. Child-proofed everything. I refuse to carry knee pads. My only concession, double-strength hose. Extras in my bag. Enough to slow a bullet. A woman has the same obligation to her knees she has to her mouth. No lettuce between the cracks.

✗

On a hair trigger.

✗

Like a dog whose ears prick at sounds out of range to the rest of us, my lap is tensed. Flashlights and batteries . . . thickets of light bulbs . . . tension increases. I scan for track lighting. Above my couch, lights glare, tropical heat, enough to dry my nails by. I get as far as three-way soft bulbs. My lap kaplunks. Drops me like a Murphy bed. In quick succession, my jaw thuds, the dilation of my mouth a full nine centimeters, woodpeckers couldn't dig a deeper cavity. The sockets in my eyes go eggcup. Seated on air, I'm squatting down. Liz Claiborne bag, Anne Klein wool tweed cruising jacket, slim jeans, the usual allotment of shoes and underwear, no jewelry, heavy or otherwise. A medium to below medium build. I

14

tip the scales, I don't go off the scales. Still, squats are seismic. Some more than others. Calves, ankles, thighs immediately kick in to alleviate the pressure. I'm no hardbody. The granite in my calves, ankles and thighs is molten. Trembling is inevitable. But never at this early juncture. The shakes are for later . . . when I really start to give out.

✗

The Hardware Store on Third sells prophylactics. At this moment I can personally vouch for that. The hand-held wire shopping basket, not a foot from my face, contains ten blue boxes of prophylactics, neatly bedded down, forming the initial H. The hand holding the wire basket needs no steadying. The wire basket, not a foot from my face, containing the blue boxes of prophylactics is well in hand.

Monumentally so.

✗

. . . October first to October thirty-first, catch-up. Odds and ends. Fall on piles of unmatched socks and well-worn bras and frayed bathing suits. Fall behind, no end in sight. Ends have more finality than beginnings. Depending on how you see ends, some things never end. History's full of loose ends clamoring to be looped. Any record's better than none. Even falsified ones. For the record: Jane Samuels is past the man who filed. First.

✗

"How are you?"

✗

My voice wobbles. From where I stand—seated on air—ankles, calves and thighs pitchforking, jaw dropped like a bridge over a moat, sockets inhaled, I claim a certain angle. Full view of the legs as well as the hands. Firmly planted legs. The hand attached to the wire basket containing the boxes of rubbers (forming the H) is supported by two masculine pillars. The legs stand motionless. His slacks prevent me from comparing what his legs are now to what they used to be before they filed. First.

15

So in conclusion: What rests between his twin towers—the so-called groin—from where I stand, it doesn't strike a chord.

Spread like a fan. My lap peacocks. Wide enough for a table with the leaf stuck in. Lap nostalgia. How can I put this without sounding like a week ago to the day, on the very eve (no less) of the fourth anniversary of my deliverance from the man who filed. First. I was whacked on the head by a rabbit? Put one way, laps are telling. But you have to know how to look. The widening of one's lap closely corresponds to the opening of arms. In preparation for a welcoming embrace, limbs split apart.

Citing history: Consider geological history. Rocks give evidence of what went before. Confining geological history only to rocks belies the basic premise of geology. Geology examines surfaces. Each and every surface has a history.

So it follows.

Aptly so.

Laps are surfaces.

Laps are geological treasures.

Historically and geologically, before there was a man who filed. First. there was Suki. In memory of the beloved cat Suki, constant lap companion, laps and cats wedded to each other for all eternity, my lap opened its trap. Cavern wide. No two ways. Take my word for it. The lap craves cat. The lap does not crave the cock who filed. First.

"How are you?"

Neither time have I been insistent. Second time, less so. No trace of coax. Not by the tilt of my tiltless head. Nor by the lean of my unleaning body. Not by my manner of sitting on air do I convey a willingness to stay for however long it takes. Harold Samuels, the man who filed. Before me. is ancient history.

x

I'm nobody's fall guy.

x

I'm past catch-up.

x

"How are you?"

x

Third time. My lap snaps shut like a car door bearing down on a digit. Still I sit on air. My head's so-so. Unusually, monumentally so-so. Bordering engine trouble. If I say so, there's one reason why I say so. In so many words, fall. Just below the surface of fall, the question on every leaf's lips: Why did I fall out of favor?

x

In Harold's other hand, an attaché case. Mark Cross, gold-trimmed. A gold-plated bar clasp. The bar is like a hood ornament, large and showy. I'm always appreciative of the craftsmanship that goes into forging things for men who pick up on how many women pick up on things like that.

High-end attaché cases.

Definitely come-ons for women who'd do anything to land a man of quality tote.

The wire basket containing the boxes of rubbers in the formation H is temporarily shelved. His free hand on the bar, Harold slowly pulls it back. The snap of the bar's grip is whiplash audible. (So apropos.) Power grips, like power handshakes, should never just fade away. When it's done right, the opening of an attaché case of caliber is like the raising of a curtain. You may not feel one hundred percent diverted from the discomfort of sitting on air, but you stop fidgeting long enough to see what happens next.

Harold stretches the moment.

Many an Oscar presenter does the same. Ripping the envelope slowly, riveting you, making of it a theatrical event.

(When Harold filed. First. he filed at a faster speed.) Why has he orchestrated this? Mark Cross finery, fine as it is, is still not monumental. For Harold to go to these lengths, his rationale must reek of rationality.

✗

It does.

✗

Attaché case extraordinaire. Technological wizardry. The clasp, both bar and bar mates, the parts the bar mounts for sealing, begin chattering. Sounds of tacks bouncing on Formica. Wombish shuddering in the butter-soft leather sac. Open mouth panting. Contractions. Is this what I think it is? Is this labor?

✗

It is.

✗

The Cross has a discharge. Or should I say the leather birth canal delivers a cane chair? By all appearances, a girl chair. The seat padded, an apron of ruffles and flounces.
  Harold offers me a seat.
  I refuse the seat.
  Just as I do with gloves on mark-down: Reject the first pair, see what's out there. Harold filed. First. My lawyer twisted my arm to file. How can I yield any sooner to Harold than I would yield to gloves on sale?
  So Harold sits.
  So I wait on air.
  Had he filed. Second. there is no question, I would have still deferred. The ruffled apron, the flounces . . . very Chiquita Banana. Sitting on busywork furniture always makes me feel like I'm trying too hard.
  I cramp.
  Dry heaves from the Cross.
  A chair so plain and sturdy it looks like office furnishing.
  My shrug says so-so.
  Drier heaves.

18

One huge pelvic thrust. Then wicker. The chair is high backed, slender legs, lacquered toenails. Armrests curving gracefully from the shoulder area.

I go for it.

Sitting on air is murder on the extremities.

✗

"How are you?"

✗

The note I hit is the note I was trying to hit all along. A knell employed by acquaintances in elevators on winter Mondays, early in the morning, the knell of people who really don't give a damn how anybody is.

✗

"I'm better than I was. I gave up smoking. It's sobering to go through an experience like that. You tell yourself you can do without something, you want it anyhow." Harold's voice never does what I do when I'm sitting on air for extended periods. It's what you look for in the dress of an employee who deals directly with your life savings. A cool to the touch voice. Once you get accustomed to Harold's vocal inflections, the austerity of them, it's not a far jump from there to thinking of Harold as a one-note kind of guy.

His chair faces mine.

The slack between us, a small card table or a tea trolley could hog and still we wouldn't be wedged. We aren't bumping knees. We are not so far apart that there's no room in the aisle for people to pass.

"Certainly looked at from a personal point of view, experience-wise, there have been difficult times." Harold's warming to the subject. Otherwise he wouldn't go on speaking. Harold doesn't believe in embellishing speech with words.

"It turned out all right though. For a while there I worried I'd have flashbacks of my first wife for the rest of my life."

✗

Though I am the first wife, I try and sit like I could be anybody.

The owner of the store introduces himself. Owner. I don't catch his first or last name. Owner presses extra keys on us. "Stay as long as you like, past closing time, overnight if you like." Owner gives us the security code.

I might have guessed.

Cross has clout.

Cross has Owner in its pocket.

Small merchants grovel for Cross.

It's not my navy Liz Claiborne shoulder bag Owner's fawning all over. Liz gets treated like the rest of us. Restricted hours. Sales tax. Refunds without receipts, forget it.

Intermission.

Curtain down.

Harold dozes. His head doesn't slump. The impeccable napper. No crud. The corners of his eyes don't crust. Or breed. All five foot four inches of me walks to the exit. Not to stretch. Not to grab a quick mineral water before the next act.

Harold's history.

✗

I'm past Harold.

✗

I'm not past flinging.

✗

One-night stands are flings. Flings are convenience foods. Hundreds of nights running don't mean automatic upgrades. The Fling (going on his second year) is a warm platter to tide me over till a real meal comes along.

Oh Suki . . .

I'm on my way to a lap job.

✗

This is New York
You have to think flings through.
Advance reservations.

Mutually agreeable times for coupling. I'm not convinced men are as hard to come by as closet space. Of the two I believe closet space to be the greater challenge. I believe there's just so much a closet can hold no matter what appointments you juggle.

We met on a walking tour.

The historical Wall Street area. If I had done historical China-town, or historical Little Italy or the historical tenements of the Lower East Side or the Historical Society's exhibitions on his-torical Wall Street, Chinatown, Little Italy, the Lower East Side synagogues and tenements, we never would have connected. He tagged along. In the Wall Street district on business, he couldn't pass my lap up. I knew exactly what I was doing. Walk with your lap out often enough, you learn a few tricks. Ladling, flashing, scooping as you go. Basketball hoop. Come play with me.

The Fling's a shrink.

Naturally he lapped it up.

X

My apartment . . .

I brush my teeth.

I mouthwash.

The breath of spring.

In fall.

The Fling going on his second year notifies me daily of any pa-tient cancellations. The slots are rarely back to back, so we're on the copulation economy plan—you cut corners to come, like pocket dictionaries, abridge the foreplay, reduce the contents of sex to the physical. Skim everything but the good parts.

This morning I booked the one to two.

The patient who masturbates into his General Electric cordless vacuum—the other brands don't have GE's sex appeal—is still un-der extended warrantee. Until that runs out, he wavers.

Fall, this way or that?

Fall's a tough call.

Once my place was Harold's place and my place. Now that it's no longer Harold's place I am at liberty to dump the furniture. Re-decorate. Fall for something new.

It hasn't happened yet.

X

21

It will.

✗

The moment I open to his knock, the Fling going on his second year opens his fly. "My wife wants me to help her select her birthday gift. Hurry. My wife's waiting. We have ten minutes." Into the bedroom on top of the comforter. He keeps his pants on, I keep my almost everything on.

It's a fire drill.

For his wife's benefit, I rush his lump into my right palm. The lump bulges because my right hand and its sidekick, the left hand, are experienced lump handlers. A steady rhythmic squeeze, release-grip-release, like a hand-held heart pump.

The color of his bulge, flaming.

My sprinkler system—lap vicinity—activates to keep the bulge from going up in smoke. My Bermuda Triangle—lap vicinity—isn't a flame-retardant in the sense of a fire extinguisher, but a parched birdhouse—lap vicinity—is a fire hazard.

(I take pains not to inflict rope burns.)

"Nora's waiting." He quickens the pace. "I should be there by now."

(The pains I've taken not to inflict rope burns are lost in the shuffle.)

The hose doesn't swim more than a few laps. The hose gushes. The hose goes limp. The hose swabs down my Macy's pillowcase. The hose tucks in. Never a Godzilla prototype on its best day, not even close—it's a dead ringer for a cauliflower.

The Fling zips his fly.

A visual check.

Meeting your wife to pick out her fortieth birthday present, your fly—anything in the lap vicinity—must never look mauled over.

✗

I would have liked a minor contraction in my vicinity, anywhere on my person. A nose plug for the cannoli, a clothespin . . . something. I would have liked a reason to linger over brandy and a good cigar.

I too must go.

Egg hunts and bunnies . . .

Fall, it falls to some of us to get a jump start on Easter.

22

Call it research. After all, I am a seasoned ferreter. An information gatherer. Consulting original sources, secondhand sources, following leads, tracking down answers, making evaluations, filling in the blanks. Investigator, detective. Pursuer of truth. Capture is rapture.

Bunny beware . . .

Jane Samuels is on your trail.

Waiting for my elevators is like waiting to go standby. There's a chance you'll be skipped entirely. Still I give it a shot. They could surprise me. One of these days, when I really need a lift, one or both of them might quit stalling.

I take the stairs.

Elevators and I arrive in the lobby at the same time. Alex, the doorman, holds the street door for me, tipping his hat.

"How are you?"

"And how are you?"

One thing I can say about Alex I can't say about myself. When he asks how I am, he asks like he means it.

I haven't got far to go.

From where I live to the street where I was bopped, a short hop. The route is straight, three blocks, no turns. My home turf. The shop people know me by name, now the local school crossing guard also knows me by name. To the school crossing guard, I'm not just another redhead in the crowd. I am the woman she saw slugged by a rabbit.

I let the school crossing guard do her job.

"The skills you acquire crossing a New York City street you can use the rest of your life." She has me by the arm, guiding me, we look both ways, crosswalk entered, step lively, here comes the corner, step up. The light turns red, we stay put. "Most misunderstood by the children is the light system. Obedience to the light system can't save them. Systems falter. Mechanical failures. Drivers are human. The human element has a system all its own. The unreliability of systems is a hard one for kids."

She doesn't look much older than a teenager. On her, the braces and the freckles act like a serum.

"Any sign of rabbit?" I ask.

The light turns, I'm led across the street, deposited on the same corner I started out on. She ferries two more people back the way we came. One of the two is me.

The one doing the talking is not me.

"Know your light system, mistrust your light system. But until a better system comes along, put up with what you've got. Kids want quick simple answers. The light system's set up for timed responses. I'm not."

Corner to corner delivery. The light delays her. Now she's mine.

"The rabbit?"

"We're all pedestrians. Life is riddled with streets, helping you get from here to there is what your school crossing guard is for."

"So?"

"One renegade rabbit, it doesn't look good for the rest of them."

Her eyes say enough said. I tell her I'll be in touch. My own private system for fall research: Never call it quits. You want somebody to fall into your hands, know when to fall back.

✗

. . . October first to October thirty-first, falling all over myself, not in the literal sense. In the sense that fall has a widespread fallout.

✗

Until a better system comes along, you put up with what you've got. On that the school crossing guard was on the right street. Next time maybe she'll clue me in on how you go about getting something out of your system.

✗

For the sake of argument, it's highly unlikely Harold will strike the Hardware Store twice in a row. Equally unlikely for me to accept the unlikely (whole or in part) at face value. Is there such a thing as a knocked-up attaché case? Was Harold a figment? Is history being made? Will the fourth fall observance of my deliverance from the man who filed. First. mark the end of an era? Though

24

some ends hang in till the last, history underscores pivotal points. Breakthroughs. The collapse of the old, paving the way for the new.

Best scenario: I march inside, I see Harold, I research him to death, capture the truth—capture is rapture—I make a clean getaway.

Worse scenario: No end in sight. Catch-up never catches up enough. Ancient history is living history.

On the lips of every autumn leaf: Here I come.

✗

Poker face.

To look at Harold sitting in the same chair, flounced and ruffled, is to see a man who will always look younger than his years. His face doesn't flicker. The perfect accompaniment to his marbleized voice. World War II: On paper at least, Sweden takes no sides. Harold and Sweden both neutral. Fewer nose to mouth lines. Smoother foreheads. Harold is a Swedish success story.

I sit opposite, molding myself to the wicker chair.

"How are you?"

Not a wrinkle in my voice.

Everything about Harold is tailored. His blubber ratio isn't enough to keep from freezing to death should he swim the English Channel. His saliva's below the international dateline. His nose . . . I detect alteration. The nose is store-bought. So he's whittled his nose.

"Giving up smoking wasn't easy. I kept at it. No backsliding either. I chewed gum, that helped. Everywhere I went, I went on foot. That helped. It was the one time in my life I declared something history and it balked."

So that's the way it is.

Harold sits cast-iron still. Seance still. Portrait posing reposed. Me too. I repose myself out of my chair. I repose myself into a cab. A stupor of serenity. How kind of Harold to say what he said. That after years of marriage, seventeen, not inclusive of the three we spent living together, a total of twenty, give or take, not inclusive of the year we corresponded, his most vivid memory of personal struggle is giving up ciggies. Worth recounting. For years to come. His courageous victory over nicotine. The man who filed. First. on me could barely bring himself to file on cigarettes. Cigarettes got to him like nothing else. Ever. I want to go on record: No cover-up.

Composed, reposed. Jane Samuels, the impartial observer. You heard me. If a researcher strangles the subject in his sleep, it invalidates the findings.

✗

I could use a little recreational shopping.

✗

The red patent leather belts in Saks Fifth Avenue look like lipstick tubes. Fire reds, corals, crimsons. A Clairol dye chart. Nipple pink. Tongue plum. Menstrual mahogany.

I make my selection.

Vulva rose.

"Cash or charge?" Two belts slung low on her hips. The side pouches look like holsters. Palms on both pouches, the gunslinger's trigger fingers are getting itchy. I hand her my Saks charge.

"The belt's you," the salesgirl says.

"In what way?"

"The color's you."

I try again.

"In what way? Do you think middle-aged women should be partial to brighter colors, that in reaching midlife, the partiality of a middle-aged woman, what colors she is and isn't impartial to, will really affect her destiny?"

Trigger fingers pull the triggers.

Lightning speed. Side pouch opened. "I do color charts, let me give you my card."

No such thing. Not till she answers the question. The one I asked, slightly amended.

"What's your opinion of a woman who'd put a hardware store on her paper route because she has research to do there, pertaining not to cold hard hardware but to personal matters such as falling out of favor, such as filed upon. First. such as getting an oral accounting, such as combing through said accounting, such as being an impartial observer, composed and reposed (for the record, strangling the subject in his sleep invalidates your findings), in light of all that—can the partiality of a middle-aged woman for bright colors bring her any closer to achieving her ends?"

She rescinds the offer of her card.

Returned to pouch.

Pouch buckled.

"Saks doesn't have to stand here and listen to this."

Tapping the receipt, telling me to sign here.

✗

I don't know what it is about Saks Fifth. Every time I shop elsewhere, I don't feel like I've gotten anything out of my system. All the way back to the Hardware Store I marvel at how therapeutic recreational shopping is. Especially in belt departments. Saks says they don't have to stand there and take it. But in reality, Saks lets you belt it out.

✗

Stuck in the Mark Cross.

Harold's mother. Broad-shouldered all the way down. The attaché case pleats from exhaustion. Its color is not so good. Is the Cross going to die in childbirth delivering a sixty-five-year-old woman? Helen yanks her arms free. She pushes down, the leverage releases her as far as her waist. Her army jacket says it all: Warrior woman.

Helen sees me.

"He's got such heart," Helen says of Harold. This is news to me. "My mother died the same day I had a mushroom conference in which I was a keynote speaker. You need field experience to know mushrooms. It was Harold who convinced me to skip the funeral."

The Cross goes from green to cream to greener. Harold uncrosses his legs. From his seat, he reaches over. He begins pushing his mother down. She pushes back up. All her bench-pressing pays off. A draw.

"He wouldn't allow me to cancel. A corpse is history. No one should ever let sentiment for the past stand in the way of mushrooms." Harold puts his shoulder to it. "His sister's the worst. No heart. She makes everything an issue. Harold's the one with heart."

His full weight on the top of her head. Helen slowly sinks over the horizon. I do not think of somebody being drowned in the tub.

Because Harold's got heart.

✗

27

First.

I am not a captive audience.

Foremost.

I am not an enraptured audience.

I can leave anytime I please, whether or not I have somewhere to go.

I can leave.

Owner passes me on my way out. He can't conceal his disappointment. No purchase, her heart's in the wrong place.

✗

On a day I looked more mousy than foxy, a rabbit did a bunny hop across my forehead. "Read my paw prints," he said. He did not batter my brains out for bus fare. He didn't make a move on my lettuce patch. "My paw prints, read 'em," he said.

✗

Do I dare say now what I daren't say then? Mr. Rabbit, you are a crank. History's got its historical figures, New York with all its history, has its cranks.

Too late.

The time to dispute the reading of paw prints on your forehead is before paw prints start flashing like a Times Square ticker tape.

✗

Paw prints to me: Lincoln Center. Bathroom stall. Proceed to the man in the wall.

Me to paw prints: Is this a psychic experience? I have the highest regard for psychic experiences. Joan of Arc, Moses, twins across the nation, to name only a few. As much as I'd like to meet a man in a wall of a bathroom stall, it's been a day. What with Harold who filed. First. What with fall in general. I'll pass.

A moment passes.

Paws to me: Have it your way.

✗

I go anyway.

Just to prove myself wrong. A man in a wall? Tell me another one. I'd sooner fall for the one about a giant rabbit roaming the streets of New York without a leash.

✗

My visit to the bathroom at Lincoln Center is under false pretenses. Unlike some bladders you can't take anywhere, bladders who won't let you sit for a minute, there are no thimble bladders in my family. The length of the line for the bathroom is sellout long. The women in ticket holders look like bouncers. You seldom run into these types anymore. They're the ones who can tough it out without face-lifts. Lots of pacing in place. Marking their territory with perfume. I'd be shot on the spot if I tried to bluff my way past these molls. Facing down loaded bladders violates every rule of self-preservation. The women guard the cells like they're linebackers. PMS-y around the eyes. Regretfully I get only as far as the Lincoln Center sinks.

I press a lever for soap.

I soap my hands.

What of the man in the wall of the Lincoln Center stall?

I reach for the faucets.

Why he whispers to me from inside the sinkwell.

"I could crawl out of this drain. I could crawl out of the woodwork. Guys like me have been crawling out of the woodwork since the Nixon years. Don't jump to conclusions, I'm not a creep."

Righteous indignation.

An articulate speaker.

Not what you'd expect from a drain at all. Drains and brains together just don't seem to go together. "Creeps crawl out of the woodwork but walls are not their natural habitat. Walls are too good for creeps."

My hands are soapy.

I know I should turn the taps on.

But there's a man in my drain talking.

"I don't want you to think any the less of yourself for listening to a drain. In my circle, talking to drains is as highly regarded as talking to walls."

I don't rinse my hands.

The film of soap comes off easily with a paper towel. I now have verification. Paw prints imprinted on my forehead are not just there for decoration. I am now the proud owner of clairvoyant rabbit tracks.

29

Hunches hint, they don't paint pictures.

No mention was made, for instance, of the corridor wall outside the bathroom. How it cracks. How it parts company. Razor slits. No wider than I would open a door if someone unexpected knocked. Now you see me, now you don't.

Now you do.

A cock in the wall. Out to there. Stiffer than my broomstick. Could this be biblical psalms come true? Thy rod and Thy staff comfort me. I've been pointed at before, this one's not accusatory. It's at the point where the tip curls like a finger, motioning me over.

Maybe I brought this on myself.

Like some women of my sex, there have been moments when I've lamented to other women of my sex how hard it is to find somebody who'll get me climbing the walls. Not to cast aspersion on the dicks of native sons—women of my sexual persuasion appreciate honest slamming—but honestly, shouldn't there be somebody out there who can get off the wall women climbing the walls?

A cock with good ballast.

Further up, look-into-my-eyes eyes.

His shoulders are also well hung.

I'm tingling, not from the bladder. In that subterranean region. A stirring. Goose bumps on my clitoral. If my feet weren't already rapidly putting one foot in front of the other, I would have remained behind.

To banter with the walls.

✗

To skip off to Hardware as if nothing happened is not the way it's going to happen. Cock in the wall is turning corner. Now that I've turned that corner, I'm more than a little unnerved. Just how many corners should a girl turn before turning to somebody for help?

✗

The school crossing guard never said she wasn't in my corner.
The school crossing guard is an expert on corners.

✗

Somehow I'm not surprised to see her keep nocturnal hours. After years of enduring indifference from various city agencies on my neighborhood's noise level, I can tell when a school crossing guard is dedicated to making streets a lifelong career.

A slow night.

Soon as she sees me standing on the corner, she pounces. She's dressed in bright orange. An occupational hazard. The more conscious you are of the night vision of drivers, the less self-conscious you get about orange.

"I was a little short with you today, I apologize. The demands of daytime volume."

"I've seen a cock in the wall."

"Pedestrians are from all walks of life. Cocks included."

"Would you say I've turned a corner?" Asked more like I'm asking for reassurance than for explanation. So I quickly say, "The paw prints are behind this. Behind the paw prints, the rabbit who raised a hand to me, I must find him. If you really meant what you said, you'd help me get from here to there."

The traffic light dies.

Two cars rear end.

There is no faster way to feel you're expendable than when the most devoted crossing guard you've ever run across leaves you to fend for yourself.

✗

Evening shopping hours. I never did get the bulbs for track lighting. When it's this empty, the Hardware Store feels cavernous. It's just Owner, Harold and I. Owner's standing next to a display on drain cleaners. I feel we'll be seeing quite a lot of each other. Sooner or later, he'll realize I'm more of a browser than a fervent consumer of hardware. Perhaps he realizes already. He doesn't acknowledge me.

Harold is directly ahead.

Next to him is one of those easels upon which one of those charts lean that lecturers appearing before small groups refer to with one of those pointers, a tool used by educators and the like to help you keep up with where on the chart you're supposed to be. Prosecuting attorneys use such charts to demonstrate ballistics. The bullet has perforated the left ear at an obtuse angle. Scientists use the same medium—charts, copiously labeled—to depict the chromosome gene structure of ambidextrous earthworms. Medical

31

students study charts: Bone structure, skeletal, neurons and so on. Charts are pictorial. Pictorial is visual. Visual gets you right between the eyes.

The chart is of a nose.

Harold's pointer directs me to the blow-up of his bump, an accurate reproduction of what his nose looked like prior to reconstruction: Bunched up.

"I axed my nose for land development. You can't have land development without axing something. The nature of land developing is such that something has to be sacrificed. Even in the absence of specific words or deeds to warrant the ax, a land developer's duty is to sever it at the root. By whatever means, new ground must be broken. The way must be cleared."

He's talking about his nose.

Why do I feel he's talking about me?

Harold's raised pointer raises a new point. Just above my nose, in the air, he writes in script. "Meat begets dead meat."

It's just like his mother said.

Harold has heart.

Harold inserts the easel, the chart, the pointer, the works into the Cross. The Cross ahhs. A Cross disposal unit. The Cross crunches. Soft burps. Coos and gurgles ensuing. While the Cross lip smacks, Harold profiles.

The hell with track lights.

Before I leave, under the approving eye of Owner, I purchase half a dozen blunt instruments.

✗

Instrumental in my purchasing half a dozen blunt instruments was word for word what the land developer who filed. First. said. There are land developers, there are land developers' wives who—through no word or deed of their own—get written out of history.

✗

Falling flakes. The sidewalks are coated. Inclement weather is especially hard on noses. Noses take a beating when the temperature drops. Noses with dragon fire probably fare better than noses without. Noses without internal combustion accumulate higher snowdrifts. The frostbite factor is hard on naked noses. Twice I'm nosed out of a cab. Once by a nose that tried to pierce my ears. The second nose bodily shoved me from the cab.

Third try, I get my wheels.

My cab noses ahead of the buses.

On the sidewalks, peddlers make everyone pay through the nose for nose warmers. Acrylics, goose down. Stuck-up noses wear cashmere. Noses to the grindstone pull their collars up. Police officers on foot patrol are not indigenous. They holster their noses.

The cab pulls up.

My building doesn't have an awning.

I slip. Nose first. A good samaritan of the male gender examines my collarbone for breaks. One thing leads to another, we rub noses. His nose is unusually, monumentally well-endowed. Thick, long, it looks like it has breast implants.

Nosiness.

Mine, not his.

"Have you ever tampered with your nose? Ever contoured your nose without due process? Had a surgical consult, contemplated the blade?"

"All my parts are in their original wrappers."

"What's your attitude on the rain forest?"

"How so?"

"Filing it to stumps."

"I don't believe so."

Right on the nose. It connotes. A man loyal to his parts, a conservationist, is a man who files. Last. He sees me safely to my door. I don't have to lead him by the nose. The elevators cooperate. A wait of no more than four minutes. I show him in. I put down the package of blunt instruments.

He puts me down.

✗

A saber on the sofa.

He's a nasal gymnast.

The sofa under the track lights (lights switched off) is like a mattress in a cheap motel. With every nose dunk, I squeak along with the sofa. His nose is an oil rig inside my south pole. Deep penetration. I cannot remember a time when a man's nose was better than his hands.

Another corner turned.

I pleasure that man's olfactories. Stroking his nose, my mouth

33

suctioned to it, but not to administer artificial respiration. I
French-kiss his nose. I lower myself on it. He tells me not to worry,
he won't smother. The spasms of his nose match my own.

Eventually he asks to see me again.

He lets himself out.

Next time I'll get his name.

✗

A hardware store is not a pharmaceutical; one doesn't hit hardware the way you'd hit a drugstore. Only if you have a compelling
reason. My reasoning is this: Now that I have a key (and security
code) going and coming is not intruding. I am welcomed. I am not
compelled to go where I'm unwelcomed. I am not compelled to
open just any door, only the ones that unlock the past. Even I can
see the chinks in that reasoning. Plenty of doors to the past don't
want to be tampered with. Compelling me to use brute force. Blast
my way the core. Capture the rapture.

I stand by what I said.

I have a compelling reason not to stay home.

✗

A piece of Sara Lee. I gain admittance without setting off
alarms. The lights are low. I have to squint to see. Knees out, lap
down, I take up more space than usual. The semidarkness makes
me clumsy. I bump, I do not crash or topple. Like everyone else, I
get where I'm going by groping.

Harold's sleeves are rolled up.

The attaché case rests on a small square table. Harold's hands
are fondling whatever is inside the case. The contents squirm, I
hear throaty sounds, female throaty sounds.

I ought to turn away.

I move forward.

A bare rump surfaces from inside the case. Soufflé out. It sticks
up in the air. The fanny is puckered. Betty Boop dimples in generous supply. Even with a Coppertone tan, this ass will never be
Brooke Shields. Harold opens a tube of zinc oxide, fingerpainting
her tush. He follows up with a steamed towel across her stern, the
kind they give you in a good Chinese restaurant after the spare
ribs.

He slaps her rump.

34

"Get your ass in gear. Put to sea. Set sail. Never swim to where you've been. Fish around. Don't drop anchor, get your sea legs, keep a girl in every port, take your pleasures where you find them, turn the tides, ride the currents, never let them hook you."

It works.

Anchors away.

The soufflé ships out.

Harold sits back in his chair. Harold closes his eyes. Harold goes beddy-bye. I pace. The hardwood floors creak. I stay the night. Treading, sitting, thinking.

Working out a hypothesis . . .

Harold is filing big-time.

Harold has cut all ties.

The land developer is a pirate.

Working out a what if . . .

What if he meets a mermaid?

It cannot be emphasized enough . . . nauticals are all wet. But once you get your feet wet, watch out for the undertow.

Big fish eat little fish.

What if Harold drowns at sea?

What if two passing ships meet?

Pirate away the pirate, what if?

The last thought before my eyes close . . .

She would have to be a good catch.

Monumentally, unusually so.

✗

Midmorning. Not at all fishy. I slept through the activity around me because it's fall. Waiting as long as I have for things to fall into place can exhaust the heartiest of wives. Filed first on. Owner lets me use the phone. I call the Fling going on his second year. He's been trying to reach me. Come quick, a slot's just opened up. I hurry home to change my underwear. I arrive at his office more than a little breathy.

The doctor will see you now.

✗

The Fling's favorite thing—dead ringer for a cauliflower—rests in my hand like a gerbil. There are step-by-step training programs for chimps to be reintroduced into the wild. Simians are taught to

35

hunt, to puff out their chests, to appear bigger than life. In the right hands, any animal can be beefed up.

Gerbil stimulation is my specialty.

I rough it up, thereby loosening it up. The gerbil retaliates, charging like a warthog. Burrowing in, thrashing. The butting of the gerbil against my vaginal walls is like a prisoner looking for a way out of a cell, testing each spot for give, fists hammering away internally, slingshots, buckshot, hitting me with everything that's not nailed down. A gerbil with heavy artillery. I surrender . . . with pleasure.

The gerbil emerges wet.

I hand the Fling going on his second year a Wash 'n' Dry to wipe the greasepaint off his prick. It's not professional to sop clients paying 120 bucks an hour in your semen. The least he can do is provide dry seating.

"When's your next patient?"

"We have time yet."

The chair Nate sits in is a leather armchair. Burly Hell's Angel arms. Wrap-my-arms-around-you arms. Nate's furniture has frames with meat. Furniture that feels like you can cry on its shoulder. The couch where I sit is the same ilk as the chair. Roomy. Half a twin bed.

"The Vacuum Cleaner basher or the Sleepwalker?" I know their labels, I don't know their names.

"The Sagger. She says her body feels like it's standing in the middle of a mud slide. Women are too self-conscious about their bodies. Mud slides are all in the mind."

He rises.

We embrace.

I come up to the base of his scrawny chicken neck. Nate is narrow, his furniture obese, his clothes hang on him. Suits with plenty of play. The flapping most noticeable in the wind.

Extra silicone gel in the shoulder pads for the man who says women are too self-conscious about their bodies.

I milk him.

"Ever treat pets?"

"The problem with animals is usually people. I know what you're getting at. The bunny who left his calling card on your forehead was upset. Be thankful it's not a permanent scar. Tell the owner for me, the problem won't work itself out without intervention. Aggressive animals are animals under stress."

He milks me.

"What did Barry say to you at the funeral?"

"He'll never look at another woman. For him, Betty was it. Isn't that pretty much what you'd expect a new widower to say? They were married for decades."

The buzzer on his desk gives us a ten minute warning.

"He's the only person we have in common. I never would have introduced you two if I didn't trust the both of you to behave yourselves."

He steers me to the leather chair.

"Christ, he just lost his wife. You're his best friend. You don't really think—"

I'm pushed to the floor. Feet placed on the arms of the chair. Nate sits. He pulls my panties. He inserts his thumbs. He circles every spot but G. He tells me to beg.

I do.

✗

The woman who is too self-conscious about her body is in the waiting room. I only catch a glimpse. Old enough to be my contemporary. Early forties. Heavier makeup around the eyes. She has the hair I want. Cascading down her back. When she stands, she leaves a little stain of mud on her seat.

God, I hope he can help her.

Mud slides are all in the mind.

✗

Fall. I walk miles and miles. If I go on foot to the Hardware Store it will take me that much longer. The time saved with a cab will give me that much more time. Is time with Harold of the essence?

I hail a taxi.

✗

Actually the Hardware Store, door to door from the Fling, is one of those short-distance cab rides where the meter fare is so low you inflate the tip to discourage the cabby from heaping upon you tired epithets like cunt, which, back in the days before cunt was a household word, used to have punch.

✗

Harold's in mixed company.

I can hardly tell where he stops and she begins. The lady sitting on my wicker has Harold's face in a jaw lock between her legs. Her cheek bones are chiseled. They come to tacks. His head from the back is balding. When I approach she pulls her skirt over him. She opens her compact. The lipstick she applies is scarlet. The outline of Harold's head shows him bobbing for apples. Lolling on the lawn.

Harold's company addresses me.

"I told him I wasn't going to be one of his movie gofers. I don't think the man's bought a ticket in the conventional manner in years." She bites off a hangnail. Spits the hang. "He'll do anything to evade the lines." She puts her hands on top of the skirt. The cranium underneath is a diamond in the bezel. Her taps to Harold's head are reveille. The action under her skirt, below the equator of her bellybutton, is bucking. Her legs clench. She comes. A terrific series of stagecoach bumps.

Harold slides out.

The slick on his mouth isn't lip gloss.

In his mouth two tickets.

"I knew they'd be there. She'll do anything to avoid seeing a movie alone. Even give up the aisle seat."

She addresses me.

"Give them the aisle seat, you trash the relationship. The aisle seat is collateral."

I am an impartial observer.

I address no one but myself.

Is this his mermaid?

Will she pirate him away?

Good catch or catch of the day?

I cannot emphasize enough . . . nauticals are all wet.

She addresses Harold.

"What are you doing?"

"What does it look like?"

"Putting the tickets back where you found them."

"Let me know how the movie was."

"Trying to wrangle the aisle seat won't work."

Nail in her mouth, another hang. Hangnail spit. Two more hangs. The moment hangs in the balance. She slumps in her chair.

I leave for a prior engagement.

If I didn't have one, I'd leave anyway. Women who brag one thing, spit, then slump, then mutter You win, you win . . . where's the punch?

✗

Susan is my prior engagement.

My all-time longevity friend. A short-lived friendship that's lived to a ripe old age. A classic case of quantity over quality. This I can't blame on fall or rabbits. Like weeds, the friendship just keeps cropping up. Susan is monumentally unusually self-possessed. And in the fall my interest in Susan grows monumental and unusual. No one else is better equipped to handle their problems.

When I get to her building—a building just off a major avenue, in the building a doorman by the name of Tony—two elevators pull breathlessly up, the eagerness of young suitors. Both competing for my body. I take the one on the right. For the ride down, I'll go left. I am not so so-so that I believe Susan's elevators hold grudges.

Only mine do.

✗

My longevity friend Susan is mixing bran and low-fat cottage cheese sprinkled with fresh Parmesan for Patches. His patches look like the patches worn by one-eyed buccaneers. Hence the dog's name. Patches rolls on his back. Susan nuzzles him. Like an imperial cupbearer, she brings him his drinking bowl. She lifts the bowl to his lips.

I've seen people like her.

Intense relationships with pets.

Deep attachments.

And when Patches drops dead her grief will not be out of proportion. Her grief will be proportioned. Within whatever framework Susan says. Her grief will not get the best of her.

I take it back.

I haven't seen one remotely like her.

Her frame is on some other plane.

"Think of your frame of mind as eyeglass frames. Replace negative frames with positive frames. Throughout the day make frame adjustments. Get the fit right for you. Vigilance is your only pro-

39

tection against what lurks around every corner. Yield your frame, you end up balling hunks you hardly know, your moral fiber will crumble, you'll ask for refunds when none are due you. You won't give a damn about voting in the primaries."

Patches licks her face. Her face is a harvest moon. Susan's body weight and size were arrested somewhere around junior high. Patches fetches his leash. Patches pleads for quick action or he will explode on the nearest leg. He tries to squirrel under the door. He gets up and tries turning the knob with his teeth. He rolls on his back and bawls out loud.

She kneels.

Fingers tracing the eyeglass route. Doing to him what she does to herself. Fixing the frame of mind, patting it into place like hair. "In your present state of mind, you are a dog. You have a bladder problem. Control your frame . . . I know how tempting it is to yield to the call of the wild; biologically we are all creatures of biology. Every victory of mind over impulse is a defeat for the City. Lurking around every corner are hunks you hardly know who'd like nothing better than to ball your moral fiber."

Patches pees on her leg.

"It's not working. Leave him be. You're asking too much of him. Fixing a frame of mind is even beyond me." The suggestion is not well-received. Her moonface looks like a bowling ball headed for the pins. Suddenly changing direction. Working her temples. Susan switches her frame. Bowling ball to cotton ball. How I envy someone who can file. First. on their frames.

I get a mop and pail
We clean the floor together.
Patches eats.

We girls swap girlie confidences. I catch her up on Harold, my how-are-you's, on the fertile attaché case, on the school crossing guard, the Fling's gerbil, and the Fling's friend, Barry the bereaved. Her frame lets my frame know my frame is in its infancy.

This is what longevity friends are for.

To outstay their welcome.

But for spite, never to file on you. First.

"I believe a rabbit attacked you without provocation, I believe the school crossing guard knows more than she lets on. I believe attaché cases from Mark Cross are on the cutting edge, I believe Harold is going to tell you how he is in excruciating detail. We live in the City. In the City's present frame of mind, logic isn't uppermost in its mind. The City will try anything to frame us. Promise

40

me you'll resist. Set your mind to it. Follow my example. Protect your fiber."

Susan is my longevity friend.
Unlike me, her pet did not die.
Her husband has not abandoned her.
Her frame of mind is adjustable.
Obviously, on a higher plane.

✗

. . . and mine isn't.

✗

. . . and tinkering with my temples won't make it so.

✗

So why don't I give it a rest?

✗

Home away from home. The Hardware Store on Third. Every small town has a center, a plaza, hangouts built to draw people, easy-on-the-eye places, show up ten times a day, nobody thinks anything of it. Hardware on Third is like a watering hole. Night, day, by the banks of the river . . . everyone, whole families, entire herds, flocks . . . communities. Thirst needs no justification. You come because you can't stay away. Hardware is on the Mississippi. Waterfront property. And I am a river rat . . . and my plane (which isn't on a higher plane, no amount of tinkering will make it so) would gladly give it all a rest.

Now is out of the question.

✗

Harold's strip of Hardware isn't a strip anymore. Behind his chair, a sleek floor lamp, beneath his feet, an ottoman, the table holding the Cross is a cocktail table, a glass top that looks like chapel glass. The quarters aren't tight. Everyone who has to get through . . . passes right through.

Cross knows things I don't.

41

Cross is privy.

As stylish as my navy Liz Claiborne shoulder bag is—meant to be worn casual or dressy—for all that, it still can't go into labor or redesign space.

"How are you?"

I'm sure the question could have been framed any number of ways. But in my frame of mind I'm more concerned with tone than repetition. Do I sound as if I couldn't care less? Do I sound overbearing? Do I say it so the man who filed. First. will know I've got better things to do?

Harold is sitting.

Neither limply or rigidly.

The same here. Neither nor.

I check my skirt. My skirt isn't riding up. No thigh flesh showing. I don't want to look my age but I don't want to look like I'm trying not to look my age.

"She did everything right," Harold says, neither limply nor rigidly. "Gave me the aisle seat, talked film talk without talking it to death. We had intercourse. She did most of the heavy work. She gave me the option of staying till morning. Meat begets dead meat, fish around. I told her not to take it personally. She took it personally." His even tone comes to an even halt. Like the best downhill skiers, Harold never takes a spill.

Listening is what I'm here for.

Wild rabbits couldn't drag me away.

My forehead has other ideas. The throb is not the dull throb of a headache. No headache ever hippity hops. Or barks Read my paw, read my paw. If the bunny had walked up to me, asked me politely instead of putting his seal on me, I would have said, Sir, I don't read palms.

I am reading something though.

A hunch comes to mind. Leave now the man with the nose will meet me in my lobby. Of course, it's only a hunch. The throb says no, it's a certainty. We compromise.

A likelihood.

✗

Still I'm a little skeptical. The man in the wall wasn't originally supposed to turn up in the drain. That stunt, coupled with the broomstick bonger in the wall, proves bunny paws aren't know-it-alls. A woman brushes past me. Here on the streets, a common enough occurrence. Do not stroll when you can make haste. My walk too. Hers is a lot faster. Springier. Jauntier. A light stepper. I've seen that sock-hop before. It doesn't come from air soles.

It comes from Bunnyville.

✗

So the paws had a winning hand. Parked in my lobby is the nose (and the man whose nose it is). Pulled up next to the doorman's station. Parallel parked. The nose that casts a shadow bigger than most people's bodies. The nose that brings other noses to their knees. Alex the doorman has his nose buried in a book. Alex the doorman will not take his nose off the printed page. Doorman Alex mutters under his nose, Someone to see you.

Undone by a tower of flesh.

The tower's other features look diminutive. They might as well not be there. While waiting for the elevators I put the time to good use. Petting his nose exactly the opposite of how you'd settle someone down. In the elevator, the nose is a trunk with a hard-on. The bridgework broad enough to rest a limo on. I mount up. Godiva (with clothes) on a hobbyhorse. Down the hallway, to my door. Borne aloft. He opens the door. I dismount in the living room. His nose taps the floor like a horse's hoof. I don't think it's a signal for a trough. Or maybe it is. I plummet to the floor. The nose stays in the air, poised above my dewdrop. Bees do this with flowers. Just before making a nosedive for the nectar, they take aim.

The nose beelines.

A mating dance.

I camera shutter like I'm on a shoot where any second I'm going to lose the light. His nostrils vibrate inside me. The fluttering of a hummingbird inside my cathedral. As the nose climaxes I do not think of him as blowing his nose.

We get around to names.

Gerald meet Jane. Jane says hi to Gerald. There's always this part where the action lags a little. What works for me may not work for women below their fourth decade.

I nap.

Sometimes I don't.

"How are you?"

There was a time, not so long ago, when I know I had a wider social vocabulary.

Gerald cracks his knuckles, unbends his bent elbows. His ten

43

fingers and toes get theirs. He strokes his nose. Routine pampering in the winner's circle. The only joint he neglects is the joint between his legs. "Joint trouble. We all went to joint therapy. My ex, the kids, my joints, their joints. Our joint bank accounts. It was a joint venture. Sure we had joint trouble, but everyone has joint trouble. Joints take a beating just standing up."

My own joints are still.

Lest the sound rattle him.

"Joint therapy was intended to help us cope with the day-to-day pressures on our joints." His hands drop between his legs. "My joint contracted joint disease. To this day, they don't know whether it's viral or what. For a while it wasn't responsive at all."

He squeezes his nose.

Immediate wingspan.

I watch it swell with the same pleasure bird-watchers get observing eggs hatch. Gerald aligns his nose. A finger about to sample the cookie batter. I am ravished. The tunneling is far less than the depth Canadian beavers dive, far less than fathoms deep, far less than tunneling through to trapped miners. But the twist and counterclockwise twist of his joint is reminiscent of Chubby Checker doing the Twist. Almost enough to bring God, for . . . the . . . love . . . of God, Christ almighty into my fist-sized agnostic twatchel.

Post coitus weeping.

The man is in touch with feelings.

Making his nose puffy. The membranes raw.

"Joint custody," between sobs, "is so named for its link to joints. The loss of child custody is believed to be a factor in joint infirmities."

He misses his kids. The kids are with mom.

Mom filed. First.

"You'll recover. Give it time. All will be normal in time."

So they say.

✗

Later.

The face in the mirror is a silent scream. Suck my dick. You're not going near the Hardware Store. I face my face down. Lots of labored mouth breathing. Skin with no skin tones. I breathe into a paper bag. The eyes in the mirror tell me you'll recover. Give it time. All will be normal . . . in time.

In the meantime.

I drop myself off at the Hardware Store like a kid getting dropped off at school.

✗

Harold's thrice-divorced father stands outside the store. Feet apart, palms pressed on the ebony handle of the big black English umbrella, the kind Americans like to think of as the umbrella no elderly English gent would leave home without. He could be getting ready to take a golf swing. Batting practice. The umbrella could be a walking stick. A prop. His umbrella could be for rain.

It's not raining.

No sign of rain.

Rain is not in the forecast.

He gives me the look striking hotel employees give scabs. "I'm speaking as an absent parent. A father on years of inactive duty. A patriot all the same. Go away."

I stand my ground.

My eyes on the umbrella. Would a thrice-divorced father whose son filed. First. poke a woman who filed after innumerable delays, if she didn't go away, yesterday not being soon enough?

He thumps the sidewalk.

"I believe the part about you and Harold meeting by happenstance. I believe an elitist attaché case has it all over a non-elitist attaché case. I believe my son when he tells me you've inquired as to his well-being."

Everybody believes me.

Do I believe me?

Jabbing. The sidewalk would splinter before that umbrella chipped a single tooth. "Even if he does answer you in full, you mustn't assume the same will go for you. You're marital history. A man doesn't have to ask the time of day of his marital history."

That, I believe, is not written in stone.

Sam bids me good day. My lap's out. But not for blood. A stick-out-your-tongue out. My lap has never been the cause of anything deep-seated. When seats are available I look like everyone else. If Sam had turned he wouldn't have caught me. I hiked up. I wouldn't give him the satisfaction.

My lap is as thick-skinned as I am.

✗

The moment I impact the chair opposite Harold I'm at liberty to rearrange myself. Cross my legs, fold my hands in my lap, rest the Claiborne in my lap, make any casual little gesture that the person sitting across from me may think random but is actually a ruse to set tone. Given the fact that poorly set tones between people refer to things not sitting well, how one is perceived sitting across from someone either tones up the tone or depresses it further. Mothers are always after their daughters not to sit with legs apart. If one's chair deportment were totally unrelated to tone and tone unrelated to things sitting well or unwell, a lot more daughters would spread their legs when they sit.

Harold is the victim of a ruse.

As I see it, the woman who did not file. First. sits like she's killing time.

✗

I do not how-are-you.

Something that goes without saying is when everybody has figured it out. Do something often enough or ask something often enough, people just assume here-we-go-again. Harold knows what I want to know.

✗

Harold rubs the bald spot on the back of his head. ". . . a game of blink." How unlike Harold, the man who filed. First. not to start at first things first. "She said she was pregnant. She didn't blink. I didn't blink. She said it was mine. She didn't blink. I didn't blink. She said she was keeping it."

Binge blinking.

Eyes doing the Mexican hat dance.

Harold's eyes are high kickers.

"Her lids didn't budge. She had eye movement, her eyes weren't stationary, but no eye was batting. Without her canopies moving, her eyes had that stitched open carp look. Her eyelids were pulled back like the tops of convertibles. Like blinds that wouldn't draw."

Good-bye Sweden.

Hello wrinkles.

If Sweden—a country with no lines from nose to mouth (WW2, on paper, Sweden isn't batty) were to do what Harold was doing with his eyes—I would jump all over its neutrality.

Harold's eyes, cockeyed.

"It was like waiting at a corner for a traffic light. Only the light never went from red to green. If mankind weren't meant to duck for cover, we'd all be born without lids. Not once have I ever treated anyone in an unblinking fashion."

That last statement, revisionist history.

Listen to yourself, Harold.

"I've always slammed lids. First chance I get, I get the drop on them. I would never neglect anyone by not coming down hard. Just like that."

Your brain is waterlogged, Harold.

Get a grip.

Harold opens the Cross. He extracts a book. No need to guess the title or author. The book's the last word on the one issue above all other issues that breaks new ground. The issue that one man has gained international prominence for fishing around in.

The name on the binding confirms it.

Dr. Spock.

✗

A first for the man who filed. First. He's with child.

And I'm not.

A first for the man who filed. First. He's monumentally, unusually wired.

And I'm not knocking it.

A first for the man who filed. First. He's pregnant.

But not by me.

Citing history: Consider geological history. Rocks give evidence of what went before. Confining geological history only to rocks belies the basic premise of geology. Geology examines surfaces. Each and every surface has a history.

So it follows.

Aptly so.

My lap's a geological treasure.

My geological treasure misses the cat more than Harold's cock. And that's only the tip of the strata. The cat stuck by my lap. Read my lodestone: Harold is only a scratch on the surface, the cat covers the surface. Geologically, the cat is the bigger event.

Rocks don't lie.

Citing history, you cite human behavior.

People lie.

✗

Incoming message from my forehead: Proceed to the bistro on Forty-eighth and Ninth Avenue.

At this moment, no better moment to haul anchor.

Harold's going to be a mommie.

And I'm not.

✗

Almost out the door . . .

I'm all for being helped across the street. In her zealousness to help me, somehow the school crossing guard's discovered my whereabouts.

"Tell me how you did it, are you psychic or something?"

She laughs.

"I came in to buy masking tape."

My turn to guide her. Follow me. I pick the tape out. I offer to pay. She accuses me of bribing her. She's right.

"A woman brushed past me earlier today. Something about her walk, you couldn't miss the—"

"The welfare of all pedestrians is my paramount concern. You say she brushed by you; did she make a threatening gesture?"

"No threatening gesture, I'd tell you if she had. She hopped. Can you put me in touch with a rabbit?"

I thought she'd say no outright.

"We'll cross that street when we come to it."

✗

The bistro on Forty-eighth and Ninth, we both hop to it.

✗

If you discount the neon, the garbage cans in front, the sign that says NO SOLICITATION, it looks like a French chalet. It feels like the provinces. Country simplicity. The smell of onion soup isn't Campbell's. Fresh flowers on every table. The birds in the cages are real. The back of the bistro is not so far back I can't see it from the front.

Barry waves at me.

Score another one for the paws.

48

He may not be himself . . . the loss of Betty, a marriage of long duration . . . the Fling going on his second year (who is in a position to know) swears Barry never flung it around with anyone other than Betty. I turn to the school crossing guard to warn her.

No school crossing guard.

The story of my life.

She filed. First.

Barry offers me a chair. Very wooden, very imitation Shaker. Barry selects wine. Very chalice. Barry is wearing a somber suit with a somber necktie. His eyebrows are furry caterpillars. They meet in the middle. His face, a jowl's paradise. His jowls hang like earlobes, you want to reach out and flick—and count the swings his jowls make before coming to a rest. Like skimming pebbles across a lake.

Barry's eyes are corpse grey.

His lap is in full view. He's sitting off to one side. Away from the table. Even to someone not especially lap sensitive, the lap he's sporting would be noticeable. In grief, some laps go out of their minds with grief. Geology is strata. Laps are geological. Strata is not impervious. Stress changes terrain. A trauma to any layer of strata hastens decomposition of layers. What used to be buried in a lap basin can suddenly surface. Mobility through layers is an ecological fact.

The focal point of Barry's lap is picket fence up. Out of respect for his bereavement, I do not mention to Barry that his loin is in steep exclamation. All through the baked clams, the Caesar salad and the chalice wine, his widowed willy is a stake.

"I just don't know what will become of me without Betty. She's irreplaceable. I'm going to set up a memorial fund in her honor."

I tuck my legs under.

The penis begins a hula-hoop dance. Many species, not just the penis, test their equipment. Some tests their wings. Some test the mike. The hula-hoop dance is like a belly dance without the belly. For a penis Barry's age—late fifties—spry is the word that comes to mind. Calisthenics like this are analogous. Shell-shocked tourists thawing out can be observed wiggling. Tourists and non-tourists alike do the Bus stop. They bounce in order not to chill while waiting for their ride. Movement is so universal it would be as unrealistic of me to expect Barry's sexual organ not to twang as it would for me to expect my lap to be frigid.

His willy is smirking.

Out of respect for his bereavement, in which he is coming on to me, I do not tell him to wipe the Peter Jennings Pepsodent smirk off his prick.

I stand.

I do not kick my chair over backing away. Backing away, I say I have a hunch my longevity friend Susan is waiting for me. (She is, I'll bet my forehead on it.)

"We were so close. I'm lost without Betty." His jowls shaking, his penis tipping its cap. His eyebrows humping each other.

He looks like a one-man band.

"You'll recover, Barry. Give it time. Probably what you're feeling is the strata of different layers. How those layers stack up . . . the momentum, rising to the surface, settling . . . in the process . . . a whole bunch of dirt that never had its moment under blue sky is suddenly topsoil."

He digests this.

"Is Susan single?"

✗

I call Susan on a pay phone to see if she really is waiting for me. Anybody can slip up, even psychic paw prints. This is not some Aesop fable, this is life.

"As a matter of fact, I wasn't even thinking of you, but when the phone rang, I had a feeling it might be you. In your frame of mind, if I were you, I'd want to be in proximity to frames on higher planes."

Susan is my longevity friend.

Once you get over how she says what she says, you understand she wouldn't be saying it if she didn't want you to better yourself. Be as good as you can be but maybe not quite as good as she.

✗

It's just the three of us.

Susan's street is tree-lined.

Patches in the lead. Susan and I try to keep up. The look he throws us every time we say Whoa says Who put you two in charge? His leash is one of those permissive ones, the reels that pull rank reluctantly. Liberal leashes. Democracy at the fire hydrant level. A dog gets to vote on matters like where and when to wee-wee, whom to sniff, to cop a feel from, whom to play hard-to-get with, whom to roll over for. To my knowledge, no consumma-

tion has ever occurred between leashed dogs. Even the more in-
dulgent owners set aesthetic limits on what goes on in public. Urination and defecation, fine. Good clean fucks, not so fine. Good
clean fucks are nowhere as sanitary as urination and defecation.

The air quality feels fine to me.

Not to Susan.

"The City always tries to get the better of me. Some days it's a
battle not to let the air quality snap my frame of mind. But you
have to allow for some bending. Better a bend than a crack in the
frame. Really supple frames bend over backwards but that's years
ahead of me."

I know what's coming.

One hand to her face, tracing the flight patterns that eyeglasses
would follow. Making the motions of fitting glasses to her face.
With her bowl haircut and uncluttered dish round face, she could
be sketched by a child. Her grin is pumpkin. In its natural state,
the corners of her mouth are always upturned. More so when she's
completed a change of frame. "I am now of the frame of mind
where the air is a feast for the eyes. Let the City dictate to you in
the smallest way, you have one less roadblock to put up when it
makes a pass for your pussy."

I was hacked by an urban jackrabbit.

The City is spooky.

You won't find me defending the City.

Her ability to adjust her frame is optometrical. A knack you
have to have the knack for. A positive frame of mind is positively
better than a negative frame. I take a few stabs at positive thinking.

"My life is blessed." Good opening, upbeat. "The Fling can't
keep his hands off me. I relish handing over his hard-ons like I'm
in a soup kitchen." Sounds rosy. This is fall. Can't frames turn over
a new leaf? "The real bonus is I get to play character roles. I get to
make myself up as I go along. Even if the sex is so-so, even if the
sex is substandard, even if he flops, there's theatrics."

Patches tugs the leash.

Hurry, light's changing.

"My life is blessed." Good opening line, stick with it. "Gerald's
nose isn't flaccid. He shoves it up me." Balance out the positive.
Don't sound like a loser. Don't sound like the plane you're on is
space cadet. Be aware of basic hygiene. "I mouthwash down there
with Listerine."

Patches finds a tree.

Patches spray paints the tree.

"My life is blessed." Repetitive but not to excess. Blessed has a certain ring. "I'm looking at walls a whole new way. There may by untapped reserves of men in plaster."

Avoid the Pepsi can.

Patches shepherding us.

"As you know, my life is blessed. I'm blessed with insight into my life. Jane Samuels is blessed to be delivered from the man who filed. First. And is pregnant. First."

Dear longevity Susan breaks stride.

"You'll recover. Don't let the City use this baby to gain a foothold with you. I can't tell what strategy specifically the City will use. But with Harold's baby on the way, you might want to strangle Harold, which signifies that your moral fiber is owned and operated by the City of New York."

I reassure her.

"Jane Samuels is composed and reposed. An impartial observer. Strangling Harold would negate the findings."

She doesn't buy it.

I continue to sell it.

"Nauticals are all wet. Big fish eat little fish. Harold could be shipwrecked. Through no word or deed of my own, he could drown at sea."

Her face darkens.

Dear Susan, struggling.

An internal tug of war, Susan's frames dueling for her thoughts. "Better yet," Susan smiling the smile of resolution, "the mother of his child could file on him. First."

✗

Thanks to Susan, I put to port in Hardware . . . in a better frame of mind.

✗

Sire Harold is in black tie. Sire Harold is standing. Sire Harold doesn't want his pants to crease him. His blinkers are on and off like emergency lights. Lids doing the can-can. Sire Harold speaks. "My duty is clear. I came, I sired. Now I'm going to—"

We both look at the old lady.

Riffling bins like a raccoon in a dumpster, riffling the way I do sales tables of interracial shoes. A racket. Fingers to my lips. Hush. Can't you tell when someone's making an unusually monumental announcement that could have far-ranging repercussions ranging from drowning at sea to the mother of a child filing. First.

Old ladies won't be shushed.

"People make heirs. They do their duty. You can't sit there and tell me you don't have the slightest inkling?"

Harold comes to my defense.

"Wife number one is a history teacher, well-versed in kings and queens who were joined in holy matrimony to produce an heir. Wife number one is seeped in history. She knows how crucial heirs are to the succession of the throne. Wife number one has at her fingertips the names of numerous individuals, on a first-name basis, who got hitched when they found out they were going to be daddies."

Old ladies . . .

They have answers for everything.

"Is she number one or two?"

I don't stay.

Places to go, people to see.

Wife number one finds a phone.

✗

The break I've been waiting for. Lady with sagging tits is in such sagging spirits she can't bring herself to see her therapist.

The Fling says be quick.

I am a commando. Liz Claiborne slung over like a canteen. Rush hour. The pavement swarms with native life. Throngs of people whose to and fro is to my to and fro what black is to white.

I plow through.

My BVDs give me jock itch.

✗

The doctor will see you now.

In the waiting room, even an empty one, Nate observes the proprieties. Walls have ears, rumor's going around they have cocks. He shuts the door. The inner sanctum is ours.

I yank the gerbil.

The gerbil shrivels in my hand. I jam the gerbil in my ear. The gerbil retracts. The shrink of the gerbil is more than the shrink of

100 percent cotton in a hot water wash. I bathe the gerbil in the folds of my tongue. Paydirt. From gerbil to sausage. I transfer the sausage to my garden apartment. Ransack me, I say.

Surprise, surprise.

The sausage cancels.

I get on the public address system. "Spermatozoa report for siphoning. This is a contractual violation."

Joystick zipped up.

"Let that be a lesson to you." Nate's pants are too loose for me to follow the status of the pretzel. When it went in it was hard. A solid piece of raw meat. The veins in its neck protruding. "Semen isn't pancake syrup," Nate says.

I could debate that.

I don't.

"I detect hostility."

"You had lunch with Barry. Was it intimate? I need to hear from you. Are you attracted to his mind?"

I tell him the truth.

"The rabbit paw prints on my forehead sent a message to my brain. Proceed to the bistro on Forty-eighth and Ninth. I didn't know ahead of time Barry would be there. He took his dick out. Major disturbances in his strata. Laps are hardest hit. I am not attracted to his mind."

A look.

"But you spoke to him, you were willing to sit down with Barry and absorb his innermost thoughts."

My turn to look.

"I thought we settled this."

"Now it's unsettled. Let that be a lesson to you."

It is.

Some psychiatrists will use sex to try and lure you into their innermost thoughts.

✗

The Fling going on his second year gives me a crushed look. We part without another word.

✗

He's next. The patient in the waiting room rubs himself against the cordless GE vacuum cleaner. Poor guy. If he'd only stop thinking of his liquid contents as pancake syrup—sometimes it pours, sometimes the spermatozoa cancel—he'd never experience the disappointment of someone who thinks you've got to dot every i.

✗

My destination isn't the Hardware Store. It's the block of the Hardware Store. I want to see if I can walk by. Somewhere out there, there's got to be a finish line.

✗

The entrance is heavily guarded. Another in-law. A different one this time. Harold's sister doesn't have an umbrella. She doesn't wear army clothes. The sister of the man who filed. First. then propagated. First. then set a date. First. isn't like her family at all. Her face is tissue paper after you've ripped the package. She lets everyone enter but me. Me she puts her arm around. "I believe"—they all start out saying I believe, I believe people with beliefs are not always united in their beliefs—"the part about Harold's impregnating someone. I support his decision to legitimize the issue. I don't find your presence incredulous at all. What I find incredulous is that so few of us do what you're doing."

She accompanies me down the block, nudging me along. I try doubling back. She blocks.

". . . incredulous that more people don't take time out to exhume the remains of deceased relationships, and throw more good years after bad. You're sacrificing time that could be better spent reading."

Shoving me gently home.

✗

I do so read.

Bedtime . . .

On my night table, a groaning stack of books. On me, a flannel nightshirt. Knee socks. Panties as modest as bloomers. The night table, three hundred pages lighter. The reader, three hundred pages heavier. Like an infant sucking down formula, the written word is my sleeping draught. My eyes start to lose their place.

Movement on the wall behind me.

Eyes turning with my head.

Above the headboard, over my right shoulder, from the interior of the wall . . . the pop of cock. Out to there. Walk the plank out. A ledge. A rolling pin. A pole for vaulting.

I read on subways.

I am the kind of reader who can have things going on around her and still immerse herself in a book. I have the discipline to rise above distractions. I do not have an attention disorder; if I am distracted, the book is not put aside. The book is a priority.

I continue to read.

Consider the alternatives and you will understand why: Close the book, end up talking to cock in walls. Talk to cock in walls, why not climb the walls? Start to climb cock in the wall you end up above sea level.

Climbing is precarious.

Elevation sickness.

Pussies who climb trees sometimes find themselves stranded. Footholds are tricky. Balance can be lost. High perches mean high stakes.

I turn the page.

The man in the wall (cock 'n' all) reads over my shoulder.

✗

Morning.

Right where it was. The book still propped on my knees. The wall behind me sealed lips. No tell-tale slits. Was the cock in the wall pure visitation? Now that I have hunches, can visitations be far behind?

Walls are said to have ears.

And eyes.

Are genitalia any more far-fetched?

Walls have been coming into their own for as long as there have been walls to listen through. Walls stand up for themselves. Walls stand by each other. Walls are the only things we've got between us and all of next door. People run into walls all the time. Is there anyone who hasn't drawn a blank wall or been a wallflower? Walls have a literary tradition. Some of our most astute thinkers see writing on the wall.

Positive thinking: End on a positive note.

That cock was no gerbil.

My life is blessed.

✗

I work around my face. Tiptoeing. Gingerly brushing my locks that will one day be a vision of cascading waist-length hair. Periodic trims to keep them fuller as they blossom with the vigor of not so firm young saplings. My household plants spurt when they get their egos stroked. My hair hears too; a single misplaced word, from the roots up, my hair is kelp. Talking my hair into cooperating is like talking to the wall. I encourage my face to sleep in. It's not just beauty rest. Never again to be what once she was, I don't need my face rubbed in it. Bathroom lights on dim. Averting my eyes. Slap the cream on. Somebody hand me Crayolas. You call that hair, it's a lynch mob.

I am growing old gracefully.

✗

No end to what I could accomplish if I stayed home.

Mismatched socks, well-worn bras, bathing suits, tops too big, bottoms too small . . . dust the fireplace (unlit since 1884), scrub the bathtub rings, no end to what's fallen on hard times. Stomach lifts, leg lifts, neck rolls . . . what I have here is a dilemma.

Home or hardware?

✗

No contest.

✗

It's raining.

New York City's colors don't streak.

But vision smears.

Maybe what I think I see in front of the Hardware Store isn't a trio of former in-laws at all.

✗

"This is your last warning." Sam's umbrella a dark parachute. Every word he says sounds underlined. "If you go in there now, it's out of my hands. The deeper you go, the deeper you are."

He's right, of course.

Harold's mother wears a khaki poncho, a rubber sheet she's cut armholes in. Pioneer stock. This woman could live off the land. "Just like my daughter. No heart. You make issues where there are none."

Mostly, she's not off base.

The cracked glass face of Harold's sister—more lines than tree bark—is a warning to all faces, skin is only skin deep, but treat skin as if it were a bargaining chip. "Incredible how the emphasis changes in the private sector. National disasters, plane crashes, gas explosions. We launch extensive investigations. Great events require endless analysis. But hardly anyone I know would have your perseverance. If not for people like you, dead issues would fall into oblivion."

Lay off, is what she means.

"Move aside. Don't make me hurt you."

Fuck off, is what I mean.

The trio parts. On their side, might.

On my side, lynch mob hair.

✗

Trios have a history.

The Three Musketeers, a trio of adventurers.

The witches of *Macbeth*, a trio of shrews.

Butcher, baker and candlestick maker, comic relief in three.

Three strikes you're out.

And my favorite trio: Three easy steps.

Third step, the finish line.

✗

Harold is conferring with the photographer. Same guy for wife-to-be number two. I'd use him again. He made me look interesting at a time when my face was not lived in. "Avoid stagey," Harold tells the photographer. "You've been to hospital emergency rooms. The pictures should capture the moment. Be photo-journalistic. Exclude anyone with food in their mouths."

Not a glimmer of recognition.

The photographer doesn't recall who I used to be. A tribute to how interesting my face has become. The mouth thicker around the waist. Scrambled egg skin. The chin metamorphosing into I-don't-know-what.

58

Into the Cross he goes.

The sound is laundry chute.

Harold and I sit in our respective seats. He lands. First. His lids fluttering like kite tails in the wind. Adam's apple doing what his lids are doing. He pulls on one ear. Tweaking. When I depress my inner thighs like that I get spud skin.

"How are—"

"We never made that much eye contact to begin with. It's only of late, after this thing's caught my eye, that the thing with her eyes really registered. You'd think by now she'd react. She's impassive. But is she genuinely nonplussed? Can lids hold out forever? Is she trying to tell me she's going into this with both eyes open? Or is she taking a good long hard look? Pulling the lid back on every can of worms, is that the message behind the lids? Startled? Wide-eyed innocence or open-eyed caution?"

My hands are Friar Tucked.

Go on, my son.

Tell the Father more.

"The issue is simple." Harold makes a cradle with his arms. "Central to the issue is continuity. I've never felt this strong a link to history." His lids going at it like they're being paid overtime. "Setting sail now, I'd be missing the boat entirely. The skipper welcomes her aboard. My ship is her ship. She can be second in command."

Adventures on the high seas . . .

Voyages into the unknown . . .

Will there be sea battles? Will someone rock the boat?

What's a sea yarn without a good old-fashioned sea monster?

Nauticals are all wet.

But they've stood the test of time.

✗

My former in-laws have dispersed. I disperse with even greater haste than I arrived. The day previous to that fateful fourth eve of, my longevity friend Susan and her dear dog Patches handpicked a guy with an exemplary frame of mind, plucked him right out of the vet's office. To my inquiry— what makes him so exemplary?— I expected a rundown of his fine upstanding qualities.

"Money," Susan said.

Her frame on a higher plane. But sometimes, not often, my longevity friend Susan is a City girl. It won't hurt for me to meet him.

You never know. Two people hit it off . . .
One of these falls, I'll fall in love.

✗

Or should I remain at my post? The methodology of field research has been handed down from in-the-field anthropologists. On-site observations give you a firsthand knowledge of dynamics. Jane's way is my way. That other Jane, Jane Goodall. Her fervor for the chimps of Gombé is legendary. Jane Goodall never shirked her responsibilities. Jane Goodall would not approve of my frequent arrivals and departures. Jane stayed at her post.

✗

One of these falls, love's bound to fall into my lap. Fall: The question on the lips of every leaf: Who is going to break my fall?

✗

It's a fifteen-minute walk. Do I live in perpetual fear of being set upon by another rabbit? On the contrary, I'm looking forward to the next encounter. I'm more fearful of never pinning down the answers. Rabbits could do for me what chimps did for Jane Goodall. A place in history.

✗

One week ago (the day before the eve of, the day that will live in infamy) notification was sent to Bill Mool. As to time, as to place, as to my description in general and specifically. A forty-three-year-old redhead, mole on my right cheek, look for suede boots, the color of my gloves will be burgundy. Any confusion in recognizing who I am, I will answer to my name. Word came back through our liaison, Susan Gold. Could I make it Tuesday instead of Wednesday, three instead of two, someplace closer to the East Side than the West—a sick dog at home—but if I couldn't make it Tuesday instead of Wednesday, could I do Thursday instead, three-ish or four-ish, my choice, four would put us closer to five (a sick and hungry dog at home) so would I mind very much between three and four, at the latest three fifteen, but if I couldn't do Thursday at no later than quarter past three, what do I suggest?

60

Bill Mool is open to suggestions.

✗

Sitting on a bar stool, closest to the door, the agreed upon time. Thursday at three fifteen. I order a diet something-or-other. A hand taps my shoulder. I turn.

"Are you Jane Samuels?"

"Bill Mool?"

"Bill sent me."

"I thought you were Bill."

"We're the same coloring."

"Bill can't make it?"

"Could you do next week, any day's good, Monday before eleven, Tuesday, early evening. Wednesday through Sunday, he could work you in, you wouldn't know you were being worked in, Bill would never let on, I shouldn't have said worked in, my apologies to you, forget I ever said worked in, it was said to me in complete confidence."

His tongue is hyperactive, one of those tongues that prowl all day, sleep all night. Moisture on the lips like when you forget to turn the bathroom taps off. One should never judge a man by his friends' tongues.

"I'm booked solid."

"He'll be sorry to hear that."

"I'm sorry he'll be sorry. I'm not Jane, that other Jane. I don't have her stamina. She didn't have to contend with a cock in the wall, a Fling who up to now got laid without innermost thoughts, an engorged nose—who knows what you can catch from snot—a widower with designs on anything that moves, and a friend on another plane. Tell Bill it's fall. On the lips of every leaf: Don't make me fall down laughing."

I am blessed.

He says OK.

✗

Thunderclaps.

My forehead is clanging pots and pans.

Read my paw: Scoot home.

My lap must know something I don't.

Already it's spreading its legs.

61

Stage presence, electroaffinity, call it what you will. Gerald's nose is a Steinway. A signature piece. There's no way anyone can get past those vibes. What big boobs do for a woman, his nose does for him. And then some.

His nose is monolithic.

That's why Alex the doorman drops his nose to his chest. Two male noses, one's a cheesy texture, citrus rather than cucumber, the other a powerhouse banana. Guess whose nose is going to feel impotent?

We wait for the stalled elevators.

Finally one takes pity on us.

Out steps a woman with red hair, red that hollers red. Curls so big and zesty they could factory-pack fragile glass in them. She takes one look at Gerald's nose and reverses direction. She presses our floor for us. The doors close. The elevator stops at our floor. The doors open.

We are detained.

She grabs Gerald's nose. She inserts Gerald's nose into her bellybutton. She comes in loud racking sobs.

How awful for Gerald.

Wearing your sex on your face must be as damning as wearing your heart on your sleeve.

To bed, to bed.

My bed is a sleek four-poster sports model. The sheets are clean. I don't change the scatter rugs after they've done mattress duty but without exception, sheets, like milk, turn sour. I kiss Gerald's mouth, more out of duty than lip lust. I lay him out like a swatch of fabric. My breasts feather-brushing his chest, my nipples look like they're dancing on their toes. I sit astride one of his legs, moving myself back and forth. I gently take his nose in my hands. The rhythm of my hands on his nose matches my rock. His nose feels like it's running a fever, it thrashes in my hands. He eases me on my back. Be still, he says. Tracing my contours. The touch of his nose, making me wet. And him larger. Tie three penises together, that should give you some idea.

It is time.

It's like being a virgin all over again. We fit, tight enough for us both to gasp, not so tight I rip. His whole head is engaged in copulation, his tongue pitches in too, his eyes coordinating the entire landing operation.

I am taken over.

I come in no racking sobs.

✗

"You don't feel disgusted by nose fucking?" Both of us are spent. Pillow talk. "You don't feel you're missing out? You don't feel you're not getting what's coming to you? I wasn't too rough? You wouldn't be the first to come all over my nose and have second thoughts. Think about it. A nose up your keyhole. After a while, the novelty might wear off."

He's done his homework.

Targeting a group.

Asking the toughies.

"I am having second thoughts, but not for the reasons you think. Snot makes me uneasy. Nasal mucous is a body fluid. Fluids should be contained."

Inhalations, no racking anything. His nose doesn't have to be sent from the room, we can talk nose in front of the nose.

I continue.

"You need to rig up some sort of condom."

"What else?"

"Your nose is oily. Is it a pore problem?"

His pants are on the floor. He digs around in his pockets, holds a tube up, squeezes a bit on my finger, jelly, the feel of Vaseline.

"I lost joint custody. My joints have never recovered."

Lubricants for his nose . . .

Kids get under your skin.

Kids can make or break joints.

It only validates everything I've said all along. The man who filed. First. is over a barrel.

✗

Gerald leaves.

I shower, I scour.

You cannot be a researcher and not have a love of orderliness. Things in their place. Books on bookshelves, coins in the coin banks, plants watered. The tidy life. The last two years have been

63

tidier than the two years previous. People speak of extended winters, I speak of falls that extended from winter to winter. Like a massive accumulation of snow, the ice age just seemed to go on and on. Socks and bras and bathing suits shouldn't even be a footnote to history. In my life, they are cardinal. We all go back a ways. They are companions. Some going on seventeen, not counting the three years we lived together and the one we corresponded. My socks and bras and bathing suits have seen it all. Years with Harold, years without him. They are vintage. They've got mileage on them. They are relics.

Relics have history.

Parting with hundreds of mismatched socks, threadbare bras, faded and worn bathing suits, would be like throwing away old love letters from the passion years. New socks are important. New bras are vital.

A new bathing suit is a must.

But they can never replace the ones that went before.

Oh Suki. What's keeping you?

✗

The phone. Is that Suki?

I pick up. Not even close.

"Betty's death just rips me apart." Barry doesn't sound ripped apart. Maybe he's putting up a front. People have different ways of mourning. Sometimes they disguise their grief so well they fool themselves.

"Is there anything you need?"

"Do you know a good seamstress? I can't figure it out. All my pants need mending." Genuine bewilderment in his voice. He really doesn't know what's been happening down under, how his loins are kicking up their feet.

I recommend a good shoemaker too.

A penis is like a submarine in international waters. It can break the surface anywhere.

The bereaved family wants to thank me in person for my fruit basket. I can't tell Barry I'll think it over. I tell him, when the moment's ripe.

✗

My love of clothes is for their historical value. A wardrobe is

64

like a family album. Cloth documents what you wore at the time. Clothes are cloth diaries. My three navy suits have been gone for one whole day. I depart for the dry cleaners.

✗

The sign in front says under new management.

New management asks for my yellow ticket.

I present my yellow ticket to new management. The man is in his undershirt. He has a gold front tooth. It is his only adornment. (I don't count religious medals.) He reads my slip with a squint. The religious medals clink. Minutes pass.

He's still reading. He trashes the paper.

"Your papers are not in order."

"My papers are in order."

"Your papers are not in order."

I try a different tact. The proprietor I am told is not available. He tries a different tact: "Through no word or deed on anyone's part, these things just happen. Clothes just ship out. That's why it's smart to keep extras, so you don't depend on one particular item." The gold tooth has gone neon. The man is filamented. "Clothes are blind items. You spare no expense, you hang them on padded hangers, you remove the plastic bag so the fabric doesn't asphyxiate, then after a season, something's gone out of how you hang together. Through no word or deed on your part, the fit's history."

Where have I heard this before?

Cut off points . . . shipping out . . . gone to sea. Clothes too.

My navy suits filing. First.

✗

Which brings me right back to Harold.

✗

And on a direct intercept course with the school crossing guard.

✗

"The light system has kinks." She has braces on her teeth. Every time she opens her mouth, I think of metal guard railings on windows.

"You've told me that already."

"It bears retelling."

(We're not on a corner. We're in the middle of a block one block from the cleaners.)

"Are you off duty?"

"I'm never off duty. Wherever I go I pass the word. Kinks in the system. We try to compensate. We keep backup plans. And backups for the backups."

"Do you tell this to the rabbits?"

"I do."

✗

I do not doubt her for an instant.

✗

I do not see how I've stayed away this long.

✗

The Hardware Store has a new look. Paddington bears. Windup toys. A bassinet. What started out as space between the aisles is now hearth and home. A cozy den, tapestries and inkwells, an entire wall in the family room is devoted to home entertainment. The hardware is still visible. It's virtually impossible to distinguish which is backdrop. Two places at once. Shoppers don't seem to know what they're maneuvering around is a domestic scene.

Cross is over the top.

Cross should be running the country.

Harold is knitting. Yellow and green yarn for when you don't know the sex. Fingers flying. He isn't even looking down at the pedals. I can see he's dropping stitches. That other Jane, Jane Goodall would note it. The chimp dropped stitches, his eyes were agitated, one foot kept up a constant tap.

"She hasn't raised so much as a brow. Leaves everything up to me. Is it because we see eye to eye? Or is there more here than meets the eye? Whatever it takes to flick her lid. Bring her lids crashing down around her. Make her good and batty. Put her on the same blink she's put me on."

Goodall kept dossiers on chimps.

She observed kinship groups. The jockeying for position. Dominance. How vital it is for chimps of lesser standing to form an alliance with the chimp who wears the pants. Jane Goodall had a keen interest in child-rearing. I share her interests. Parental responsibilities, the duties of each parent, how the parents interact.

"How are you really?"

"She's not going to make me history."

✗

The bounce of my step—all the way home—intoxicated.

✗

Alex the doorman looks like a wall walked into him. The nose vicinity. The center of his face is a rampart. A fortification. On his nose, a turban of gauze. Very Foreign Legionnaire. My eyes are fixed on it. Total lock-in like I do with bugs to see if they're taking up permanent residence. I reach out, a gesture of sympathy.

My hand is knocked away.

The same sex offender who accosted Gerald's nose in the elevator. Now she's picking on me. Her eyes are cocked. Her buxom curls are heaving breasts. She walks over to Alex. She kisses him on the nose. Alex nods, the sight of his nose in motion sets her in motion.

Legs parting for a breeze.

Her pelvic rubs his pelvic.

"Hey sister," I guess she means me, "leave some for the rest of us."

It all makes sense.

If a guy's going to pack a rod, big barrels are better than pea-shooters. Anyone who's ever tried to put on or take off a few inches will tell you every inch counts. Nose augmentation does for a nose what steroids do for biceps. The bigger the nose, the further the reach, the further the reach—as bears with a sweet tooth have always known—the closer you get to the honeypot.

She advances on me.

I advance backwards.

She keeps coming. Unbuttoning her trench. Ninja legs. Black nylons. Breast plates. The trench is lined in bordello red satin. Her visuals are meat eaters. I stop moving. I have it on the highest authority, running away from women will make women give chase.

The sound of cavalry.

67

At least it's a distraction.

A delivery boy enters, carrying clothes in a body bag, asking for Jane Samuels. I never doubted it for an instant. My papers were in order. The reunion would have been consummated if Alex's consort didn't throw her arm turnstile out, thereby separating me from my clothes.

A hostage situation.

It's up to me.

"Not if he were the last nose on earth would I saddle his nose. I would never fraternize with Alex's nose. You couldn't pay me enough. I wouldn't wipe my ass with his nose." English. Plainspoken. Or am I saying something incomprehensible? Words she could never acclimate to as one might acclimate to snow country.

I wait for the turnstile to drop.

The turnstile doesn't drop.

The delivery boy leaves. People behaving like their papers are not in order, papers shredding into confetti, you don't want to be anywhere near. Alex pokes his nose in. Meddling. He runs interference with his nose. Slow striptease. The gauze begins to unravel.

Down goes the turnstile.

Up goes her skirt.

I run after the delivery boy. It takes more than a little doing till he slows down. As well it should. The typical bearer of an average-length nose won't go to any length to keep his nose out of other people's business. But to keep his nose out of harm's way, the typical bearer of an average nose will go to the ends of the earth.

Clothes and I return to the lobby.

Alex is face down.

In the best tradition of anvils, Alex's nose is forging away. Guess who on. He introduces us. Marilyn Beats is on her back. Her panties are down around her ankles. His nose is having sexual intercourse with Ms. Beats. She is focused. I've been there. Resounding blows. Bang, bang. Dicks jamming themselves into little sockets. Pleasure and pain. As much as I tell myself it's consensual—the hands clutching Alex's head are forcing him deeper down—still I wince.

She takes it for what it was.

A small humanitarian wince.

She says thanks.

Our language gap is bridged.

68

If only the elevators were this reasonable.

I catch up with them on the sixth floor.

✗

Thorough gynecological examination of my clothes shows no baggage damage. My garments go into the first available slot. A desegregated closet. At any given time, jeans hang with silks, silks with cottons, cottons with wools. Only polyester would find my closet intimidating. The one loner is my Special Occasion outfit. The dress with tags still on. Saved for something significant. Not to be squandered on cocktail parties. Or gallery openings. Proms, maybe.

A Marlene Dietrich number.

The dress waits. Off to one side of my closet, aloof, biding time. All dressed up and nowhere to go. I've played it by the book, hedging on heels. Convention has it, do not flaunt your stash. For special occasions, the heroine is supposed to rush into her closet screaming I don't have a damn thing to wear, tearing everything off the hangers, spending hours trying dresses on, dumping the rejects on the floor. No frock is good enough. The more sublime the occasion, the better the scene gets.

I don't want to miss my big scene.

Having the dress I hedge on heels.

I look, I don't buy.

In all honesty, it's easy to hedge on heels.

Heels are a pain.

They pinch at the ball.

The soles are thin.

Seams rub.

Walking hurts.

If the right heels came along, would I defy convention? The well-heeled do.

There's a class distinction in conventions. The well-heeled keep wine cellars of drop-dead heels in reserve. It doesn't seem to hurt their prospects any. They are swamped with Special Occasions. But what's conventional for the well-heeled is unconventional for the rest of us. What I said, for the rest of us, still goes.

Save yourself for your big scene.

✗

The phone rings. A rap to the window. A tap to the door. I start for the door. The window castanets. I start for the window. The phone cries, Me first. I start for the phone. The taps to the door sound like the door is being kicked in.

My forehead is mum.

Behind the door, a voice. "Take the night off. It's Harold's baby shower. Think of all the reading you could get done."

Message on the answering machine:

"I'm issuing you a direct order. House arrest. Make no issues where there are none."

The window-tapper is gone. Just as well. Three times, overkill.

Harold's shower.

I'll have to think about it.

I do think about it.

Heels are a pain.

I sit. An urchin chair. Adopted from the street like a stray. Identical to the color of Suki. Chocolaty. Not knowing where the chair's been, the company it's kept, its age or history, it's a safe bet every time I sit, I wonder. What does the chair know I don't? How did the chair keep landing on its feet? Next to the chair, the phone. An heirloom from the past. Black and white. Circa 1950. It rings in a Bronx accent. Whether or not I watch it, it rings. My hand ready to pick up on the third ring (never first). It won't ring on demand. It pretty much rings whenever it damn well pleases.

It's fall.

Who falls into what classification interests me. Phones that don't kiss ass fall under no one's spell.

✗

At nine, Nate calls.

"Are you alone? Nora's at the Doll Hospital learning how to patch things up."

"Where are you?"

"Phone booth on the corner."

I tell him give me a minute. Phone down, skirt off, silk blouse off. Camisole on. I douse my face in mineral water, the chin gets half a dozen point-blank. I smear my lipstick for that just-kissed slut look. My hair, between lives—kelp, prairie wheat in the dust bowl—gets fingered all over the place. I hold my stomach in, no change in complexion color. I breathe as if I'm natural. I alert Alex the doorman. He apologizes for Marilyn. She thinks his nose is the

70

last word on dicks. She's worried about rivals.

Men fall head over heels.

✗

A thorough examination of Nate—the bedroom lights are candlelight—shows no baggage damage. The Fling's ding has the flushed look of a child's cheeks after a tour of duty on the playground. His slack balls are taut. From door chimes to click-clacks. We give each other tongue lashings. His tongue, on a lesser scale, doing what Gerald's nose does on a panoramic scale. My tongue is a pit bull in his ear . . . a velvet glove on his gerbil.

Speaking of which . . .

. . . the gerbil is doing a swimmer's stroke to reach my sanctuary.

Speaking of which . . .

. . . my sanctuary is barricaded by my hand for good reason. Sex twice in one day, two different men, not being reason enough.

Speaking of reason . . . Nate is being unreasonable.

"Listen to just one of my innermost thoughts," Nate trying to make sex into something it's not. "I can talk and screw at the same time."

"My hand stays. Take your hand off mine."

"Minds like mine offer new vistas. Jokes that are really funny, knee-slappers, mind-bogglers, the things I could tell you about my childhood, starting with the womb, or we could start with my dreams and work from there."

"Tell it to your wife."

"She doesn't want to hear it either."

Jane Samuels has heart.

Let it never be said I won't fuck men who bore me, braggarts sure what they have to say for themselves is the last word, guys who call their minds Castle Milieu, stimulating conversation—only I'd have to drop everything—watering plants, sorting through socks, the mismatched pairs, the bras, frayed cup size thirty-four B, the bathing suits from the year one.

Jane Samuels has heart.

I mercy fuck.

But I stay clear of castles where men hold forth . . . unless, that is, they've filed on me. First.

Call it saving myself grief.

Call it jaded.

Call it time management.

"Do you want a professional opinion on why you don't want to spend time in a castle where wonders await you?"

"No."

Stalemate.

Which is broken when I get a wild craving for pancake syrup.

x

Nora is at the Doll Hospital learning how to patch things up. Nate wants to be home before her. The man who has said, more than once, women are too self-conscious about their bodies dresses with sleight-of-hand speed. A subway whoosh. So many loose folds to his clothes, in the event of an air disaster, he could parachute to the ground. Desert sheiks would take him for one of their own.

I do not read myself to sleep.

Tonight I'm history.

x

Every morning is a morning after. (Fall is one big morning after.)

Sluggish.

Overnight I lose my virility.

Eventually I come to life.

One lousy cell at a time.

Cells as surly as people who won't let you by no matter how many times you say excuse me. Resentful when you limit their caffeine. No cell of mine is a morning person. I've never known one to spring to life. I try breathing. First thing in the morning, cells hand-dipped in vats of oxygen.

They're terrified of what I'll do next.

My policy is to play fair. Hold my morning activity to a minimum. Ask nothing of my body I wouldn't ask of myself. Simplify morning life and you do what a good breakfast is supposed to do. Morning mulling is allowed. The perimeters are strict. Do not think about the quality of your life. That kind of thinking is for later.

For now, brevity.

I will shop for food.

I will Citibank.

Tonight I will silver screen.
Hardware . . . and what else?

✗

What else phones.

✗

What else is a who else.

Susan, my dearest longevity friend. My matchmaking friend. Plane on a higher plane. Susan's dog is alive and well, Susan was Lou's first wife, still is Lou's wife. Lou has not filed on Susan, the child they are not having is the child they are not having . . . together.

"Did you two hit it off?"

"He was a no-show. A friend came instead."

"And?"

"He wanted to reschedule."

"And you fell for that? What he really wanted was his pal's opinion. Are her tits holding up? What's her skin resiliency rating—sun-ravaged, weather-beaten, creamy and whipped—are her bazookers holding up? You were screened. The City's Charter has codes. Under these codes are provisions. Those provisions cover blind-date subterfuge. The City will use any and all means to disrupt our lives. The City, as you well know, has outposts in the suburbs. Everywhere, the pace has picked up. Scandal, homicide, blind-date rescheduling, the City's got a hand in it."

Literary metaphor: The City as jungle.

Biblical precedent. The bashing of Sodom and Gomorrah.

"If you defend the City, it's the City putting words in your mouth."

I don't defend the City.

"My life is blessed. I have errands. A blessing to wander through fruits and veggies. A blessing to make withdrawals. Citibank is my bank of choice. Shall I call you back?"

No, she says.

Will I walk Patches, just this once?

I give her a City answer. "No."

She turns it into a yes.

"He'll be downstairs with Tony at four."

73

Susan will call right back and apologize. I know she will. The phone will ring momentarily. Susan will say, Never mind what I said, I've switched my frame, negative to positive, my fingers following the route eyeglasses follow. Amidst urban decay stands the last of the urban moralists.

She doesn't call.

I dress. Slipping out of my nightgown, slipping into a pinched-at-the-waist dress. My face and hair are disposed of. Lots of lipstick to ward off my chin. The Jane Samuels we all know and love. The one who hears the words on the lips of every fall leaf: In fall, the whole world falls into vaudeville routines.

✗

Alex's nose is flushed. Less afterglow than friction. Nasal fornication is like walking barefoot. It takes a while for the soles to toughen. Also for the nose to feel like part of your face. Till then you can't keep your hands off yourself.

I say good morning, Alex.

I keep going.

I don't get far.

Pointing to his chapped nose. "I ejaculate with my nose."

Pointing to his private parts too, "Two faucets. Double staying power."

"Good for you."

"Do you know what that really means?"

"You're a stud?"

"Better. I've finally found a woman who's made all the difference in the world."

"I have to go to the A&P."

His nose U-turns, Alex follows.

✗

. . . A&P and me.

The real reason isn't food. It's research. A&P carries people food and pet food. And people food that is not limited to people. I'm here to stake out the lettuce and carrots. I'm not prepared to wait hours, maybe it won't take hours. Maybe the A&P is a magnet for East Side bunnies. Though I've patronized this store for years, it wouldn't be the first or last time something's gone on behind my back. Harold filed. First. But in seventeen years, three, give or take, living together, one year of correspondence, a land developer can squeeze in lots of covert maiden voyages.

From behind me . . .

"Did the tomatoes live up to their reputation?"

My relationship with A&P's produce manager is long and . . . fruitful. He has a gift basket business on the side. His specialty is funerals.

"They tasted off the vine. Some people have a green thumb for flowers, you have it for produce. No matter if you don't grow them. You've got the eye for them."

Jack shows me around.

At carrots I say, "Your carrots are bulbous."

At lettuce I say, "Your lettuce heads are heady."

"We can't stock them fast enough. Best-sellers third week in a row."

He's old enough to be my father's older brother. I don't want to give him an adrenalin rush. How do you ask somebody if they've seen bunnies shopping at A&P without sounding like a fruit?

"Rabbits would kill for a taste of this. Whoever said rabbits are dumb bunnies didn't have the honor of being singled out—"

He Janes me.

"Jane, Jane, Jane."

"Jack, Jack, Jack."

"Jane."

"Jack."

"You're the second person today."

"I'm the second person what today?"

"That's told me how smart bunnies are."

"Braces on her teeth, freckled, yea high?"

"That's the one."

✗

Later, I'm going to look her up. Later, I'm going to corner the school crossing guard.

✗

In a way, all historians have an affinity for hardware stores. Anyone with a sense of history will gravitate toward extension cords. Extensions give us our bearings. Hierarchies, with their ranks and grades and divisions, are structured extensions. Extended families are loosely structured extensions. The past is an extension of the present. Extending that—the future too. Extending that—some would say you've overextended yourself. Bring on the finish lines, put an end to it, say some.

Hardware may come and go.

Extension debates . . .

Not so.

✗

The tempo of Harold's pace is shuffle. I sit first. It feels second. A waiting room kind of aimless scuff-the-feet walk. His turns have edge. A shuffle with a nervous tic. I sit on the tip of my seat.

"Finally wrung it out of her. The waiting period's over. Completely. In the initial stages I was wrapped up in how she put me on the blink, much more so than cigarettes, now there—when I almost couldn't take them or leave them, I was able to leave them, here it's a whole other sea. No one should have to go through a goddamn love affair. Father and seed. It's better I know now when I'm single. And it's better she knows now when she's single. Once she's married, she's given away her hand in marriage. She can't go around offering her hand in marriage."

Extensions . . .

One form or another.

How much will the man who filed. First. extend himself? Why does wife-to-be number two want to extend her hand in marriage after she's married? And lastly, if I may, wife number one would like to extend congratulations to wife-to-be number two on whatever she has in store for Harold.

✗

Owner sees me to the door. Owner is mountain man large. Owner, whose first and last name I don't recall is escorting me to the door because I had the audacity to call him over and ask him to look around and tell me what he sees.

He said screws.

He said lights.

He said extension cords.

He said a bassinet.

When he said bassinet I asked him if he had recently received a blow to the head. It was then that Owner escorted me to the door.

✗

Citibank tries harder.

There is no other bank where the automatic tellers have such a human touch. And what a touch it is. A stinging swat on the wrist. At the bottom of most withdrawal receipts, on the average every other, a handwritten Kate Pemberton comment.

And I quote.

"Citibank will get on you for not balancing your statements."

And I quote the every other time before.

"Kate Pemberton has an army of tellers pouring over your Christmas Club account. Think we'd ever yield you to Manhattan Chase, think again."

She's customer manager.

Her methods may not be to everyone's liking. She wants it known. Nobody files on Citibank. First.

I make my withdrawal.

Sometimes it happens I do not get a note on the every other schedule. This is not one of those times.

And I quote.

"Extend us this honor or you sleep with the fish."

✗

Do I Kate Pemberton the school crossing guard or do I Jane Samuels her?

✗

It's out of my hands.

Soon as I arrive at her corner she Pembertons me.

"There's nothing more pedestrian than trying to corner your school crossing guard. Our training specifically covers confrontation. Telling people systems are not infallible gives them the jitters. Explaining systems is a thankless job. They don't pay me enough to stand idly by while you knock the living daylights out of me."

I set the record straight.

"It's nothing like you say. I merely want to meet a rabbit, any rabbit will do, not necessarily Mr. Read My Paw. You said we'd

77

cross that street when we came to it." And for good measure, "Be my extension bridge."

She sets me straight.

"Crossing guards get it from all sides. What you don't understand is we're on your side. Think we enjoy telling pedestrians there's no magic?"

I counter. "Rabbits are walking the streets of New York."

Counter to my counter. "There is no magic."

✗

Magicians would agree with her. Their magic is fake. The woman sawed in half isn't really sawed in half. The bunny pulled out of a hat hasn't been pulled out of thin air. Real magic is not a stage trick. My attitude toward magic is threefold: First I agree with the school crossing guard. There is no magic. Second, I disagree with the school crossing guard. There is magic. Third, I reserve judgment. Events unfold. As of this telling, it's too soon to tell.

There is mystery.

✗

At four, walk Susan's dog. My movie ticket (the festival circuit) isn't till this evening. I could go home or I could not go home.

✗

Alex looks a little weighted down. It's not the fatigue of standing on his feet that's pulling his head to his knees.

I advise him.

"You should prop up, Alex."

"Could you?" He hands me his book, he sits down at his station, I fuss with his nose, balancing the book under it, stepping back to look at the floral arrangement. I reach to make an adjustment.

The elevator comes.

Out steps Marilyn Beats.

Caught in a compromising position.

I could lose my nose over coming to the assistance of my doorman's great-in-the-sack face penis. I run for the stairs. Crying out for all to hear, "I wouldn't sit on his nose, not if you put a gun to my head."

78

Until now, the walls have never welcomed me home with open arms.

My living room wall, opposite the fireplace (unlit for forever), is animated. Two skinny arms, the pelts on them pepper grey—arms for utility rather than arms to send me running into the arms of—stick straight out like pop sculpture in those galleries representing artists on the fringe. Touching those arms with my bare skin wouldn't drive me up the wall. But embracing them would. Out he comes. Well, not exactly out, three quarters of the way out, the other quarter stuck inside the wall. I make it a policy to call the exterminator squad only when the vermin are really creepy. His teeth are rotten. He could use a shave. His posture is poor. He's homely. He's bestial. He's ill-kempt. He's downright trollish.

I go for the phone.

"I've let you down." The same voice as the Lincoln Center guy. The one in the drain. This man is so ungainly it may spoil drains for me the rest of my life. The phone is in my hand. The phone hangs like July hair. If he were really a creep wouldn't he try to yank it out? Wouldn't he behave like scum? Wouldn't he do more than just foul the air and say please put the phone down?

He's naked.

Distastefully so.

His stinger's not out.

"I can tell you're displeased with my appearance. It's your own doing. You've been coming on to walls for years. Walls aren't made of stone. Not all off-the-wall women want to climb the walls but when they do you can be sure word eventually gets around. Initially you saw me how you wanted to see me. Where expectations are highest, walls refract. It was me at Lincoln Center. In the drain and in the wall. It was me who turned the pages of your book."

Just what I need.

Hard days and nights at the Hardware Store, the last thing in the world I want to come home to is a giant naked gnome accusing me of making him feel he's not good enough to climb the walls with. "I'm sorry your feelings are hurt." I don't sound sorry at all. "It wouldn't have worked anyway. Pussies get stranded in trees. Heights hurt. Rock climbers aren't made of rubber."

He walks to the fireplace.

In full frontal view, there's so little there I'd like to get him a fig leaf.

"Let me make it up to you." Arms out. "Climb the wall with me. You have nothing to fear but a fractured neck."

He's no dumb bunny.

For a moment there I was afraid my English, plainspoken as it was, had drawn a blank wall. He may not be handsome, but obviously he's got a command of the language. I shake my head no. Just because they understand your fears doesn't mean they're going to be as fearful for your life as you are for your limbs.

Unfurling.

Coming to life the way New York comes to life for me. A cock the size of which I'd have to have surgically removed. My knuckles match the condom-white speckles of my couch. "You want to climb the walls, I know you do. You've had off-the-wall sex, you're curious about what the walls have to offer."

A drip in my pants.

It's not humidity.

The beeper on his wristwatch blasts. With that, he retreats to the kitchen. I watch him slip down the drain. I immediately run the water. I throw lemon slices after him. I atomize the air with Pledge. In literature I believe it when the beast gets the beauty. In real life I believe what's said about the eye of the beholder: Refraction. In my life I'm ambivalent about men who climb the walls.

There is no magic.

There is magic.

There are events unfolding.

There is mystery.

✗

The parent ring.

When my parents phone, the ring from the phone that doesn't kiss ass is distinct from all other rings. Any unschooled ear can pick out the ring. The schooled ear can even distinguish father from mother.

His is dong.

Hers is yoo-hoo.

✗

80

Yoo-hoo phones.

"I'm going to put your father on the phone. When I put your father on I want you to ask him why he sneaks out in the middle of the night to sit in the kitchen sink. Ask him why he sticks his potato finger down the drain. Ask him if it's prost. (The entire family, uncles, aunts, cuz, all have this urethral phobia.) No one in the family is body function bashful, there are frequent bulletins on ear infections but everybody is coy about potato finger prostate.

Dad picks up the extension.

"Look who's talking. Every chance she gets she rubs herself against the walls." Dad's not given to exaggeration. If that's the way he says it happened, there's no question it happened that way.

"Probably the wisest thing to do would be just to think. Think about what you really want. What makes you really happy. Be objective." For my age, I sound smart for my age.

"What kind of answer is that?" Dad asks.

"She has a point." Mom says.

"What kind of point is that?" Dad asks Mom.

"If it makes me happy to rub walls, I should. If it makes me unhappy to see your swizzle stick stuck down a drain, you shouldn't."

For her age she sounds too smart for her age.

As my mother's daughter, I know what the attraction is to walls but that doesn't mean I approve of her risking her neck. My father's not even remotely like the guy in the drain and/or wall. He's fireman tall. He still turns heads. Why would he want to leave a rent-controlled apartment for the sewer system?

I clarify my point.

"Walls and drains are off-limits."

They throw enough kisses at me to feed a family of four. A nice way of saying discussion closed, thanks but no thanks, the next thing you hear will be click.

The next thing I hear is click.

✗

Events unfold. Still nothing's prepared me for this twist. I could pack up and move in with my parents, be there night and day to supervise, monitor their every move, or I could not panic, keep my apartment, eat what I like, see other women's husbands and make it with men with facial deformities on or about the nose.

I could go to Häagen-Dazs.

✗

Ice cream between innings. Ice cream is not like sherbert between courses. It can't clear the palate. It doesn't erase the things we dote on or the things we don't. But when it's premium ice cream, ice cream between innings is an inning unto itself.

✗

Häagen-Dazs ice cream has panache. Everything about it— weight, buttermilk content, price—is telling you if it's gonna go, it's taking you with it. The Häagen-Dazs near Carnegie Hall is well lit, the storefront lighting you wish for when you go into department stores to buy lipstick that's never the same color when you get it outside. I can't speak for all the Häagen-Dazs personnel in the boroughs or outside the city limits, but the personnel in this Häagen-Dazs is uniformly eighteen, uniformly prodigious and equally Popeye the Sailor in the forearms.

✗

Getting past Alex was simple.
I snuck through the back.

✗

The Häagen-Dazs waitperson presently on duty has his shirtsleeves rolled up. Arms greased with tallows used by weight lifters to delineate meat off the bone.
"Rum raisin. Two dips."
His serving forearm ripples.
"Make it a cup, sugar cone on the side."
He scoops the way construction guys dig. Forearm show-offy. Does he really think it would enter my mind to let his scooper rum raisin me? He is a dick-head. He can't distinguish women who want more from women who take what they can get.
I pay.
A dime change.
"Keep the change."
It's only a dime. Dimes aren't worth a cent. He pockets the dime. Reaching into his back pocket. The top of the arm where the bulge is throws back its bulge, a pinup shot.

82

I am the dick-head.

I can't distinguish between pure profit motive and impure thoughts.

✗

In more ways than one, harebrained.

Alarmists are constantly looking over their shoulder. Alarmists would think walls parting is the end of the world. Alarmists will get their heads examined the instant they start seeing rabbits. Alarmists worry needlessly. But like all non-alarmists, in retrospect, I sometimes see where I should have heeded the warning. The decision to just observe events as they unfold can be the difference between living with guilt (you are a harebrain) or saving your parents from a life-threatening menace.

✗

I call my folks.

✗

Mom answers.

"I'm in a pay booth. I'm coming right over. Just be there."

"Now's not a good time."

"We need to have a mother-daughter talk." Chewing my lip.

"Talk."

"It would be better in person."

"I said not now."

"When would be convenient?" Whining and chewing.

She says hold on, she has to get her daybook, she comes back to say Dad's looking for the book, Dad gets on to say Mom says you sound upset.

Now I'm mad.

But not so mad I can't think. It's clear to me they can't see me because Mom is getting off on the walls and Dad's pecker is down the drain halfway to Peking.

AT&T asks for money.

I gave my last change to dick-head.

"Eleven thirty tomorrow," Mom shouting over a recorded voice demanding all my small change.

Shouting back, "I have my mammogram."

83

We agree on dinner.
Tomorrow I'll badger them.
Give up the cock in the wall.
No more squeezing cock into drains.

✗

Days like this make mornings look good.

✗

I still need track lights.
My need for track lights is so great that if I don't get track lights my need for track lights will interfere with the course of my day. Track lights will put me right back on track. Why I'd want to stay on course (days like this make mornings look good) is of course an extension of who I am.
I am not a filer.
I do not file. First. on days that make mornings look good.

✗

Owner, whose first and last name is Owner, isn't waiting by the entrance for me. Off to the side is his cash register. That's where he's waiting. He springs up, he calls me by name, Jane Samuels, wife number one. A big oxish man, a natural at eclipsing the sun. His bald head has no trace of having ever been a lush plain. On his head there have been no seasonal changes for a long, long millennium.
He wants me to halt.
I grant his wish.
"Ask me what I've seen today. Start with the bassinet."
I tell him instead.
"You saw a bassinet, rooms full of furniture, Harold was knitting, probably he did that in his chair, a ruffled and flounced number. You may have asked him how he was, many people spend their entire lives telling others how they are, it takes a certain persona to listen. This is fall. Who falls into what category is an interest of mine. For example, I can't listen indefinitely straight through. Whereas that other Jane, Jane Goodall, could take it and take it and take it."
Whispering confidentially.

84

"Just between you and me I was flustered by the rooms. You asked me earlier if I'd been hit on the head. My head does feel so-so."

"Unusually, monumentally so-so?"

"Nowhere near unusually, monumentally so-so. Give it to me straight, am I seeing things?"

"That would make two of us."

"I called Mark Cross. I described the attaché case I wanted, you know what they told me?"

There's a researcher in all of us.

He did what I should have done.

Checked original sources.

"They said to keep it quiet. They offered me hush money. More than I'd make in six months. I'm still distressed, just not—"

"Monumentally, unusually troubled."

"I think I held up pretty good," Owner hugging me. Squashed by Owner, you do not fight it. "You and me both."

I set out looking for Harold.

"Mr. Samuels isn't here. He's getting married."

Owner waives the track lighting fees.

Six bulbs.

A savings of seventeen dollars, the three dimes we spent living together, one year of loose change correspondence. Owner bear hugs me again. Another vote of confidence.

I must look like I need it.

✗

Harold's getting married . . .
I'm dog-walking.

✗

Susan's block starts out (reading left to right) with a fortune-teller, three residential buildings and a thrift shop on the corner. Put Susan together with thrift shop cartons and gunnysacks of used clothes, she's like one of those dogs in a drug bust. Her hands are pros, dredging up cashmeres like bodies from lakes. The trees along her block are not boulevard trees. They're control group trees. The group that didn't get the medication. Susan's building is where left meets right. A middle-size building, like a middle-size child. Not too tall, small, not too brick or too glass. You look at the

85

building you think functional, you don't think architectural.

Bathroom art is kitsch.

Her block isn't kitsch.

Harold's getting married . . .

I'm dog-walking.

Walking Patches is not like feeding someone's goldfish. First I sanitize. Mouth freshener. Patches doesn't begrudge any drop of food that goes into anyone's mouth more than he begrudges ice cream. The dog is smarter than he lets on. I will not talk down to him; whenever feasible, a developmental play period will be provided. Above all, I must try to stay out of the state of mind where my life is dog-walking and Harold's life is walking down the aisle.

I must think positive.

My life is blessed.

Harold's getting married.

✗

Tony is the building's two-legged watchdog. Tony and Patches are minding the building together. Tony releases the dog to me. Slip of the tongue . . . referring to the dog as a dog is impersonal. It would be like referring to wives by number. Patches is wearing a knit coat that duplicates in navy and white his patch pattern. His walk is heel-toe, his cantering is show horse. Sidestepping dog shit. He walks like someone wearing new shoes. On a windy day Patches would rather hold it in than despoil himself like a dog. Where other dogs water trees like they're putting out forest fires, Patches takes aim. It looks like cake decoration.

The fifth tree.

Urination as intricate as scroll.

I good-dog him to death. Man's best number one dog is the phrase I may have used. I don't remember the phrase, I'm startled into new phrases by a vision on a low branch just overhead.

Suki, is that you?

Suki, that is you.

You are Suki.

The ghost of my dearly departed cat—the true love of my lap—crouches down on the branch, ready to spring. Her eyes are sunlit pools, her coat in death is fudgier than in life. Her claws are out. "You've replaced me with a dog? I thought you and I had something going. Put yourself in my shoes, see how you like being just a memory."

I pull Patches away.

Suki jumps.

The tree branch shivers like a park swing on a windy day.

Harold's getting married.

I'm dog-walking.

Suki appears and disappears.

It's not magic.

It's geology.

Patches looks at me with the kind of look he usually reserves for dog shit. Christ, I was taking a leak. I was relieving my bladder. We battle it out, I drag him back to Tony. He sits with his back to me. The canine cold shoulder. Tony makes no mention of my height. A smaller version of myself. Half-mast. All the tugs of my heart, tugging my lap.

I patrol Susan's block.

Back and forth. Alert to every breeze. Still no Suki. Branches giving me the brush off. Lady, you're barking up memory lane. The Easter egg lump on my forehead begins a Gene Krupa drum solo. Leave now, meet the Mount Rushmore nose. Take it or leave it.

I don't take it.

I don't have to take it.

Suki means more to me than a nose scuba-diving my coastline. More than the cock who filed. First. And married. First. And got fertilized. First. From the corner of my eye I catch Tony pointing me out.

I am not a tourist sight.

A tourist sight is a must-see. A tourist sight doesn't get filed on. First.

✗

Tony must have alerted the proper authorities. The first and only husband of Susan singlehandedly takes me by my frame of mind and piles frame of mind and me into a taxi. A sheriff of the Old West running somebody out of town. Lou pays in advance. Lou slaps the cab. The cab guns it.

✗

It's a measure of the state I'm in that Gerald's nose, plainer than the nose on my face, is overlooked until I hear him call my name.

The temp doorman on duty casts a salacious look. Then blushes. I don't know what for. We're all adults here. If a man likes same-sex sex, a man's nose can be as erotic to another man as a man's penis is to another man. And maybe a nose of Gerald's dimensions transcends. Can a heterosexual guy really look upon a nose like that and not experience the slightest quickening of his member?

The elevators pull a work slowdown.

Fifteen minutes to get to my floor. Gerald makes it feel like days. "Talk to me," he says. No response. "Why don't you talk to me?" And then those three most overworked words in the English language: "How are you?"

"How are you?"

"I asked you first."

It's a delicate moment. I hate good men who are good listeners at bad times. By bad times I don't mean inconvenient let's-make-it-some-other-time times. I mean the time's not right because the way things are between us, I prefer to keep them that way. Forcing talk is like forcing love. It's harder than shaping history.

I token talk.

If talk is cheap, token talk is bargain basement. "I'm going to a festival film. Some director introducing his first feature. It's sold out."

"You haven't told me how you are."

"I really want to see you again." (God is my witness, not token talk.)

"I really want to see you again too."

See.

Thinking you can lose someone because you don't talk is like thinking someone can be kept by doing your words and deeds right.

We have elevator sex.

No foreplay. He kneels. I sit on his clapper. The roasted marshmallow position. I jiggle. It's over.

Tender kisses of farewell.

It's not till I get into the apartment I remember we didn't use a condom. Conceivably, I could conceive. Second.

Or catch a cold.

Leading to strep throat.

Snot in the crotch.

My life is blessed a thousand times over.

✗

Small film screenings are like preview linen sales. Snob appeal. History before it's made history. The advance word of mouth on the one I'm attending: The director's sunk his tuition money into the budget. About what I spend annually on facials.

He's supposed to have promise.

I promise I'm not making this up. Supposedly he makes us take a look at ourselves.

My longevity friend changes her frame of mind more often than I change underwear. Of my two parents, one climbs walls, the other's going down the drain. Former in-laws are my own personal Homeric chorus. The Fling wants me to tour his milieu. Barry the bereaved is boring holes in his clothes with a periscope that isn't.

I don't mind taking a look at myself.

Not at all.

It never hurts to look.

Not at all.

The words on the lips of every fall leaf sum it up: Falling is a shock to the system.

✗

I arrive at the designated time. Just in time to see the director waiting on stage. The houselights aren't turned up enough. He wants to see his audience. When the lights brighten he says they're too bright. Adjustment of lights takes longer because the director directing the lights wants it just right. Coming from anyone else, it would be pretentious. From the director, it's a nice touch. His clothes are of the moment. Black shirt, black slacks. Sterling silver buckle. Loafers, no socks. Not the attire of the up and coming. The attire of the up and arrived. To be seen in anything less black would be a major career setback.

He takes one question.

No question in anybody's mind this question would be raised. It's the question on the lips of every fall leaf: Where did I come from, where am I going?

Not verbatim.

But in so many words.

"I was involved with a woman who valued my opinions. It took a while before I saw what she was doing. She wanted to make contact. Promote our relationship from historical trivia to historical significance. She really wanted to relate. She wanted communication."

89

Light applause.

The audience gets it. A message film. The lights go out. I can't say at which point I dozed but it was somewhere around the part where the girl turns to the guy and says, "Talk to me."

✗

Midnight.

A couple offers to share their cab uptown. I don't know how it happened but I end up sitting between them. Sectioning them off like a loose-leaf divider. He has flattop hair. A lawn that's been mowed and spiked. It's the kind of bed of nails you wouldn't want to picnic on. His wife monopolizes the rolled-down window. I've met her type before. They read on airplanes.

On planes, he's the nonstopper.

"Fifty minutes into the film, he loses me. That business about history . . . he didn't take it far enough. She understood she was being played along, he understood he was playing her along, nobody made a row. That business about history . . . she wants historical designation, she's not getting what she wants, I kept waiting for it to disrupt their relationship. When it didn't, I felt set up. A conflict of ideologies without the clash. I never got a sense of what held them together. On his part, even less than hers. He shut her out entirely. That business about history . . . he was saving himself. Based on what? She was the one with more substance. More vitality. More upstairs. She did all the talking. True, not everything she said was worthwhile, but she had her moments."

The cab pulls up.

I pay my share.

I get out on his side.

The wife's head never turned once.

✗

Did the movie fulfill its promise? Have I taken a closer look at myself? The next best thing . . . I've taken a closer look at others.

The wife of the nonstopper.

Does she have somebody on the side? Is she offering her hand in marriage? Are children involved, if so you have to make allowances. Children change the picture. What's her history? Why doesn't she talk? Is she wife number one or one hundred?

Her husband.

Is he really dense? Or is he deliberately baiting her?
The mode I'm in . . .
By any other name, how-are-you?
I'm juiced.
I'm hopped up.
I'm ready for Harold.

✗

I'm full circle.
Sneaking into Hardware like the tooth fairy. The newlyweds are asleep in bed. The groom's mouth is slightly opened, unsightly but not monumentally overly unusually so. The bride looks awake, even in sleep, wide-eyed. Lids rolled up into her head like the carpet when dance fever hits. Soft curls on her face, no bone structure. She's all baby fat. Eyebrows tweezed to thin arches, ample bosom, a young diva. Her fingers are pudgy, the kind most of us outgrow. She may still have trouble picking up certain objects, I'm not sure she can even tie her own shoes. Those eyes of hers are big and dark. I feel stared at. I don't like the feeling of being watched. When she sits up in bed, I like it even less.
It's I who turn away.
"Nothing's new under the sun."
Settling back sounds. Even breathing. She's asleep. A full day's excitement, the wedding, the reception, the baby on the way. Sleep disturbances and stimulation go hand in hand. Thoughts that couldn't be further from your mind come out your mouth.
Nothing new under the sun?
You might as well say there's no magic.

✗

Home, the pre-mammogram hours.
Rest. I must. I can't. All the usual fabric softeners don't work. Not warm milk, not cocoa, not touching toes. Not Snickers. Not. Not. Not. Not because of Harold or Mrs. Harold. Not because of the ghost of Suki, my dear and departed.
Mammogram mayhem.
Judgment day for tits.
My feeling about breasts is all women should do a monthly self-exam. Should they be bumpy, my feeling is women shouldn't rest till they find out what's buried in their front yards. Mammograms

are about going through customs. Inspectors dying to catch you with contraband. I always strip-search myself. My sacs held up to makeup mirror lights as powerful as the ones they put under cars to look for sexual dysfunction. I frisk my corned beef for lumps. On the forms I am ready to declare every nugget.

(Telling everybody what a nice pair you've got does not persuade a radiologist to curve your grade.)

So-so in the head. Monumentally, unusually so.

I can live with that.

So-so in the lap.

I can live with that.

I can very well live without so-so in the tits.

✗

So here's what I propose:

Heels are a pain.

They pinch at the balls.

Seams rub.

Walking hurts.

First thing today I strip-mine the shoe stores for a comfortable pair of heels. A clever piece of manipulation. Make heels representative of lumps. Unsuccessfully seek heels. Patterns and planting seeds are historical fact. Before the American Revolution there was the groundwork for it. By failing to find a suitable pair of heels, I've set the stage. Foreshadowing the next scene: You shake me down for lumps, you're not going to come up with a single heel.

It's fall. Sometimes life does fall into step.

These are my boobs.

This is not a nose we're discussing.

The backup plan for my system is mammogram diplomacy. Smile on the way in. In return get smiled at. Thank yous on the way out. My phone with the Bronx accent doesn't have tits. My phone doesn't have to kiss ass.

I do.

✗

System backups fail. Systems fail. The school crossing guard insists it's not a two-way street. Faith in your system makes no difference to your system, systems collapse left and right, indifferent to faith. On days when I do not have a mammogram, I might be

inclined to agree. No two-way streets.
Mammogram morning.
No two ways, there are two-way streets.

✗

Nine A.M.
I come to life one lousy cell at a time. Cellular relapse. CPR with
a cold plunge. Bright colored clothes for today, more superstition.
Bright for a glowing report. My plants get extra pats on the cheeks.
Effusive over my garbage disposal. I don't manhandle the elevator
buttons. I apologize to Alex. Forget what I said. You nose is too
good for my ass.

✗

An hour into looking for heels I am dragging my heels.

✗

Last stop before my tits get frisked.
The French shoe store on Fifty-seventh Street has exotic prices.
Designer shoes too good to touch cement. At their rates, there's always an empty pew. I hold the door for the person behind me. As I
walk ahead of whoever's behind me, I swing the door wide.
Enough for the person behind me, even the person behind the per-
son to ride on the coattails of my swing.
Behind me, Marilyn Beats.
Her curls are doing stunt pilot loops. Her perfume has kitchen
spices in it. Her Ninja legs taper to napes. Marilyn Beats has a
square brass knuckle chin. And bad mama hips. Nice if you can
carry it off. She can.
"May I help you?" The salesgirl is French, her skirt short
enough to be a wide belt.
"She was here first." Marilyn Beats in a little girl voice?
Is she having a mammogram too?
"I'll wait." My mouth is dry.
It's a tiny shop. Nowhere can you sit and not be conspicuous to
a fault. Marilyn tries on a pair of ankle boots. She strolls past.
"What do you think? Go on, tell me what you think." Her meat-
eating banners aren't flying. The hands on her hips aren't fists. For
all practical purposes, a cease-fire.

93

It helps that the salesgirl is French.

The way the French linger in cafés prepares them for women lingering in shoe stores. Marilyn sits next to me. She nestles in. She sighs. Her mouth is a pout. She sniffles into a tissue. Dropping clues like a crop duster.

Are those tears?

"They look fine to me," I say of her ankle boots.

"What Alex is today he owes to me. He had his nose fixed at my insistence. He's not the first man I've brought along."

Salesgirl moving to a discreet distance.

Cats clean their paws, their heads turned away, yet nothing gets past them. The salesgirl pretends not to listen. Combing her hair, hanging on every word.

"What I really want is a man to change my life."

That's it?

That's the most Marilyn Beats can come up with? It's not New York material. This is a woman whose twat roosts where people breathe in and out. Conventional females don't get bonked in the lobby of their buildings. Nor do they put strange men's noses in their bellybutton. Just to make sure, I repeat it back. "You want a man to change your life?"

"Yeah."

The short black skirt the French salesgirl is wearing is made out of material that moves with you. Material that keeps up. Material that's fresh. No gingham for her. Maybe the salesgirl can help Marilyn revise her act.

Meanwhile . . .

I have a date to go topless.

✗

The Breast Center for the Above-Forty Set has a building all to itself.

It doesn't help that the lady holding the door for me (she's on her way out, I'm on my way in) is holding back tears. The elevators lie in wait for me like those men your mother tells you never to go home with. The stairs are no better. Shadows this thick. The receptionist either has a cold in her eyes or she's had a good cry too.

Other than that . . .

On the classical music station, the sharpening of blades. Cloying incense to cover up what? Between now and the time someone

94

actually lays a finger on me, I have to figure out a way to ask incendiary questions in the least incendiary way. Smart consumerism: Tell me please, when was the last time your machines were inspected, where's your documentation, for my edification, could you explain the basis for this low rating?

✘

Her nameplate says Dawn.
"Dawn, forgive my asking—"
"Don't ask," wiping her eyes.
"I merely want to know—"
"You don't want to know." Coursing tears, splashing into a cup on the desk, like a pail under leaky ceilings to catch the drip.
"It's regarding the status of the machines."
"What do I look like, chopped meat? Behind this receptionist's desk is a human being who could use a little sympathy."
Uh-oh.
Saying it's a two-way street, you have to play like it's a two-way street.
"I care what becomes of you as much as I care for my own two flawless breasts, no history of malignancy in the family, a history of spoiling my fellow man. Forget inspection certificates, it was callous of me, not befitting someone with no history of breast cancer, a legacy of chests for all mankind to rest their weary heads on."
I am summoned by the authorities.
Where my breasts are stripped to the waist.
Where like any beast under scrutiny, I try to make myself smaller than I am.
Fall: Where you can fall into enemy hands.
Where they never heard of the Geneva Convention.
Where breasts are turned inside out like pockets. Where there is no plea-bargaining. Where you smile till your mouth hurts. Where your eyes water. Fall: Where Empires fall. Where the mighty fall. Where the best laid plans—

✘

"Everything looks fine, no change from last year."

✘

95

Where it's payback time . . .

"Whatever's the matter, Dawn, I want you to know I'll be thinking of you."

Dawn takes my check.

Dawn's hands are shaking.

"It's a man," she says.

Uh-oh again.

"When am I going to meet the one who'll really change my life?"

✗

Coincidence?

Far be it from me to proclaim man-who'll-change-my-life a grassroots movement. The numbers are too low, I haven't taken a public poll. I leave that to other researchers. It's not a one-question deal either. More like a battery to determine whether this is a revival of an age long gone. The woman waits for the man, oh me oh my. Or in the spirit of the times, the woman leaves no stone unturned. Smart consumerism. She brings home the best prize that money can buy. Or maybe this heralds a new age of dissatisfaction in the broadest sense.

I spoke too soon.

Marilyn Beats could be ahead of her time.

Marilyn Beats could embody a mixed bag of times.

✗

Moving right along.

Dinnertime I'm committed: Mom and Dad.

In due time, Hardware.

Additional time distribution: An obligatory pay-my-respects to the bereaved family. All this week, receiving well-wishers. Barry and his sons wish to thank everyone personally for their fruit baskets. And that time of year: Linen sale at Macy's. My fall tradition.

And time to spare. . .

What better time than now—on this day of titty reprieve, this festive time, this unusually, monumentally momentous breast affirmation time—to celebrate.

A new bra?

Make it a bathing suit.

One without a history of seventeen years, three spent living together, a year's worth of postage stamps. A bathing suit to lay the

96

groundwork. The American Revolution had groundwork. Before the official rebellion, little acts of rebellion. The rallying cry of all women filed. First on: I want a bathing suit to change my life.

✗

Fresh from the triumph of my breasts, I rush to Saks.
When I get there, I belt out, Which way to fun-in-the-sun?

✗

The dressing room sign above the mirror reads: Do NOT REMOVE UNDERGARMENTS WHILE TRYING ON BATHING SUITS.

An honor system.

Sister, you do not want to compromise another sister's clean crotch. Sister, clean crotches are a diminishing tribe. Sister if your petri dish so much as brushes against the patch you are honor bound to give wide berth to, chain letters will follow you all the days of your life.

Enough already.

So my crotch has been around the block a few times. My crotch is sexually active. However it is a crotch under constant adult supervision.

DO NOT REMOVE UNDERGARMENTS WHILE TRYING ON BATHING SUITS screams the other sign above the wall hooks.

Saks Fifth has red-lettered it. A lot louder than DO NOT LITTER. As loud as NO SMOKING. But trying on a bathing suit with panties is like reading subtitles with somebody's head in the way. Obstructed views spoil the view.

DO NOT REMOVE UNDERGARMENTS WHILE TRYING ON BATHING SUITS says the third sign on the door.

There are women who can estimate anything. The number of jellybeans in a jar. The number of hairs in a tub. The size of a man by his finger size. I am not one of them.

DO NOT REMOVE UNDERGARMENTS WHILE TRYING ON BATHING SUITS. The fourth sign is on the ceiling.

System failure. The honor system is subject to the same perils as the light system, the same perils as the two-way street system. I peer, I twist my panties this way and that, is the bikini bottom too small, are those hips or new land formations? I try rounding myself off to the nearest cent. It doesn't add up. I cheat. Right away I see how unflattering the suit is. Right away I hate the suit.

Right away I buy the suit.

No whammies on my crotch.

The time couldn't have been put to better use. A new bathing suit I loathe but in no time could love. I might even discard the bathing suit relics from the past. Given enough time, this new suit could spark a revolution. It could end my bondage.

Throwing out old bikinis.

Installing the new.

Emancipation by bathing suit.

✗

A cab: Next stop, Hardware.

Time to myself in the backseat.

Out of context time.

The historical researcher holds quotations sacred. Taking something out of context can color people's perceptions of what a passage really means. Conscientious historians labor hard to avoid distorting history.

Going out of context differs.

It is not a reference to quoting. Going out of context is the means by which historians distance themselves (the objective view) from the context of the times, placing events within the larger context of other times and places (the overview).

What is coming out of context?

Who comes out of context? Is the practice of coming out of context derivative of going out of context or quoting out of context?

I come in the cab.

Sitting straight up in the backseat. Concentrating on the meter, I come. At precisely four bucks on the meter, I have an orgasm.

Now . . .

Within the context of what's been said about out of context, it's my opinion that coming in the backseat of a cab (no hands, no fingers, you've got to give me credit, only a meter to focus on) is part of the heritage of out of context only when a bona fide historian does it and nobody else. My coming out of context plucks me out of time and place. Thus plucked, I have the vantage point, hovering like a spirit outside myself, free of restraints (in context, you get caught up). Ever the historian, I utilize coming out of context in constructive ways, analysis and such.

Thusly . . .

When I see Jane Samuels on her way to Hardware (yet another

time) I say from the vantage of overview, "Jane, it's fall. You've fallen into some very questionable habits."

✗

Bustling.

The Hardware Store is big as a belly in its sixth month. Expanded not just in the front or back, a rubber tire around its middle. There's an influx of people. A random sampling shows two out of two are carrying Mark Cross attaché cases. Will events be duplicated? Will history repeat itself? Might I not walk in someday and see others of my species? A herd of us sitting on air. Might they not ask of Cross people, "How are you?" If these Cross people are spouses who've filed. First. then that would make the air sitters spouses who've been filed. First upon.

Questing as I quest.

The quest for historical perspective. And the biggest quest of all, finish lines. History is the perfect vehicle for time lines. Epochs, eras, centuries, all are marks denoting starts and finishes. Resolutions. It was never history's intention to crush the historian with the weight of history. Finish lines are the number one compelling reason for anyone to finish what he starts.

Start to finish . . . that's the long and short of it.

✗

I see Mrs. Harold before I see Harold. Her belly is triplets big. She waddles to where Harold is standing. He's changing the honeymoon sheets. Yes, it is odd for an ornate bed to be superimposed (or the other way around) on bins of wire and can openers, books on How To and How Not To. Monumentally, unusually out of context? Coming from someone who comes in the back of cabs, no.

He kisses her.

No kiss in return.

"Nothing's new under the sun. Smack me."

"You're the mother of my child, I'm not going to smack you."

"If you don't smack me, I'll find some other man to smack me. My hand in marriage to anyone who'll flutter my lids."

He backhands her.

"Harder. My hand to any man—"

"Your hand's mine. I've got the papers to prove it."

His next smack would spin my face. My lids would fan my face.

99

COLORADO COLLEGE LIBRARY
COLORADO SPRINGS
COLORADO
WITHDRAWN

I would blink back tears. Mrs. Harold, nothing. The fat pockets on her face are heavy insulation.

"Nothing's new under the sun."

"All new."

"Nothing."

He defers.

"Change my eyes, you change the way I see the world. Frozen lids, frozen outlook. Now start thawing. Pinch my ears."

Her voice is what Harold's used to be.

A monochromatic no-color color scheme.

He bites her lobes. She doesn't yell ouch.

"It's possible to change your outlook in other ways."

"Is not."

"Is so."

"Is not. Not now. Not ever." Face too. In all aspects very Swedish (on paper at least, WW2, Sweden is neutral, Sweden doesn't wrinkle like the rest of us).

"Outlook has nothing to do with lids." Harold finishing with the sheets. Neat hospital corners.

"Looking at it from my eyes, everything changes in the blink of an eye. If it doesn't impress my lids, it doesn't impress me."

He picks up a pitcher of water.

The contents tossed.

No blink.

She hands him a knitting needle.

He jabs.

No action in the eyes.

Mrs. Harold turns to me. "What I want is a man who'll change my life."

✗

Somehow it doesn't surprise me in the least.

✗

A marriage made in heaven? I think not. If this Jane—Jane Samuels—conferred with that other Jane—Jane Goodall—then this Jane would say to the other Jane: Jane, correct me if I'm wrong, taken as a whole, Mrs. Harold's frame of mind is on some other plane. In and of itself, historically commonplace. You can't have planes without plane diversity. Take my dear, dear longevity

100

friend Susan Gold, a rare frame indeed. Susan is a frame-of-mind switcher. What some people do with their remote, flicking from channel to channel, she does with her mind. Mrs. Harold acknowledges flick power, you could not fail to pick up on the frozen lid, frozen outlook, nothing new under the sun, so on and so forth. What I'm getting at, Jane—and this is right up your alley—when a female chimp makes a monkey out of a male chimp, does he ever get to turn the tables?

✗

I have obligations.

Thanks to my fruit basket (Jack at A&P does a bereavement basket of fruits and nuts to die for—no pun intended) the family of the bereaved are dying to see me. I walk the ten blocks. The sun is out. One out of every four people is wearing leather. On Madison Avenue more leather. I turn left. I turn right. I stop to price a leather jacket. I announce myself to Barry's doorman. He remarks on the sun being out.

✗

The smell of ripe fruit.

Fruit baskets outnumber people. I stop counting at thirty. I'm offered fruit pies, fruit tea, fruit loaf, fruit granola, dried fruit, compote, fresh fruit drinks, and mango ice cream. I say no to fruit pies, fruit tea, fruit loaf, fruit granola, dried fruit, compote, fresh fruit drinks, mango ice cream.

"Might you have fruit Danish?"

The mother of the deceased says no. Barry's boys are teenagers. They offer to go to the bakery. I won't hear of it. Barry asks me if I'm sure I won't have any fruit pie, fruit tea, fruit loaf, fruit granola, dried fruit, compote, fresh fruit drink—name your poison—and mango ice cream.

"I'm sure."

The mother of the deceased looks like she's on the verge of tears.

"Mango and orange juice, please." To please her.

Immediately everyone is cheered.

"Ice in your drink?" The mother of the deceased, I remember now, Marge.

"No ice."

101

"Fruit salad on your mango?" Marge is hopeful.

"She doesn't want fruit salad on her mango." Barry answering for me.

"Grandma made that fruit salad herself." The taller of the boys can't be more than sixteen. If I'm not mistaken, he has the beginnings of a jowl, unless he's got a wad of bubble gum, fruit flavored, in his mouth.

"I'll put some in a jar for her to take home." Marge gets up to serve.

Barry waits till she leaves the room. "We told her to keep out of Betty's closets, give it another week, whoever heard of disposing of worldly goods this soon?" (The wrong question to ask someone who's bought her very first bathing suit in seventeen years.) On his sofa, surrounded by both sons, he reaches for their hands. "We ended up having to sedate her."

(How much longer before I can get the hell out?)

"Maurice, go see what's taking Grandma so long." The younger son takes the older son with him.

Barry and I are alone on the couch.

I move to a seat off the couch.

"Betty was ill for two years."

"It's terrible to linger."

"I did all the housework, the shopping, everything that needed doing, I did."

"Terrible, just really awful."

"You learn to forgo. After a while you get used to it, you don't think you can, but you do, no sacrifice is too much."

Marge brings out the serving tray.

Maurice is carrying a fruit jar.

The older boy, another one.

I eat and drink like I'm on the run. I get up, word perfect. Got to go. Marge gets up like she's going to detain me.

"Let her leave," Barry detaining Marge. To me: "The good-byes, you know how it is."

"We could play Scrabble, how about Scrabble, Grandma?"

She'll never fall for it, she'll tell Maurice too much concentration.

"Only if Jane plays." Marge crosses her arms in front of her.

Jane has heart.

Jane plays, we all play.

The Scrabble board is all set up. We take our seats at the game table. The first go-around I make the word *leaves*. In the middle of placing the letters for *autumn*, second round, the table on which the board rests bounces up, knocking *autumn* off. Just prior and immediately following the bounce that scattered *autumn*, rips of cloth.

Something is thumping. . .

From down under.

With our bare hands we hold the table to keep it still. No one looks under the table to find out what it was, Marge starts to, but Dennis, the one with the jowl that turned out to be a wad of gum, won't let her.

Maurice takes the rap.

"My foot fell asleep."

Marge, still feeling the effects of the sedation, says, "Foot my ass, that was your father's penis."

✗

Thanks to Barry's elevator, my getaway is quick. It's been years since I played Scrabble. I've always maintained (still do) I can read anywhere, on subways, in bed with a cock in the wall reading over my shoulder, tapping me on the shoulder to let me know when to turn the page. The discipline it takes not to lose my place on the written page was easily transferred to the board game up till (but not inclusive of) the time my knee felt something wet and slimy in content and completely out of context to Scrabble.

I lost the game.

But not by much.

✗

Barry's doorman remarks on the sun. Less of it, a drop in temperature, can't you tell? I turn right, I turn left. I continue to tally the number of leather jackets. At fifty-nine—all leather, denim leather combos, also leather vests—just one leather short of sixty, the count is called off. What counts is I didn't stop voluntarily. I was stopped dead, surrounded, cut off, put under siege. I tell my former in-laws I want out. The resumption of counting is not the reason. Counting leather jackets is mindless. It can lead to counting out-of-state license plates, in-state pregnant women, and double columns of trees without the ghost of my dearly departed cat.

The trio does not move aside.

"I'm on my way to a Macy's linen sale."

To no avail.

Helen is wearing combat fatigues and boots that must have seen action somewhere. She floats an inch above the ground. Swaying but not adrift in the wind. Sam's umbrella is tucked under his arm like a loaf of French bread. He too is an inch above ground. Floating in a tethered sort of way. With Yvette's cellophane wrinkles, she looks old enough to be her mother. Last count, all three are not on ground level.

Is there magic?

There is mystery.

"It's probably none of my business, but are you wraiths?"

"Looking to make an issue out of it? You have no heart, admit it. You would've told me to cancel my mushroom conference, in which I was a keynote speaker. You make issues where there are none. The death of my mother was untimely, coinciding as it did with my mushroom conference. Don't deny it. You would have urged me to forgo mushrooms. What you fail to understand, the corpse was history. No one should be a prisoner of war to history. You have no heart."

I persist.

"I'm on my way to a Macy's linen sale; are you wraiths?"

Nobody's telling.

Sam's raised umbrella is a large black finger in Helen's face. "Spoken like a true soldier of fortune. I couldn't have said it better myself. A man doesn't have to give the time of day to his marital history. You won't find me rehashing what went amiss with us. I will take issue with one thing, however. Had it been the other way around, your mother wouldn't have gone to a mushroom conference."

The issue is clear . . .

On the lips of every fall leaf: My tree and I were once so tight, how will I make it on my own? Barry, for example. Should he delay mushroom gratification? Can you squirt and grieve at the same time? Two weeks since the demise of his wife. I've known people who grieve longer over being filed on. First.

A clearly contestable issue.

Yvette's face is cracked paint. When she smiles she starts to peel. "If your own family won't make an issue out of you, who will?"

Macy's is having a linen sale.

Not being a wraith, I walk to the subway. The in-laws take no

issue with my going because it is they who have disappeared.
First.

✘

Macy's is crowded. Linen really brings them out. Even the escalators have lines. Moving slow, but still moving. Maybe twenty people ahead of me. One person below me. Slithering up. Someone crawling out of the woodwork. He's not some stranger off the street, he's my man in the wall. Einstein weedy hair, the leather jacket is crusted over. Crust unknown. I can barely see the tops of his shoes. For him the floor is foam. He's sunk down. In-laws above ground. Homely men below. When he walks, it's trudging through sludge. His pants are filthy. Not for a moment do I see what I saw in him. The man is a ghoul.

"My mother can't keep her hands off walls. Are you by any chance screwing someone by the name of Irma?"

We get on the escalator.

Same deal.

He sinks.

"The wall holds close to a thousand New Yorkers. Your mom could be involved with anyone."

"My father's fixated on drains."

"Lots of people off the wall get to a point in their lives where they feel walled in. Your dad's looking for a way out."

Off the escalator . . .

Pressed against the nearest wall. It gives like a waterbed. He puts my hands on the one place on his entire body that might be of some interest to me. I hear the sound of velcro. Out it comes. Out to there. There is a murmuring over his shoulder. Where there's a linen sale, you will find ladies in hoards. A group converges. In the tens of tens. He dives into the wall. He speaks from behind the wall.

My eye contact is on his cock.

Protruding like an Uzi.

"My name is Marty Nesterbaum. I'm forty-four years old. Most of my life has been spent in the streets. Thanks to your tax dollars I now live in a safe, clean environment. But the homeless need your support to keep it that way. People off the wall like yourselves cannot allow the legal system to dump creeps on us. The creeps own the street, they mustn't get hold of the walls."

A glistening cock.

105

Tension is tense.

"I'm indebted to you all." He puts on a rubber. "Permit me to repay society."

Is the thing massively refracted or what?

"Creep," women call out.

One heckler crosses herself. "I could never. Not like this. Not with somebody who's reduced it to the level of taking a bite out of a sandwich."

A shouting match begins. Off the wall women accusing other off the wallers of being insensitive to the homeless, brain dead between the legs. A group attacks the wall, women with grey hair, support stockings, orthopedic shoes. And panties off. More than traffic can bear. Reinforcement cocks show up. The numbers are about even. The women climb the wall. I visually follow them to the top. Lollipopped on dicks. In orbit looks on their faces.

And down they come.

Falling leaves. Soft landing. The crowd underneath, their net. Pandemonium. A racket as loud as a Springsteen concert. Free-for-all. Like Macy's was giving away linen.

Women who didn't get a turn want one. Women who've had a turn want seconds. Tragedy is narrowly averted by the appearance of hundreds more. Male organs out like coat hooks. The women enter the wall. Revolving door brothel action. In the wall, lots of pig squealing.

I abstain.

Those few of us not participating resume shopping for linens.

✗

In the confusion I left my jars of fruit salad. I could go back for them, but I don't. They were heavy. Lugging the past, shouldn't I be able to unload something?

✗

The guardian of linens stands in front of the dressing room. In Macy's you get to try linens on for size. The guardian distributes samples. My sealed packages are confiscated. She'd do well in bathing suits. In no uncertain terms, she makes it clear that any crotch discovered naked on unauthorized linens will be melded. Her glasses are thickly rimmed and black. Her shirt is starch white. Her shoes as flat as they come. She wears no makeup. The

106

prison warden look.

A booth becomes available.

The dressing room has a cot. I drape the cot in the floral sample. I go for a dry run. A restful night, a fitful night. I sit up and pretend to read. Rough sex, passive sex, artificially enhanced sex, marathon sex. I run the gamut.

A knock at the door.

Do I want to see another pattern?

"Stripes. Bring bold stripes."

She drops them through the door slot. The stripes look a lot stronger than they feel. They snap in two during the nap test. At least the flowers made it to marathon before they wilted.

"Hoops and rings," I call out.

Instant delivery. The hoops and rings make me dizzy. She offers plain sheets. But blank sheets remind me of stationery. Stationery reminds me of years of letters attesting to my undying love of Harold, his for me.

I don't buy.

As good as the sale is, the sheets don't get me climbing the walls.

✗

Heavy street traffic in front of Macy's. Extra supervision of that traffic. The school crossing guard's orange outfit is more orangy than hunters wear in hunting season. The rush hour surge, plus the linen surge. She herds a pack of us across the street. I bring up the rear, she drops back.

"I was offered a desk job today. Processing traffic violations. I wouldn't have to see the violators, only the violations. It would cut down on human contact."

"You accepted?"

"You'd be glad to see me go, wouldn't you? Then you could work my replacement over. Draw her out, see if what I've told you matches up to what she says. It will. The system doesn't change just because the crossing guard changes. No matter how tenacious you are, there's not a crossing guard around with a nice word about systems."

The issue needs clarification.

"You've been systematically ignoring my pleas to meet rabbits, preferably the one that cuffed me. I'm prepared to cross this intersection a dozen more times till I get a satisfactory answer."

The dozen comes to thirty.

"I would have resigned from the system long ago if I hadn't discovered alternative systems. Backups for any system require their own backups. But alternative systems are self-contained. They are the closest things school crossing guards have to easy street."

"Out of context?" I ask.

"Far out, I told you, easy street."

"How far?"

"Loophole far."

"So rabbits are an alternative system of some kind?"

"There is no magic."

"Is there—"

"There's easy street."

✗

Fifty crossings more. Me on her heels. I keep hitting the same wall: There's just so much a crossing guard can spill.

I bring the following to her attention:

It's I, not you, smacked on the head. Me, not you, with psychic flashes.

She brings to my attention:

Who better than your school crossing guard to tell you when to stop the inquisition before you get hurt?

✗

In ten blocks I will be at my parents'.

✗

In ten blocks I am at my parents'.

✗

The building on Twenty-third Street is vintage. The lighting in the halls looks gaslit. The main entrance has a door knocker. The elevator is sunken treasure. Metal gate, a decorative cage. Anybody just missing the elevator can see who it was that didn't wait for them. I press six. At three, I get off. It's faster on foot.

I use a key.

The door is double bolted.

108

I knock on my parents' door.

Mother answers. The doorway picture frames her. Old Master. With her white apron, her long braid, long enough to be sat on, she is of another time. You almost expect to be asked for a calling card.

"We were beginning to worry."

"I was talking to a crossing guard. Where's Dad?"

"What about?"

"The pressure she's under. Where's Dad?"

"She should talk . . . he went to Häagen-Dazs."

"He's not down the drain?"

"You make it sound like down the tubes."

"Isn't it?"

"Around our age, it catches up with you."

Dad enters. Even when he's not making an entrance, he is. White hair, a slim six feet. His color looks like year-round tan. Put him in jeans, he looks as young as sixty.

"That's the third time today," Irma taking the ice cream away.

"You go to Häagen-Dazs three times a day?" Me taking the top off the ice cream for a finger lick.

"Frank likes to watch the girls dish it out."

In all fairness, I can't object to my father leering at Häagen-Dazs personnel. But if you give parents an inch, they take a leg.

"I would rather see you spending your time reading."

"Frank reads. He's always reading. He reads with his eyes closed. There is no illiteracy in my family." One of Irma's lifelong concerns, book passion.

She goes into the kitchen.

Dad and I set the table. He does silverware, I do plates. We both do glasses. In the three times he's entered and left the kitchen, my trips have synchronized with his. No unbecoming conduct with the drains. No embrace between Mom and the kitchen walls either. One quick rub when she thought I wasn't looking.

Dinner is served.

The usual: Eat more, I made it the way you like it, no onions in the salad, chicken breast sauteed in onions.

"What's in the Saks bag?" Irma passes the salt to Frank, Frank didn't ask for salt.

"A bathing suit."

"Are you going on a cruise?" Frank using the salt he didn't ask to be passed. Irma saying enough salt, Frank.

I clink my glass with a spoon.

"Everything out in the open. I want it all on the table. Which one of you is going to go first?"

I wait them out.

Irma says Frank. Frank says Irma. I say Irma.

Irma waits me out.

I cave in.

"At this time I am not at liberty to reveal my sources but if you're feeling walled in on all four sides because of being old, impending death any day now, your friends kicking the bucket, memory loss—let me help you."

They are not jumping at the offer.

"There are viable alternatives. Participation in alternative systems is not one of them." I don't want to lose my parents to easy street.

A period of silent eating.

Broken by a period of silent drinking.

"There is no magic solution." From someone deeply immersed in the inexplicable, ranging from Harold to Bunny Boy to all of fall, this is the height of hypocrisy.

Frank breaks.

"Irma shouldn't have snitched."

"You were leaving bloodstains around the rims of drains. I suspected the worst." Her prostate aversion, she won't say prostate. "This would have blown over by now if you hadn't snitched on me for snitching on you. A fling with the walls, nothing more."

My seventy-year-old mom . . .

Flinging?

"Come for breakfast tomorrow, just the two of us," Irma puts more chicken on my plate.

My seventy-year-old mom . . .

Flinging?

"Eleven. Make it half past," Irma says.

Flinging . . .

My seventy-year-old mom?

It's one thing to think it, quite another to hear her say it.

"You look pale." Dad passes me the salt. Mom tells Dad table salt is not smelling salts. I say tomorrow at eleven, just the two of us.

"Half past eleven," Irma corrects.

Frank begins to clear the table. Mom brings the Saks bag to my seat. I take the hint. Kisses back and forth, mostly air kisses. She opens the front door before I get there. I take that hint too. They're in a hurry. It isn't a television program they're rushing to see.

It's sex.
Alternative sex.

✗

Last stop before home: Hardware.

I have a big day tomorrow. Brunch with Mom, Hardware, cruising more trees, if you're there Suki, I'll find you. I also have a hunch (a gut feeling, not from my forehead). The school crossing guard is . . . a rabbit. What I base my conclusion on is this whole concept of alternative easy street systems. One can feel walled in on all four sides, why not all four corners? But bunnies? Is there historical precedence? Four corners of the earth is part of our heritage, as is four walls. The earth is getting smaller. At any given moment, especially day in day out confrontations with irate pedestrians—nobody likes being told systems aren't what they used to be—the corners, one, two, three, four start to close in on crossing guards. But rabbits?

Cite history, you cite human behavior.

Cite human behavior, you cite contradictions.

Walls are real; bunnies bogus. The power of Harold's attaché case, real; bunnies bogus. Psychic paw prints, real; bunnies bogus. Gerald's nose, Alex's nose, really real; bunnies bogus. Men in drains, real; bunnies bogus.

I'll make the school crossing guard confess.

Fabricate if I have to. This is fall. The words on the lips of every leaf: Here's where we separate the leaves that reach a finish line from the leaves that fall without rhyme or reason.

But why bunnies?

✗

I can hear the noise a half block away.

Noise spilling out on the sidewalk from Hardware. Perhaps Harold is throwing a party. A bash to celebrate bashing Mrs. Harold severely enough to flip her lid. They will both live happily ever after. Here on in, a love feast for both their eyes. Their lives, blessed.

I pick my way through.

Cross folk, the owners of Cross attaché cases, are camped out all over the place. I dare not ask anyone how he or she is, but the look I give them says let me in on it.

111

So they do.

"We're having a competition. Who can get the most out of our bags." A wrenlike woman, her scarf wrapped four times around her neck, taps her bag and orders up a six-pack of diet Coke. She gets Dr. Pepper. She smacks the bag. I wouldn't quite say she went up in a poof of smoke. In fact, it was only her scarf.

"You have a Cross case?" The man is in undershirt and tie. Nice tie, I say. "Let's see what you can do," challenging me.

"I'm wife number one."

"I've got several of those myself. Go back where you came from," waving his tie at me.

The wren woman with no scarf has a sharp beak. Her beak faces me while talking to him. "It always starts with one number one. Expect a steady trickle. I've been married four times. Filed on all four. First. The longest stretch was husband number one, seventeen years, three we lived together, one year of—"

"Letters," I say.

"Trial separation." Bird eyes looking at me like I was her worm. "You were in it for the long haul and didn't make the long, long haul. The trickle of number ones always begins with a forerunner, then builds to a gush. Day or two, mark my words . . . first spouse is like the first born. They never forget." Crinkling her nose.

This is fall.

I want to fall through the floor.

✗

Mr. and Mrs. Harold are in the other wing. I didn't know there was another wing. Apparently so. The light is faint, I have to squint. I follow the sounds of body heat. The bed sheets are in disarray. He is about to enter her. The standard missionary. It could be an all-nighter. If I'm going to ask, it has to be now.

"How are you?"

He climbs off her. On the night table, his Mark Cross. I hear the hum of machinery starting up. Harold puts his head in the Cross. Whispers, like players in a huddle.

This is fall.

The next time I think I want to fall through the floor I will not think it in a room full of attaché cases.

✗

112

Banished.

The good news is I'm back home, no hassle with Alex, no fuss with the elevators. I just appeared out of nowhere. Not a scratch on me. Citing history: There are lapses in every record.

Not magic.

Not necessarily mystic.

A lapse.

Followed by me getting ready for bed.

Eventually it will mean scrubbing my face, giving my skin an opportunity to breathe. Years of grime were removed from the Sistine Chapel, enhancing the art. Antique stores are full of tables restored to their former glory by stripping. My face is the other side of the art story. As makeup is removed, the object of beauty loses something in translation. My buddy the phone buys me time. It rings, I pounce (not on the first ring). Every minute spent on the phone is a minute I am not face to face with the chin permutating into I-don't-know-what.

"Are you in a better frame of mind?" It can only be my dear longevity friend Susan.

"Much much better."

"You're not just saying what you think I want to hear? I've caught Lou at it, it's all right, really it is, don't worry about bringing me down to your level, I have my system."

I'm tempted.

Set her straight, systems fail, even backups fail. She would only say it's the City putting words in my mouth.

"I bought a bathing suit."

"What's the matter with the ones you've got?"

I don't answer.

"You're holding out on me, I've caught Lou at it, pocketing change he hasn't got coming to him, sometimes as much as a quarter extra. He finds money on the sidewalk and doesn't give it to charity. I know for a fact he borrows pens and doesn't return them. His moral fiber lacks fiber."

"The bathing suits I've got are old."

"You should have said so in the first place. Now tell me what happened when you walked Patches. Lou told me Tony told him you were feeling up all the trees on the block."

"Suki."

"Suki's dead."

"I saw my dead cat."

"In what frame of mind were you?"

113

"Harold was getting married. I was dog-walking. But I did see her."

"I believe you believe you did."

"You didn't say that when I told you about the attaché case, and Harold moving into Hardware."

"That was then, this is now. How shall I frame the words? If I say too much I splinter your frame, too little, your frame thinks we're on the same plane, and we're not anywhere near. My frame's plane is head and shoulders above. Ask Lou."

(By tomorrow her frame could be reversed. Tomorrow I could actually tolerate her again.)

"Come over for breakfast, I'll buy bagels."

"Slot's taken." She asks for an afternoon slot. I offer her the one o'clock to one-ten.

"You don't make it easy. I'll take it."

"Say hello to Lou for me."

"Soon as his frame of mind comes to its senses."

If that isn't a closing line, what is?

✗

My face: Naked, it looks better than my hair.
I sleep in my bathing suit.
This is fall. Once in a while, I fall asleep with a smile on my face.

✗

My sleep is uneventful. My forehead mute. Nothing hops to mind.

✗

The day begins with a bang.

Nate calls to say his first patient canceled. Nate calls a second time to say his second patient canceled, third patient called Nate to say she'd be tardy.

He's on his way over.

Show me a lousy A.M. cell, one cell at a time coming to life, and I'll show you a lousy A.M. tumble. I fall back to sleep after arranging for Nate to be cleared through lobby security. I've left the door unlocked. Nate lets himself into the apartment (and into me) like a latchkey child. He mopes around inside my little nookery, entertaining himself, turning my nipples like knobs, fooling with my earlobes, mousing around inside my pipes. A juice spill splatters my pink tiles. He lets himself out. Skips off. I almost call after him, don't forget your lunch money.

✗

The day began with a bang . . .
Less than a beaut.

✗

I have heard nice things from him about his wife.
So.
If ever there is a cardiac event in the cockpit, I am to dial 911 and if his wife of whom I have heard nice things about confronts me, I am not to name names.
So.
If ever he crash-lands, his wings become disabled, his fuselage cracks in half, I am to dial 911 and if his wife accuses me of totalling her husband in bed I am to swear on my life we aren't even on a first-name basis.
Anyway it will never come to that.
So jubilant will Nora be that her cheating husband didn't drop dead, so glad will Nora be that her cheating husband survived the wreck, she will forgive all. But if she should ask, I am under oath. Deny everything.
Because.
The woman about whom I have heard such nice things from her husband, must never think, NOT FOR A MOMENT, her husband thinks she's a complete zero in bed.

✗

Everyone gets rescheduled. My mom, Susan, the crossing guard, Hardware. A conservative estimate would be a one-hour delay straight down the line depending on how fast my face can do an about-face.

✗

I breakfast in my new bathing suit, I shower in my new bathing

115

suit, under my jeans and turtleneck I wear my bathing suit. It looks no better than it did yesterday. Turning to the side in a bathing suit is thought-provoking. With most thoughts directed toward the abdomen. My stomach was never flat, when I sit the roll doesn't shoot out as far as my knockers, but there is substantial reason why I never look down when I'm sitting naked. The suit has earned its place in history, not by being figure flattering but by being here with me. The suit is an inspiration. Tonight I'm going to formally introduce it around. Throw a scare into my seventeeners . . . the socks, the bras, the relics.

Let them know they could be next.

✗

Just as I get to the elevators, they close. They know they're supposed to open when the button is pressed. Doors don't have options. The law governing elevators says elevators obey buttons. The penalty for not obeying the law is the person pressing the button with both thumbs kicks the door.

Then stairs it.

I'm not alone. Neighbors on the steps outnumber the people taking elevators. Two-way traffic, the middle lane for passing. At this hour nobody is weaving in and out. Everybody leaves enough stopping distance. We've all been down this route before.

Eight floors later. . .

Alex stands on the receiving line.

In turning to look, he turns slowly. Too quick, his nose could knock the wind out of an innocent bystander. He needs practice. My chin nearly gets it in the neck. At speed he could have severed me at the root.

"Watch where you aim that thing."

"It's like writing with the hand that isn't dominant. I can't quite get the grip."

"Keep at it. You'll see."

"Marilyn's shaped my nose with her own two hands. No one's ever taken the time and trouble. I was the rawest of raw material." He swings around to greet someone coming into the building. I duck out of the way, and out the door.

✗

What ever happened to take me as I am? Or what you see is

116

what you get? What ever happened to boy meets girls, girl leaves well enough alone?

✗

A glorious fall day. Leaves stir in the pocket park across the street. A small pocket park for those times you can't get to a big pocket park. I survey the trees. No Suki. I pet a dog in the park, nice doggie, pretty doggie, my what big eyes you have. Still no Suki.

History will repeat.

✗

I repeat, history can be a long or short time coming.

✗

Like a reporter covering her beat, I beat it to Hardware.

✗

The Cross people at the Hardware Store are sleeping off last night's party. The whole store feels done in. Reduced in size by half, each Cross person is plunked into his case, each case bathtub size. Making a big deal of this sort of thing in fall undermines the meaning of a Jane Samuels fall. My fall is separate from every other season. A lot should fall to the imagination. And much of what falls to the imagination really is real. In a Jane Samuels fall, doubt (not all, but some) is what falls through the cracks.

Harold and honey are sleeping.

They must have been at it for hours. In the sack, Harold never filed. First. Just as I am about to leave, an alarm clock inside the Cross goes off. Harold wakes, shuts it, wakes Mrs. Harold. Her eyes have been opened all along. She sleeps like a silent sentry. No weariness in her eyes.

Harold's eyes look like he slept in them.

"Nothing's new under the sun." It does grate after a while, even to historians who would agree. History copycats itself, but to be told so repeatedly . . .

It would file on the nerves.

"You're having your first child. Children make all the difference

117

in the world." Harold's voice has undertones and overtones. His approach is reasonable. But in some systems, no matter what you say, the system turns a deaf ear. It's like words and deeds. Do everything right, a land developer still makes you into a wasteland.

"I turned you around, now return the favor. Before I put you on the blink, you were an empty shell of a man."

Good for wife number two.

"Just look at me now." Careful Harold, you're walking a thin line. Sound miserable, you will only discourage her. Remember you want to do to her what she did to you. "I'm flipped in the lid. Issues that were never issues are suddenly grave new issues." He realizes he's laying it on too thick. A quick change, you can see it in his eyes. "I have a whole new outlook, wouldn't have missed it for the world." Hand on her tummy, head down listening for the baby's heartbeat. Her belly is so far along the watermark is show-ing a full reservoir. "Tell me what you need. Just name it. But don't make me hit you anymore, or pinch you."

She yawns.

"Hit me, pinch me, jab me." Her neutral tone is desert without dunes.

"Please." Harold's tone is hilly.

"Nothing's new under the sun."

I close my eyes as Harold puts his hands on her lids and yanks.

"Harder, harder." A vocal command, Mrs. Harold still in neu-tral. She doesn't have range.

I open my eyes.

"Nothing's new under the sun. Find a man to change my life."

✗

Dawn, the receptionist. Marilyn Beats. And Mrs. Harold.
All the same frame.
Do I want a man to change my life?
Talk to me about it after fall.
What I want right now . . . a finish line.

✗

Two blocks from the Hardware Store. My stride in full stride. Mom's place in fifteen minutes. I hold vigil over trees as I go. No Suki. No bunnies, no wraiths, no men coming out of walls. Only a group of children up ahead handing out leaflets. Maybe they're

118

working on a class project. Something to do with community. Helping to make the world a better place.

"You wear fur?" She has pigtails and a chipped tooth.

"No." No lie, I don't.

"You wear fur?" A boy with a Tom Sawyer face.

A swarm of them circling me. Pigtails and Tom Sawyers and Little Bo Peeps.

"How would you like it if someone—" Skinning motions with a rubber knife.

A metal band is slipped around my ankles.

I've met these types before. Citibank, Ms. Pemberton and her SWAT team of tellers. Give them a cause, then get out of the way.

"You wear fur?"

"Is it money you want, a contribution? I'm not going to buy my freedom, you release me now or—"

"You'd hit a kid?"

This sets off a discussion. Is it worse to hit kids or wear fur? Are people who hit kids more likely to wear fur? When somebody brings up whether or not I deserve to die, I protest vehemently.

"I'm going to count to three, release me by then or I will sing to you. Do you want a song with historical content or just multiplication, two times two all the way to fifty times fifty?"

Strong-arm tactics.

Meet force with force.

Be prepared.

Anything could fall into your lap.

That's the beauty of fall . . . you never know when the Big One's going to fall.

✗

On my way to Mom I was detained . . . for all the right reasons. I was liberated . . . by the times table.

✗

Mom's brunches are what people used to eat before they worried about what they ate. Leftovers from breakfast are a foregone conclusion. Tavern fare, hearty food. Not meat and ale but close. The pancakes have fillings, the fillings are filled with itty bitty bits and pieces that add up. Chew well, and don't forget liquids to keep the batter in your mouth from coagulating.

119

✗

The first twenty minutes of my food intake is monitored. It's what I'm used to. Mom did it in the high chair, she does it now. At the twenty-minute mark Irma pushes her chair from the table. She marches into the kitchen, her waist-length white braid coming loose, strands of hair down her back. I follow her, plate in hand so it doesn't look like what it is. What it is is tailing my own mom. Just as she scrutinized everything that went into my mouth, I will keep an eye on her. Nothing that has been said thus far is anything you wouldn't hear between any mother with access to walls (but not to men in walls) and any daughter who keeps her social life distinct from walls. There's been conversation.

The big topic did not fall out of our mouths.

"Come and get it," she calls.

It couldn't be me. I've already gotten it.

Out they pour.

Hands I wouldn't shake hands with. Webbed fingers, gnarled fingers, surplus fingers, hands large enough to be cheese boards, arms with tree knobs up and down their arms. They move through the walls like it was a transit system. The walls are stiff enough to support the ceilings but onion skin enough to see the multitude of homelies who have yet to exit. The first wave hits the leftovers. Never mind using spoons, forks, or napkins. Slurpy eating, guzzling, barnyard sounds. Dad didn't know the half of it. Mom's not just talking to the walls and rubbing against them. Mom's feeding the natives. Charity begins at home. At least they don't overstay their welcome. The look I give them is pure Pemberton. SWAT the buggers.

I tackle Mom.

Someone has to tell her hip injuries from falling pussies do not heal well when the pussy is in her seventies. Daughters should stop mothers from having sex before sex becomes sexual exploits.

"Are you having sexual intercourse with the walls?"

Mom tackles the question.

"Thirteenth-century English bestiary books are full of creatures like the ones in the walls." For years now my mother has been collecting coffee-table editions. In fact, I was the one who gave her the one on medieval art. "Sotheby's knows." How my mother knows about auction houses is easy. She's like me. We both have other things going on besides. Besides, the more you have on hand, the less you're going to feel the Big One if the wrong Big One falls into

120

your lap. It's a system. Besides are backup for systems besides the ones you've got. "Sotheby's solicits beasts. A 148-page manuscript of beasts from thirteenth-century Northumberland was sold by Sotheby's for $5.85 million. Colored-ink drawings on vellum. Even paper beasts get people climbing walls."

She gives me a conspiratorial look.

"I'll show you how it's done." Removing her apron. Unbuttoning her blouse. Her hair braid is history. With her silver hair loose, she looks less like a mom, more like a harlot.

Force with force.

Strong-arm tactics.

I am not going to watch my mother have sex. Moms potty train, moms teach their daughters how to cook a roast. All I know about where babies come from came from Mom.

"This doesn't jell. Not one thing in your history explains what you're doing. It's totally out of context." I sound like the mother I want her to be.

"Don't knock it till you've done it. Have you ever gone out of context?"

When your mother's life is riding on it, never tell the truth. "Never. Not in the context you mean. You've known Dad all your life. Dad is family. How can you be unfaithful to the past?"

"Nothing's new under the sun."

At least she hasn't said she wants a man to change her life.

"I need a lifestyle change."

"You can't treat history like this. The ties that bind—"

"Snip, snip."

I'm getting nowhere. "Just how far up the wall do you go?"

She blushes.

She gets over it. Off comes her skirt, her slip. My mother is in her panties. My mother does to her panties what she did to her slip and skirt. "When your father's not around," her eyes heavenward, "up there to the ceiling. When he is around, in the dark of night, three's not a crowd."

I bang the counter.

Bongo fists.

It brings them to the surface. I've read of small rodents who stomp the ground to bring worms up. Raindrops, when they come down hard enough, can also bring things up. Vibration attracts all kinds. Beasts emerge. A riot of color and types. Beasts with horns on their heads. The horns between their legs stiffly out, held like they're taking a sobriety test.

121

She lifts her breasts.

Beasts suckle. They put their hands on her round buttocks. She touches them where they like to be touched. They lift her off the ground. They cradle her like a babe. She asks for the bottle to be put in her mouth.

I grab for her.

They grab harder.

Citing history: Lose the battle, win the war. I will return. For now, though my cause is just, it's a lost cause. I let myself out. Just as there are some things better left unsaid between parent and child, there are some things better left unseen. One is catching your parents humping each other. Another is seeing your mother fuck medieval art.

✗

And furthermore. . .

It could be as simple as letting her get it out of her system. Her behavior doesn't meet with my approval. How I express my disapproval is a matter of common sense. Come down too hard, I invite open rebellion, possibly elopement. Confrontation can ruin a mother-daughter relationship. If I lose my parents to the walls (or drains) I don't want the break to be permanent. By keeping open the lines of communication, I let my parents know their daughter would never file on them. First.

✗

Reverse direction. Walk back uptown. Twenty-third Street to Fifty-sixth, Susan lives between Eighth and Ninth. A detour in between, I won't be long. Just stop by a corner where a certain someone is helping the people of our fair city by telling them what they least want to hear: The system sucks.

✗

Lime green. Coral reds.

The school crossing guard is brighter than the brightest traffic light. Her slacks and jacket are divided into big squares. She would be wasted behind a desk. I can't keep my mother out of walls, maybe I can keep the crossing guard out on the street. The last thing I need is for her to go where the pressure's off. My one rabbit connection could hop out on me forever. Somehow she has to understand a desk job is a loaded gun. What's my angle? I have no angle. I have a blank wall. Only a blank . . .

"Sitting behind a desk, processing citations, what kind of life is that? We need women in uniform. You'd feel too walled in. Even with a view, they can't put in a single window without putting in a wall. Walls first. Then windows. In square feet, there'll be more wall space per inch than windows per foot. You thought you had it rough with the four corners closing in on you, think again. Anything can crawl out of the woodwork. It's not a patented system. Theoretically, corners, drains anywhere. But the wall is where men in the wall really reside. Why put yourself in a desk job where wall pressure adds an extra corner? What all four corners combined couldn't do, the fifth corner—the wall corner— can do with its eyes closed. Once you start making it with wall men, think what that kind of sex does to your pathways. It would cloud your judgment. Your only thought would be of your own pleasure. The next orgasm, how many on the head of a pin. Basically you would fuck like a rabbit but roaming the streets as one— to alleviate the four-corner pressure—forget it. The fifth corner would make you a love slave. And that's the one corner above all corners you don't want to be backed into. You'd never be able to file. First."

Damn.

I shouldn't have been so graphic. Her face is the red of her suit, which brings out the green more, but in signals means stop. I've gone through her unspoken red light. Right in front of her face too. No faster way to put up walls between people than to ignore their traffic signals.

She files. Of course.

I respect her for it.

My head's so-so.

Monumentally, unusually so-so.

I blatantly violated her colors.

✗

She hasn't seen the last of me yet. After what that rabbit did to me, it's hard not to want somebody's hide.

✗

123

Susan's doorman waves me on, dispensing with the formalities. Tony's been briefed. That's how the doorman-tenant system is supposed to work. The elevator is empty. I press six. Delivered to six. Doors open. Once again, system reliability. The Big One, though, can fall anytime.

I don't have to knock.

Patches' bark is my knock.

"Let's talk in the other room." Susan looks drained of blood. Her olive skin, nearly white. She ushers me into the bedroom. The apartment has two definitive rooms. The slumber room off the main room, and the living room. Kitchen, bathroom, and foyer are finger foods. The living room is called Lou's room because he spends so much time there. A desert motif. Twenty-five cacti representing exactly what cacti represent.

We sit on the bed.

Susan leans against the headboard. Knees up, arms around her knees. Hugging herself to herself. The perfect bowl of her hair is windblown. "Just now in the laundry room there was an assault to my frame of mind that was worse than any assault of New York City air." Clenching, her arms wrapped cinch belt tight. "There wasn't a washer to be had. The accountant from the fourteenth floor removed his load and gave me his machine. He used his own quarters to start me on a new cycle." Is this another moral tale? Yet another lesson for me to draw upon when my library books are overdue? "I didn't swap my tits for a free washing machine. It wasn't like that. All he wanted was a peek. All he got was a peek."

Not a moral tale, a dark tale.

I try to reply in terms that are on her terms.

"All frames of mind falter. That's the way the system works. The light turns green, you walk, you never make it to the other side. Or you marry, seventeen years later, your kitten's a cat, the cat ships out, the husband grows into a land developer. Systems are like beaches, the erosion—"

A stiffening of her shoulders.

"My system allows for a weak frame of mind. It was never designed to eliminate inviting offers, accountants slipping it in, using the washing machine to support my back, accountants mounting me, fucking me against the washing machine like a Mix Master. Those aren't just City temptations. Break the holy marriage vows, ball the pizza man who delivers door to door, spread your legs in subways, it's pussy collusion. I'm every bit as pussy as you are. But my moral fiber is not the beach yours is. My moral

124

fiber doesn't erode. The accountant was an emissary of the City. Singled out by the City is what I've come to expect. Now the City is stepping up the action in the crotch. A full-blown campaign. The biggest frame-up of all. Thinking with my dick."

Adjournment to the bathroom.

Susan prepares a color rinse for Patches. The last one lasted only a week. Toilet seat down, I sit on it. She takes out a mixing bowl, mixing water and color in proper amounts. I help her unfold the plastic cloth, like the drip cloths moms put under paint easels for the kiddies. Patches hurries over. I don't know whether he likes his spots painted or it's the cookies afterwards.

She hands me a brush.

We each do a side.

"You've outflanked the City before, you'll do it again."

"Did the City tell you to say that? Are you so pussy-whipped you'd lead your dear longevity friend into a sense of false security?"

"I'm not the City's pawn."

"You aren't the girl next door either."

We dip our brushes, carefully brushing them against the sides of the bowl. Picking our spots. Patches' spots, you always want to pick the roundest ones. A jagged spot, the lines are harder to follow.

There's an art to spot picking.

"The City did tell me." (I'll hate myself in the morning.) "But you saw through it." (I earnestly say.) "The City couldn't fool you."

"Confession is good. Confession helps build moral fiber. Confession is food for the soul."

"Books are food for the soul."

"Confession is better. Did the City also make you say books are good for the soul?"

"The words were put in my mouth, yes."

Finally Patches gets his cookies.

I beg off.

"Must you go so soon? If you must, then remember the rule of thumb, put yourself in the frame of mind where you wouldn't do anything your mother wouldn't do. Don't do it for me, do it for Mom. If that's on too high a plane for you, then think precisely step by step what your mother does. And do likewise."

(That really rankles, she doesn't know about Mom. But still . . .)

Good-byes are said.

125

Door is opened, door is closed. Elevator comes, down I go. Hello Tony, see ya Tony. Out the door . . . Hardware here I come.

✗

Fall . . . the things that fall out of people's mouths. I confess when I confessed to Susan—yeah the City is telling me what to say—I lied. Right away I felt better. In the frame of mind I'm in, I don't need anybody rubbing my face in a spot that isn't even a sore spot, but rubbed enough could become a sore spot.

I'm not the girl next door.

So?

✗

My body heads for Hardware.

My mind to another spot besides the one I'm in.

Filed on. First. wasn't my first experience with files. Everyone in research has mental files. All kinds of facts and figures filed away for that time when retrieval is necessary. My system is to access when it's not necessary. And to do it at random. No one would ever think of having just one change of clothes. The idea behind that is never to be caught short. Clothes lack staying power. Not only do they get threadbare, one season to the next, they hang like strangers. Even if you've put a roof over their heads, they've got a wild streak. Or your friendly neighborhood cleaners may well turn out to be an underground railroad, smuggling designer clothes to faraway lands. Extra thoughts, like extra clothes, are insurance. Money stashed away. A kind of safety cushion. The thoughts you have, besides the ones you've got, provide you a way to fall right side up after a big bad one falls in your lap. Always have a little something going on the side. I would not recommend this to any but those who are at ease with quoting out of context, and its affiliates, going out of context, and coming out of context in the backseats of cabs.

Just let it happen.

As it's happening now. . .

My life is blessed.

The head's so-so.

Engine trouble's monumental.

Bottom line, my files are mint. You are only as good as your files.

126

Besides on the Hormone Oxytocin

After the sex act there is a rise in oxytocin. Inject a female rat with oxytocin during ovulation and she will display her genitals 60 to 80 percent more than females without the hormone. She will solicit mounts like a rabbit. Inject it in an asocial rat, a rat without a history of cuddling, a rat whose brain is not primed for changing his mind, and the hormone will fizzle.

How effective oxytocin will be as an aphrodisiac, a socializing stimulant, a fraternizing compound, a bonding agent to increase a parent's nurturing depends on natural inclinations. Those not predisposed are not the best candidates for oxy-tocins.

The hormone has an agrarian background.

Five minutes of vaginal stimulation in sheep that have given birth will release enough oxytocin into the bloodstream to make a ewe a model mother.

Scientists are researching the brain for receptors that aid and abet oxytocin. Someday it is hoped they will have a better understanding of what it takes to ma-nipulate a frame of mind.

The immediate applications of besides aren't always immediate. Some besides are indeed way beside the point. And others are like chimps. When chimps were first studied they were said to be a minor point until it was discovered chimps are man's mainstay. The beauty of my method is its spontaneity. I surprise myself. Like people that go around lifting cars off victims trapped underneath, the rush is energizing. Besides thrill, it's no small consolation knowing that if your entire mind filed. First. (thoughts shipping out without a thirty day notice), your files would take up the slack. Falling upon reserves is the crux of my system. Beams hold up buildings. Besides are supports to the beams. It's stood me in good stead. To this day, I've never lacked for a single solitary two by four.

✗

Hardware . . . arrived.

The Cross touch is the Midas touch. Not gold per se, but the power to alter what is before us. With all the wealth in the world at their disposal, Gucci is topped by Mark Cross. Gucci does not have the wherewithal to pull a chair from an attaché case. Somebody over at Mark Cross must have raided a treasure trove of besides.

The store's roof is raised.

Cathedral ceiling, birds on rafters.

Harold is nowhere to be seen. I enter a new room. Cast in blue. Undulating seawater. On one wall is an aquarium that hangs like a tapestry. Shimmering fish, iridescent, changing in the blink of an eye.

127

A voice from the opposite wall.

"Say it, say it, say it."

Wife number two is seated on a floor pillow. She looks heliumized. She offers me a cushion. Green satin, fringes, no ruffles. The seating arrangements are satisfactory. I cross my legs under me. Divas, before they slim, have her Buddha bloat. Wall to wall breasts. Like an extra pair of knees.

The same request.

"Say it, say it, say it." Pared down. Despite the insistence of her words, detached is what I hear. Still, I don't want to traumatize her guppy so I say it.

"How are you?"

She lifts the bottom of her maternity top. She anoints her barge with cocoa butter. She picks up a hand mirror. She flosses. "I tire more easily now. I've doubled my intake of calcium. I put on a few pounds. This isn't the first time I've had a change of circumstances." Her face smooth as her voice. No tonality. Child-chubby hands, not a day over twenty. "Being a blinker all your life, you probably take blinks for granted. My gaze doesn't have the whole range of movement. Until the lid flicks I can't share in the emotions that go along with it. It's no use telling me it doesn't work the way I see it. Everything is outlook. Outlook is ocular. Your trigger isn't jammed. Naturally our outlooks are going to be different."

She isn't inanimate.

Yet she is.

I'm not the last word on lids. But as an amateur, just an offhand guess, oxytocin deficiency. Something tells me there are street rats (with the scars to prove it) who are more convivial. Dip her eyes in oxytocin, she might still be resistant. She is no ewe. Lacking certain hormones, it has to show up somewhere.

Besides do provide.

It's up to me to make the links.

Mrs. Harold waves her doughy hand. Am I dismissed?

"To the man that makes me blink, I will personally grant my hand in marriage. You are dismissed."

I don't get very far.

Outside the blue room, Owner ambushes me. He's all hush-hush, bending over to talk, making his body our soundproof booth. "They haven't sent the money yet. One, two days tops, that's all I give them. Either Cross comes across or I go public. Just substantiate something for me: you've seen the others?"

I nod.

"Say it, say it, say it," Owner says.

"I've seen maybe dozens of people with Cross bags. Theirs operate the same way as—"

"Don't bother saying it."

x

I wouldn't have said it anyway.

In the midst of Owner telling me not to say it, my forehead is a bugle boy. My lap tugs, a mother tugging her child. Pointing due east. It's moments like this I can't wait to get home. Read my paw: Home is where Gerald is. Just to see what will befall, I tell my forehead, say it, say it, say it.

The paws say the last thing I expect them to.

"Three's not a crowd."

x

The day began with a beaut. Is the day going to end with a three-way bang?

x

Traveling time, I make great time.

x

Have I presumed too much? I presumed Gerald would be waiting for me in the lobby. I am correct. I presumed a lap job. But I have only to look at the joint on Gerald's face to see it's not engorged. He's got it covered. A muslin slipcover over his nose, not unlike those that falconers put on peregrines. Under the hood the joint is creasy. Is it joint disease? Is his nose out of joint? How dare he show his face around here looking like that? Alex's nose is turned up, the universal nose gesture of superiority. Rubbing Gerald's nose in it like my dear longevity Susan. That alone is reason enough to invite Gerald up. In the elevator I have second thoughts. The slipcover flattens more. Ground zero. Chambermaids in the best hotels don't make beds that smooth.

A variation of how are you:

"What's the deal with your nose?"

129

"I dropped my kids off at their mother's. The mother of my children has a boyfriend. He hugged my kids." His nose taking can't-catch-my-breath breaths. Right before we reach my apartment his nose starts to squirm like a kitten in a sack. "I'd like to raze her. I'd like to give it to her good. I'd like to break every joint in her body."

Smoke under the hood.

I can hardly get my key in the door fast enough. Gerald rips off the hood. Cock on his face. The falcon goes for the kill.

I . . . prey.

✗

Darted in and out of. Gerald's nose the anteater. My vaggie one big anthill on the outside, inside is the ant colony. We both come within seconds of each other. More snot in my crotch, no condom. On top of a yeast infection, I could catch major germs. Gerald sleeps. I sleep close to his nose, a cowpoke on the open range snuggling up to her horse. In bed, at last. The tapping on the wall wakes me. Something creeping on my ass, unremitting. The tapping associated with open-up-and-let-me-in. I am awful at those blind tastings. Guess the wine, no peeking at labels. But I do know when a cork is looking for a decanter to cork.

I can smell this one a wall away.

Marty Nesterbaum opens my cheeks, someone opening the King James. He enters me. Gerald wakes. My face, in his face, covering his eyes. I suck off his nose. During wine-tasting I don't feel compelled to taste every single wine. In real life I don't buy it when a homely gets his gal. (My mother is not a gal.) So why don't I shoo the man in the wall?

Because three's not a crowd.

✗

Still later.

Marty came and went, Gerald soon after. It may take hours but this is one of my finest hours. Individual introductions. My bathing suit to hundreds of socks, holes in toes, most missing their mates, bras so old they can barely hold themselves up, seventeen-year-old bathing suits from a previous life.

I line them all up.

"Listen up, see how this grabs you. I've given you free room and board. For over a decade you've been treated royally. Free-

130

loading every chance you get. Exploiting me for your own benefit. At every turn, reminding me how far we all go back. As if that were some kind of lifetime ticket. Safe passage is a myth. No such thing. Get it out of your heads. Any minute I could file. First, last and always, geological history is not one long era. Read my lap: Dinosaurs die out."

I sleep in my bathing suit.

Night took its time getting here. The day began with Nate. Not a beaut. The day ends with a three-way and a spark of rebellion.

A beaut.

x

Night into day . . .

A restful night.

Uninterrupted bliss.

Last night made my day.

Most notable the bathing suit speech. This time next fall, I could have drawer space. Yesterday began and ended with beauts. Today begins with breakfast in bed. Cappuccino yogurt, fresh-squeezed juice, herbal tea. For one whole half hour I don't think of my mother. I don't think, period. (After the one whole half hour, it's a Mother's Day blitz.) Her relationship to the homeless has always been above reproach. Do not encourage them; when approached by the homeless, have a coin ready—exact change—drop it in the receptacle, take off fast, pay as you go. Now my mother's putting out. By rights anyone in a wall should be boxed in. Instead, when City Hall deposited the homeless into walls, they somehow got refracted out to there. A twist. Are mothers and daughters any safer leaning against their own walls than going unarmed into the streets of New York? It's been contrary right down the line. What probably happened, things went awry. Someone forgot the homeless were people too. They have sexual appetites. Far be it from me to get into the ethics involved. The three-way with Gerald and Marty was safe. Minimal risk of injury. How long will it be before someone falls from the ceiling? The possibility of litigation alone should make the City revise its policy.

The whole thing smacks of politics.

Win votes by getting rid of the homeless. Win votes because people off the wall are fed up with being accosted for handouts. What it comes down to is numbers. If the number of people fornicating with walls turns out to be greater than the number of

131

people abstaining and the number of people who are relieved to see the homeless anywhere but on the street is greater than those opposed to radical solutions, then stuffing the homeless into walls is political genius. As of this moment, based on one parent climbing the walls, the other taking the drain route in, and my touchy-feely with Marty, if I had to vote . . .

Sure.

It deserves a chance. From what I've seen so far, if nothing else, we can't do worse by the homeless than we've already done.

Sure . . .

Except leave my parents right where you found them.

✗

Too much too soon.

I can't keep up with myself. Morning syndrome. Thinking is a cold water plunge. I am dangerously awake. The diver coming up too fast, cells that don't know whether to laugh or cry, the body wants up and out. It's go now or climb the walls. I bathing suit it again, in the shower, singing in the shower, blow dry the suit, wearing a damp suit, I dab on lipstick, the oil slick on my face is cream at forty dollars an ounce, the face powder covers the cream, no amount of concealing will subdue my hair, raging forest fire, flames licking, just have to let them burn themselves out, I don't need a silk dress, I need a terry cloth for the bathing suit. Jeans, flannel shirt on, boots. Bag. Can't leave without the Claiborne.

Should I answer the phone?

I'll tell whoever it is to make it fast.

"Noon today," Nate spits out. "On the couch, my office."

Sex with him is abridged. Arrangements for abridged sex should not exceed the act itself.

"I guess."

"You guess? Will you or won't you?"

"Will."

Fling good-byes me, good-bye back.

I'm pumped. Steps two at a time. Alex, get out of my way . . . must walk this off . . . the state I'm in . . . the Big One could fall into my lap and I'd ask for something bigger.

✗

First hour: Aimless walking, walking just to walk. The window-

132

shopping is so I won't be completely unproductive. Next hour: Better, more relaxed, I can plan my day like the rational person I am. For the next day or so, no visiting the crossing guard (breathing space), let her begin to wonder whether it was something she said to me instead of the other way around. Hardware and Fling, that leaves an entire day, unless the chimps, Mr. and Mrs. Harold, prove so eventful—finish line just around the bend—that staying becomes imperative. Not being on the scene when a Big One is about to fall into your lap is missing your big scene big time. I don't have the heels for it, I've got the dress. If I had the heels to go with the dress, I couldn't carry on about nothing to wear (a big scene all its own), all in anticipation of the Special Occasion, the name I've given to the Big One falling into my lap. Let it be good . . . let it be heaven-sent . . . let it—

Dad, is that you?

✗

Park Avenue between Thirty-first and Thirty-second. Ten forty-five in the morning. Across the street stands a man in front of a young woman. Blocking her. She executes a basketball maneuver, feigning one way, going another. He flits to another female. The pattern is repeated. His color is high. He's tall like my dad. Same white hair like Dad. Hunting jacket, same. I hurry off. I can't say I will never be the daughter of a homely who pops out of the woodwork. I can say when a parent is at that midpoint, coming on to off-the-wall women before he knows how to drop through the sidewalk, my first thought is he wouldn't want his daughter to see him. Second thought, his safety. Pick the wrong off-the-wall-woman, block her path, make her feel her back's to the wall, you're asking for trouble. Even off-the-wall women who are receptive to climbing the wall are dangerous. When you promise to get somebody climbing and you have no wall to back you up, you're making false claims.

✗

Unholy trio.

Wraiths.

This time I hear them without seeing them. My preference would be to see them. It's objectionable to have meddling in-laws. It's more objectionable to have ex in-laws meddle invisibly. I may

133

be so-so in the head but I am not so monumentally so-so that I don't know what you hear but can't see can make any head not the least bit so-so feel that much more so-so.

Yvette's voice is to my left.

"Your parents could be a danger to themselves. Are they forgetful? Do they get lost? Any change in sleep patterns? Do they get winded? When was the date of their last physical?"

To the right . . .

"My daughter can take any issue and make it into a bigger issue. You don't get a face like that from ignoring the issues."

Dead center . . .

Sam stomps an invisible umbrella on the sidewalk. "The Helens of this world have ruined it for the rest of us. They say they take issue with nothing and yet they issue orders around the clock: Put your mushroom in me, make your mushroom bigger, push your mushroom farther, get your mushroom out of my sight."

I put my hands to my ears.

"Stop squabbling."

My own personal Homeric chorus sings. "No wonder he filed. First. She wants to hear herself think."

✘

The wraiths are gone.
Gone to wherever wraiths go to when they are not of this world.
I'm gone too.
Hardware on Third.

✘

Cathedral ceilings right where I remember them. Rafters, no birds. The Hardware Store is heavier on hardware. Lighter on living quarters. The Cross crowd is sitting—surprise, surprise—on chairs with flounces and ruffles. Most are reading, glancing periodically at their watches, looking up expectantly every time someone comes in, the way pigeons do for crumbs. The wrenlike woman is in a group seated in a circle. The group is fast on their feet. Now it's me in the center of their new circle.

I know the script.

"Say it, say it, say it." In a group voice.

Lady Wren tells the group to hush. It takes a while, she loses patience, she opens her Cross, puts her head in, each person in the group loses his voice. She turns to me. "What you're doing is commendable. So many divorces end bitterly. People not speaking. Treating each other like they were history. For some time now we've waited for our number ones, the people we filed on. First. to parade through that door. If they don't it will be a first. How dare they treat us like we've fallen off the edge of the world? You're so nice, now say it, say it, say it."

I refuse.

She puts her head in the Cross, leaning over. I come up behind her, I tip her in, the Cross crunches. I say what I've always longed to say: The End.

Spoken prematurely.

Mrs. Harold springs from behind. I am spun around. In her tent jumper, she's a duplex. The attaché case she's carrying is the size of a lunch box. "I'll make a deal with you: you get me to blink, I'll marry you. Harold's totally inept. This morning alone he executed forty-five ploys. Nothing fazed, not in the least. You could be the one. The one who makes a difference in my life. We could marry, a small private ceremony. I know just the photographer. Harold could be best man." Talking at me, rather than to me.

Harold comes over.

"Pay no attention to what she said," a fierce growl. "How people look at life is not a direct reference to the eye. Lay one hand on my breeder and you will be barred from hearing how it all turns out. For the rest of your life, what became of us will be inconclusive. Now say it, say it, say it."

"How are you?"

Whispering.

"I want to put an end to this. It can't go on much longer. Somewhere, sooner or later, all things end. In the end, the kid's the end-all, be-all. The mother's only the means to an end." He leads her away. From the back, her service entrance is trashed. Her spread is lava. I don't want to see it end like this, without the end in sight. Neither do the Harolds. There is a consensus. End it will. I'll be here, seeing it through.

To that end:

Harold's at his wit's end . . . is this the beginning of the end?

✗

Owner's busy on the phone.

With the minimum amount of coins required for the minimum

amount of time to get across a message succinctly, I call the Fling from a corner booth.

"I said I would. But I'm not. No lunch on the couch." In a therapeutic setting, repeating a patient's words allows the patient to hear how he sounds. Nate repeats. "No lunch on the couch. I said I would but I'm not."

Me played back to me.

I don't sound like I'm saying there's nothing more I'd like to do than make beauts with you on the couch but alas schedule conflicts do not permit. I've-had-a-better-offer is what it has the ring of. He begs me to visit Castle Milieu. In acreage alone, ten. Jokes, riddles, dreams.

"No."

"Is that a firm no?"

"Yes."

Phone connection, disconnected.

His hang-up files on my hang-up. First.

It's not enough nowadays to let them pour their sperm into you almost at will. They also want to get you in the clutches of who they really are.

✗

To the naked eye I am a redhead in penny loafers hurrying back to Hardware at a pace that says Fuck with me you're history. To the naked eye I'm the face that believes too little makeup is better than too much. To the naked eye it would be impossible to guess while rushing into a store I've got other things on my mind.

Besides.

Besides provide. Besides provide in spurts. Sometimes you coordinate them to your schedule, other times you just let yourself drift. Open your mind, files fall at your feet. When that happens you don't file on your files. The reason you keep extras of anything is to keep one step ahead of everything. My body looking for the Harolds. My mind on other things besides.

A Besides on Lobes

The neurobiology of emotion: Behind every sunny disposition, a left frontal lobe. Behind every doleful person, a right frontal lobe.

Frontal cortex brain activity is at the forefront of studies trying to determine how we end up being who we are. The data suggests that pronounced brain activity on one side or the other affects temperament. Experimental findings by Dr.

Davidson and Dr. Tomal of Vanderbilt University show that those with more right side going for them are not as social, hopeful, or exuberant. The worldview isn't to embrace the whole world.

Dr. Tellegen, a psychiatrist at the University of Minnesota, allows for different phases in life. Brain chemistry changes in adolescence, midlife, and old age. Traits, however, appear relatively stable.

Dr. Davidson does not rule out the possibility of being able to turn on the juice of your left frontal lobe. Changing your mind, getting into the frame of mind where life sings, might one day be feasible.

I find the Harolds. Both are inside their respective Crosses. Her little black bag is king-size, Harold's bag is suspended like a hammock, swinging him to sleep. Chimps at rest.

Me too. Besides that? I want to think.

✗

Applying besides isn't the point. Each and every besides is meant to be cherished. Having a little something on the side is peace of mind. Still, I can't help but search for meaning. Linkups. A researcher is programmed to look for daisy chains, to make sense somehow of material, to put the out of context into some context. First oxytocin, now lobes. What do both have in common? Frames of mind. All of us are two-lobed people. Now if we could only wire ourselves (Susan's system is a wiring system) then we could be the people we want to be instead of the people we are.

For now, it's a struggle.

Standing between Mrs. Harold and her blink is Mrs. Harold. She has a mindset. But she's also had a vision. She's expressed a desire for something besides what she's got.

Citing geological history: Everyone has layers stacked against them. The heap has a top of the heap. How you stack up . . . well that always depends on what else is going on besides.

Citing history: A lot goes on besides.

✗

The tree check in the park across the street from where I live turns up one squirrel, no cat. I decide against asking Alex to keep an eye out. Alex would do it gladly. Once his nose fixation wears off, maybe I will ask.

He holds the door.

Looking a little down in the mouth at the nose. The sigh emitted from his nose is tea kettle. The tip of his nose is pulled low like a slouch hat. The sides of his nose, deflated. Around the nostrils, grout of some sort. If he wants to tell me, he will. If I wanted to know, I'd ask. The elevators are somewhere in the upper stratosphere. The last time one was around when I needed it was when I pressed the button ten minutes in advance. Some would say this is the price one pays for living in a building occupied by neighbors. I say the elevators are heels.

Alex leaves his post to join me by the elevators.

"She's given me the ultimatum." The whistle of his nose picks up. Wind on a deserted street. "Until Marilyn none of my clothes were imported. My nose blossomed under her tender touch. She made me what I am today." His nose revives, striking a body-builder's pose, bulge and tight gut. Bodies like his only come by noses like that by way of high technology. "Camaraderie isn't enough. She wants somebody to change her. Make her different than she's ever been. Bring her along the way she's brought others along."

The elevators, my wings.

Now I can finally put miles and miles between lobby and me. If only Alex doesn't press the hold button. Alex presses hold. The closing doors open. I feel I'm being held against my will.

"Let go of the button, Alex."

"But I like her just the way she is." He releases the button, pulls his nose out of the line of fire before the doors castrate it. All the way up, linkups. What are the patterns here? Who fits where? My mother wants a lifestyle change. Marilyn, unspecified changes in herself. Wife number two, a change in outlook. Yours truly, a change from past to present. Working against change: lobes, hormones, what else besides? Everything else besides. Representing change (at the flick of a frame) dear longevity Susan, although that may change.

If we were chimps, I'd say we were all a barrel of monkeys.

✗

My apartment is better than it was. After it got filed upon. First. it suffered bouts. Dust balls, bigger than my fist. They came like locusts. Faucets with nose drips. The false fireplace reeked of false smoke. The bedroom closet, large enough to sleep two and a half, vomited for weeks after Harold cleared his clothes. Each surface—

wood, tile, glass—had its separate sound. By day, a racket of buzzes and trebles and screeches. By night, a bunch of crybabies. And then the bouts stopped, a gradual recovery. Not that the apartment wasn't expected to recover. So-so isn't touch and go, so-so you don't get, nor do you expect, a turn for the worse.

The phone for a change . . .

Not yoo-hoo. Not dong.

Fourth ring, I pick up.

"Is this a bad time?"

Coming from Susan the question is an inquiry into my frame of mind. I frame my answer: "I was just thinking about the neurobiology of emotion. Tinkering with your lobes to adjust your frame of mind is still a long way off for most of us. It should not deter us, however, from seeking outside help. Offer our hand in marriage, issue an ultimatum, consult walls. Recent research on oxytocin only underscores the point. When it comes to framework, the natural inclination is to be who you are, rather than who you want to be. So when you talk about the various antifreezes and how they work on the brain, you're really taking about how receptive your receptors are. What it comes down to is this: Making up your mind about what you're going to wear is far easier for most of us than changing our minds."

Pause. It goes on so long I ask her if she's still there. She tells me she is but that doesn't tell me much.

"I need to see you."

"When?"

"Right away."

"Where?"

"Anywhere."

"Häagen-Dazs near Carnegie Hall?"

I take her hang-up for a yes.

✗

Elevator or stairs?

I walk.

Alex or back door?

I back door.

✗

Häagen-Dazs.

Where people pay a premium price for licking something off the face of the earth. The girl behind the counter looks like the flavor of the month. Strawberry hair, the tint of her aviators, strawberry. Her lips are fresh fruits. The forearm is stacked. A forearm that could do nude scenes without bothering with a tan. Nowadays there's nothing little girls aren't made of. She probably says yes as much as I do.

Susan comes in with wet hair.

Her bowl's tilted. The moonface is half a moon. "I confessed to Lou. The accountant emptying his machine, paying for mine, the tits, everything. Confession is good for the soul. But the City got to Lou. Just as it's gotten to everyone. It's taken his frame of mind and done something to it. Until this morning, he worshipped my strong frame. Did he confide in you, at anytime has Lou ever told you he feels framed by me?"

I pat her hair into place.

"I'm only guessing. In the long run, long-running marriages are like long-running shows. The leads show signs of restlessness."

Her bowl blows.

"That's the City talking. Lou and you are of low moral charac-ter. Without the benefit of my friendship, God knows what gutter you'd end up in." Her fingers fly along the eyeglass frames she doesn't wear. Twice, three times, some keyboard action as well. Then a sigh of relief. "Nothing the City does, nothing either of you say will snap my frame of mind. I will never climb cock, after cock, after cock." Susan orders a single scoop. French vanilla. Her eyes register the girl's forearm. Her eyes do not slide all over it. As do mine. As do the people behind us. So sound of mind is Susan she can pass on forearm.

"You confessed to Lou."

"Confession is good for the soul."

"Lou was upset."

"Not at first. At first he showed solidarity."

"He comforted you."

"Solidarity, you know."

"He held you in his arms."

"He held himself at arm's length, you know."

"You've lost me."

"He got an erection, surely you know there are many ways to show your love and affection and solidarity. We are man and wife. Lou is never on a higher moral ground than when he reaches out to me with his pride and joy, letting me know how prideful and

140

joyful he is that I stood my ground."

"After you confess, he gets a monumentally, unusual hard-on?"

"It was different this time. He went at me, oh it's too personal, I can't tell you the rest. You're owned and operated by the City."

She's rubbing that spot again, the spot that isn't sore, but rub it enough, it gets sensitive.

"Lou did confide in me." (Maybe the City does own and operate me.) "He said these confessions of yours are just your way of getting him up and keeping him up."

"No, not my Lou. As morally degenerate as he is—"

"I confess. (That'll show the City.) "He didn't confide in me at all, I just put myself in his place, just as an experiment, just to see . . ."

Her fingers working her temples.

". . . it won't happen again. The last thing I want is for Lou to file. First."

We hug. Girlie solidarity. One thing she can count on from her friend Jane Samuels. When it has to do with filing. First. Jane Samuels does not lie.

✗

Susan leaves before me. I've promised to help. Whatever it takes. Lou Gold will not file. Last. First. Or ever. I stay behind, dawdling. It's not that I don't want to see my parents, it's the fear of what I'll see when I get there. Yet I refuse to phone ahead. Give them time to hide things from me, they will. But going by my mother's recent invitation to watch her fuck medieval art, I don't know what's left to hide. I really shouldn't complain. There are children whose parents have serious cardiac problems, respiratory difficulties, arterial and rheumatoid disease. I am fortunate. For all their problems, my parents really don't have any.

I stop dawdling.

✗

Step on it. The cab guns it. There is no magic. The seconds flat it takes us to get there is because when I told him to step on it, I said it like I had a cigar between my teeth. A carry-over from old gangster movies. Citing film history: Cab scenes are classic.

✗

141

No knock.

I let myself in.

I get my bearings.

The noise I'm hearing is from the living room. The living room is down the hall to the left. The shutter doors are closed. I open them. On the ceiling, next to the crystal chandelier, a new chandelier. My mother, Irma. Her unbraided hair is long enough for me to stand on the sofa, grab her by her hair, and pull. But I don't want to be the death of her. Startle anyone . . . an early grave.

She looks down. "I'll be fine. Go see what your father's up to. He's been in the bathroom for hours. Ask him if it's—"

"Prostate."

"Don't say that word. Ask is all I'm asking."

I knock at the bathroom door. No answer. I try the door. Locked.

"Another minute."

"Mom wants you out."

I put my ear to the door. Water down the drain. I go back to the living room. Mother calls down. "As soon as he's out, look for blood. Last time he tried to flush himself down the kitchen sink, I saw tracings. How does a man that size expect to fit in a drain?"

She doesn't know.

Irma's beasts are wall people. She has no idea they come out of a lot more than the woodwork. I'd rather she learn it from Dad. I don't stand directly under her, the sofa will serve as a soft landing. I move the coffee table, then I move the sofa. "I warned you. Stuck up there like a cat in a tree. I know how you got up, just tell me how to get you down." Dad joins us. He's in one of those holiday robes. Red trim. A large valentine heart over his heart. He reaches up.

Mom slaps his hand away.

"Back off. Do you hear me, Frank? I'll come down in my own good time." A slow-motion suction peel, the other arm free. Most of the human Band-Aid is still adhering. "Check the drains," Mom reminding me.

I inspect the tub.

Droplets of blood. Something has to be done before my father mutilates himself or gets wasted by some off-the-wall woman with her back to the wall. The sound of plopping. I rush back. Belly down on the sofa. A gentle landing. She sits up. Frank puts himself between us, shielding her nudity till she dresses. She emerges fully clothed, pleated skirt and white shirt. Her hair braided. The parochial school look.

"Will you be staying for dinner? Frank, set another place."

Frank does not move.

Frank stares at the ceiling.

"Maybe your father and I should be alone tonight." She rises from the couch. I am shown the door. The door is closed in my face. I didn't want to stay for dinner anyhow. The literature on safe sex can be mailed. What I really ought to do is rap with my walls. Get some advice on how to protect my father from bodily harm while he solicits off the wall women. Find out what to expect should he become a homely homeless. The guidelines. For example, would he be able to eventually confine his hard-ons to his own four walls with his own wife? Will mother find her husband more stimulating in the wall than out? Is there any going back to what they were?

Our parents' past.

It shouldn't be trashed.

✗

Somehow I got home.

Elevators, slow as ever. Alex still blabbering.

I recall taking the stairs.

✗

Thumps.

I tap the walls. Then both fists, then books in both fists. Signals to the beasts I'd like them to step forward. The walls ooze. Homely men and women. "Marty Nesterbaum. Could you check out the walls along the Lincoln Center? Tell him Jane Samuels needs to talk."

They look at me like lady you are off the wall.

"Our contract with the City does not include messenger service." His goat legs are sunk a good inch deep into the floor. His skin is tuberous, swollen nodules, not a pretty sight. For all his mutations, he's still a middle-aged man.

"We agreed to stay off the streets. We agreed to vacate the shelters. We promised not to beg. Or eavesdrop. In return, the City gives us walls."

A woman's head is under my needlepoint.

Moles on her nose. Pointy nose, cackle voice. "It was a fair swap. Here in the walls, we're finally safe from—"

143

"Marty Nesterbaum. Einstein hair. Mid-forties. I need his help."

"—the dangers out there. For the first time, we're productive members of society. He who lives in walls lives to make people climb the walls. He who lives in walls doesn't live walled in. We can travel the walls nationwide."

I stick her head back where it came from.

"First they resent us, now they beg us for help." She couldn't be more than fourteen. Fragile face under my wall clock. There's beauty in this beast. "But can we trust them to keep up their end? No creeps in the walls." She dances inside my wall. Legs and arms kicking out. "Let me get you climbing the walls. Please." Cartwheeling next to me, sunk the regulation inch into the floor. "I can get you high. I've gotten people climbing dome ceilings."

I read to her, a book on how time flies.

The beasts retreat. The walls solidify. The girl falls asleep next to me on the couch. Her head in my arms. Someone comes to claim her. "Nice lady," he smiles. Teeth missing. Patchy hair. "I'll comb the walls. I'll find your friend."

✗

Stuffing the homeless into walls.

Was someone eating a stuffed burrito at the time? Or thinking about stuffing a Christmas stocking or suffering from a stuffed nose? Stuffing envelopes, stuffing your tummy on soup and salad, stuffing small things into large things, cramming large things into extra large things. Was someone feeling stuffed to the gills? Or was stuffing the walls just a way of sorting through stuff that's been piled up for ages? When you think of all the stuff on people's minds—all the things they have to deal with, agenda stuff, career stuff, personal stuff—stuffing things into places is a sure-fire way to get caught up. People overburdened with stuff will begin to feel like they've had the stuffing kicked out of them.

Extreme measures for extreme times.

Maybe stuffing the homeless into walls has less to do with politics and everything to do with clutter.

✗

A knock at the door. Beasties don't knock. A wraith in-law knocked the night of Harold's baby shower. Not since. Any knock I'm not expecting is a knock I'm not going to throw the doors

144

open to.

Marilyn Beats.

Smiling into the peephole. The peephole phony smile. Make yourself look like a person other people will let past the door. I unlock. I stand in the doorway. There is such a thing as being generous to a fault. I once stood by while she had an orgasm on Gerald's nose. I'm not going to expose my walls to her. Despite the incident at Macy's, it's my feeling walls are a pilot project. Not everybody gets in on the ground floor.

I don't return the smile.

"Your number's not listed. Alex wouldn't give it out. Could I maybe talk to you for a minute? I'll only be a minute." She and I both know that's a lie. "You haven't collaborated with Alex have you? Ever since I announced I wanted a man to change my life, he's been floundering. I made him what he is today. He's my handiwork. Yet he can't come up with a single thing he'd change about me. Now he's asked me to define what I mean by change. Change in the physical sense or the metaphysical. Change in appearance or change in attitude. He wants me to elaborate on the size of the change I have in mind. Small as a change in the juice I drink or a chunk of change as in a change of address. Slow subtle change as in highlighting hair or overnight change. Change for the sake of change or—"

The minutes are piling up.

I close the door halfway.

"You needn't worry. I have no intention of spelling anything out for him."

Sticking her foot in the door.

"Men willing to be treated like projects should be willing to treat women like projects. Each person should care enough to repair the other. In my mother's day a woman's work was never done. Then it was about housework. Today it's about improvement. Self-improvement. Now that's work. Working on a man is doing his work for him. He should reciprocate. Repair work—when it's on somebody else—is still taxing. But more important, it's rewarding for the relationship. Fixing somebody up is like fixing up a place to live. It's your taste. You've put it together. Why would you ever want to leave?"

The door closes.

I know this for a fact. The door is securely closed.

She knocks again.

"What now?"

"Would you have some Tampax? I've run out."

I go get a box, I give her the entire box, she gives me a summary. "All across America couples are filing, left and right, filing, filing . . . it wouldn't happen if they fixed each other up beforehand."

Thank you, Marilyn Beats.

My mother bangs walls, my father inflicts penis wounds on himself, the Fling is pressuring me, my dear longevity friend is stalked by the City, her dear, dear husband is about to split, the Harolds, the wraiths, the homeless . . . now I have the Marilyn Beats plan for landing a man for keeps.

Open a door, you can never be sure what the impact. One can plan ahead, one can have contingency plans, one's words and deeds above reproach, and one day you find a note. "Don't wait up."

The notes I stick to every wall tell Marty I won't be gone longer than thirty minutes. To please stick it out. There's food in the fridge.

And . . .

"Please wait up."

✗

I just hate when neighbors of mine exhaust my supply of Tampax. Sending me out at the height of the evening to replenish my menstrual wares.

Open a door you can never be sure what the impact.

Flying to Hardware.

And that's on foot.

✗

Too early for late-night people to officially start their evening, almost late enough for people who retire early to call it a day. It's the hour when barging in unannounced feels like imposition to some and not to others. Since the hour's never stopped me yet, I am not about to begin now. I don't regret the thought however. Jane Goodall, out of consideration for her chimps, was considerate.

The Hardware Store sits between a Greek luncheonette heavy on the pita crowd and a bakery that believes in the product selling itself after the windows have been turned into a medley of marzipan cows. The Hardware Store is covered in cobblestone, either from the days of horse and buggy or the days of fake fur, fake marble, fake boobs.

I let myself in.

Thankfully spared the indignities of knocking at the front door. Forced smiling is like forced talking, which isn't at all like being forced to take piano lessons. Forced piano lessons are good for you. I move toward the back where it's lit.

Harold stands in the passageway.

Rumpled pajamas. At last an article of clothing my skin can relate to. It could be the light. The corners of his eyes need excavation. Jane Goodall wouldn't kick me out of the academy. But she would protest at disturbing any chimp. Jane Samuels would say to Jane Goodall, No problem, Janie, the chimp is only drinking coffee, black, no sugar. He's looking right through me. Read my lap: I'm a trifle. Totally beside the point. I am wife number one . . . don't wait up . . . don't wait up.

The coffee sloshes.

Or is Harold sloshed?

He raises the mug unsteadily.

"In the blink of an eye, I could lose her hand. If it's after the birth, no dust in my eye. Dust in my eye, if it's before the birth. In the blink of an eye, I'm a single parent. Full custodial rights."

The chimp does a chimp dance, hee-hawing, grabbing his chimp loins.

A frolic cut short.

"Harold." The voice of Mrs. Harold coming from way in the back. "Change my outlook. Or don't wait up."

I tiptoe out.

Quickly closing the door. I test the lock . . . to keep the creeps in the street.

✗

Walking at a clip. I'm thinking of getting a skateboard.

✗

Only in predawn hours are the elevators in my building starved for someone to press the buttons. At this hour the night's still young. I wait. They wait me out. What they're really saying is . . . don't wait up.

✗

147

When Marty finally shows, I'm in the shower shampooing. Marty steps out of the wall tiles. Hands on my breasts. Each of his fingers has a full head of hair. "Looking for me?" His cock is one-twoing, someone limbering up at the barre. He puts a condom on.

"I just want to talk." The sound of toothpaste tube squishes, suddenly his man-of-war is a licorice stick. The condom slides off. "My father has all the earmarks of wanting to be homely. He's making overtures to drains. He chases nubile women." I rinse. Marty hands me the conditioner. "Could you hang out with my dad?"

His member swinging side to side like it was a windshield wiper. "Old guys like your father are the worst. They think drains and walls will take away their feeling of being walled in. In that, they're not misinformed." He works the conditioner into my scalp, the windshield wiper is on high speed. "Living off the wall is just about as confining as it gets. Walls are liberating. The average person in the walls travels more than the average person off the wall. Sex is sexier." He rinses the conditioner from my hair.

I'd do anything for my parents.

I soap his dick. Primitive man gutturals. Penis knee jerks. The stretch is a beaut. "I know you don't want your space invaded by creeps. My father is not a creep." His beaut winds round my neck. Cobra collar. "My dad's a war veteran." Anything for Mom and Dad. I condom the cobra, unwinding it. Thick hemp. The thing feels like laundry rope for sheets and bedspreads. Anything for my parents. I feed him into my well water, no undue haste. The well wants to stay well.

We hit the ceiling together.

Floating on a bed of shampoo bubbles. Marty drifts on the ceiling. His body glides into the bedroom. He sleeps suspended overhead. My descent is smooth. I sleep next to my bathing suit. On or about sea level.

✗

Yes, I climbed the walls with Marty Nesterbaum.
No, I am not taken with Marty Nesterbaum.

✗

By morning . . .
The man in the wall has vanished.

148

My hair is war-torn. Trampled by the troops. Unfit for human habitation. I am a rubble head. The hotline to Clip Art operates like a crisis center for hair. Each time I use it, I get the runaround. Not today. Today I will be more than a head of hair in crisis. I will be woman in peril.

I dial. I'm put on hold. I redial.

"Don't put me on hold."

"It couldn't be that bad." Spoken by a person who's obviously never had a bad hair day in her life.

"It's a hair deathwatch. Unless you get me in to see James, I'll need a hair transplant. Have you ever seen a hair seizure up close? It can clear a room. A Special Occasion is upcoming, you know what those are like—dress still has tags, heels are a pain—but," building into a sob, building on the sob to an outcry worse than when you break a nail, "I'm doomed, a life without decent hair is a life of trial and error."

Recorded music. She's checking the appointment book.

"This afternoon at two, it's the best I can do."

"James at two." I did it. There is magic.

"Not James, this is no same-day laundry service."

"Then—"

"Our hair consultant will give you a hair consultation."

Don't let it be Alissa, God not Alissa.

"Alissa will see you at two."

I know the answer to this before I ask. "Anyone else available? Marcy, Babs, Tammy, anyone?"

"Alissa."

The hotline lady tells me she has an incoming call. Decide now. I decide in the affirmative. Clip Art thanks me, I thank Clip Art. Clip Art and I conclude. Nobody hangs up faster than anybody else. It's a tie.

✗

By morning . . .

The man in the walls has vanished.

Hope of seeing James has vanished.

My forehead is conversational.

It comes to life. For a so-so lump on my forehead, nothing about it has been ordinary. A soccer kick delivered by a rabbit sounds made up. But the witnesses, New Yorkers who've seen it all, gave written testimony. "A real rabbit wouldn't have walked on his

149

hind legs. A real rabbit wouldn't have been as tall. Rabbits don't talk. Nonetheless, the rabbit was not a phony." We were all taken in. I give the school crossing guard till tomorrow, then I move in for the kill. A confession, names, addresses, the works. Every day the lump looks a little less lumpy. I'm healing. Yet with every decrease of lumpiness, there is an increased look about it. I wouldn't say third eye, would I say eye-shaped?

I would say lively.

✗

The forehead is running off at the mouth.

"Have I ever steered you wrong? I didn't steer you wrong about the guy in the bathroom at Lincoln Center. I didn't steer you wrong the time I told you there was a nose loitering in your lobby. And I'm not steering you wrong now. The zero who must never, NOT FOR A MOMENT, think she's a zero in bed, knows who you are."

Bedroom phone, accent of indeterminate origin, not the Bronx, rings.

I won't answer.

No good can come of a confrontation with the woman of whom I have heard so many nice things. If ever the woman of whom I've heard such nice things should inquire, deny everything. Admit to flinging, do not admit to the Fling. Nate who?

Again the forehead starts in on me.

"Spare the zero a moment of your time. Have I ever steered you wrong? Pick up the goddamn phone."

Against my better judgment . . .

I take the call. I say to the woman of whom her husband speaks so highly of, Wrong number. The woman-spoken-so-highly of says, I'm the wife of the Fling. I say, Wrong number. She says, Just listen . . . I want to apprentice. I want to sharpen my skills. Learn how a pro does it. I want a tutor. A vaginal mentor to teach me how to fuck my husband. I am a zero in bed. I don't have the aptitude. I need instruction. I know you know.

Forehead having a fit.

"Say it, say it, say it."

I say it my way.

In a voice as warm as Nora's (she could be talking to a friend, hers is not the voice of someone speaking to the slut who drinks bodily fluids she's not legally entitled to), I warmly reply, "I had a

150

hunch this day would come. You'll have my decision by noon."

She offers her home phone number. I don't hurt her feelings by telling her I already have it.

✗

Some mornings start out with a bang. Less than a beaut.
And some mornings soccer you over the head.

✗

Ice pack on my forehead. I stand in front of the false fireplace, elbows on the mantle. There's no better place in my apartment for a landmark decision. Except the closet. All the things people think while soaking in the tub can be thought while soaking in the closet. The closet is a natural ashram. A think tank. A place to sort stuff through. I take my shawl with me, the far reaches of the closet are drafty. Deep dark woodsy, the smell of cedar, scurrying creatures I dare not give names to. The dark isn't thick enough to get lost in. But it's quality dark, the kind that helps me focus.

Questions come to mind:

Should I accept the role, what exactly would be required of me? Does it call for full frontal nudity? How demonstrative do I have to get? Hands on? Where on? Will Nate's flinging be curtailed? Will Nora be discreet? Do I have to go all the way with her? If I say yes, will there be hard feelings if yes becomes no?

Vaginal coach.

Never having done research in this field, I'm curious. Call it researcher's blood lust. Any hint of a taboo subject, a subject that's classified info, right off I want to declassify it. Capture the rapture. Nothing beats a good old-fashioned intellectual challenge.

Exiting my closet is rough going.

I climb back over my shoes. They nip at my heels. The bites aren't love bites. My shoes are isolated from bras, socks, and bathing suits. Yet the word's out: Jane Samuels treats shoes like a commodity, she treats socks and bras and bathing suits like shrines. Not all shoes are heels, but most of my shoes have elevator personalities.

I walk to the phone. A quick rehearsal of what I'm going to say. I dial Nora's number. I say what I've rehearsed.

"Before I come to a decision, I have to know how you intend all this to play. My banker Kate Pemberton is an ace. Bank boners are

151

her whole life. Because of her, Citibank has a SWAT team. Teller errors have to answer to Kate personally. As far as closing your account, forget it."

The warm voice is toasty warm.

"There will be no bad guys. SWAT teams are out. The account is committed. My investment's safe."

The zero is no cunt.

Smart too. The zero in bed was not a zero in understanding that the banking bit was an inquiry into her style.

"I accept your offer on one condition."

"Name it."

"Two o'clock is out. I have a beauty parlor appointment."

We set up a meet.

Time: Twelve forty-five.

Place: Fifth Avenue, Seventeenth Street.

Call complete.

I dress.

I hold my homebody face down for a thirty-second count. I kill it off with cream, blush, lipstick.

✗

I thought I'd have second thoughts.

I thought I'd end up calling back to cancel.

But Nora's a zero in bed. If ever Nate filed. First. it would make her feel like less than zero. Zero is bad enough, minus zero makes you unusually, monumentally so-so.

✗

Alex buzzes.

The forehead doesn't have a clue. I employ conventional means. Conventional means means I ask Alex what he wants. "Lou Gold," he replies. "Says he wants to talk to you regarding his frame of mind." I give Alex the go-ahead. When my longevity friend's husband needs counsel, I do not put him off. Besides, I know the elevators. I still have time for juice and muffin . . . and other things besides. A woman just has to have something else going besides what she's got going. It's the brain chemistry of the thing. You need more than one thought in your head. My mouth on a muffin, my hands on butter, my mind on . . . pigs?

152

Besides on Pigs
In this country alone there are more than 3,000 Vietnamese pigs and piglets.
Potbellied is how they look. Potbellies can understand commands as well as any
dog. They cuddle. They don't shed. They use a litter box.
But they are swine.
They root around.
They eat like pigs.
They live to thirty-five years.
For thirty-five years you can wake up to pork. For thirty-five years—

I answer the door. Friends shouldn't put friends off for hogs.

✗

A frame of mind can be visualized any way you want. A house frame. Eyeglass frames. A picture frame. The skeleton of a skyscraper.

His looks like road kill.

Lou has an enlisted man's face. Close-cropped hair, outdoor blond, square jaw. But around the eyes, road kill; in the eyes, a total wipe-out. Those aren't eyes. They're pits. His squint lines are shallow graves, his outdoor blond looks washed out, his posture, how he carries himself, is a tottering frame, one push, it tumbles down. He sits on the chair with the ripped bodice, the orphan rescued from the street. Furniture disposed of like disposable diapers. Society filing. First. on helpless wood.

I serve tea. He asks for decaffeinated. I drink mine straight up. He requests milk and lemon.

"Be perfectly candid with me," Lou takes a swig of tea, "as much as a frame of mind admires another frame of mind for its strength, be perfectly candid, don't you think the admirer can come to dislike the very things he's admired? Be candid. If the qualities he's admired are a constant reminder to him he's not nearly as admirable himself, wouldn't you, looking at it from his frame, begin looking forward to the day when the frame of mind you so admire is humbled, bringing it not exactly down to your level, but only a notch or two up?"

I refill his tea.

He empties it in one gulp.

"Be nothing but candid. How would you feel living in connubial bliss with someone who brags about not blowing the pizza man she was in the frame of mind to blow?" A rattling of teacup and saucer. He switches hands. Same rattle. "I don't deny complicity.

153

In my old frame of mind, I liked the competition. Women wanting it from other men were women who were going to get it from me."

Lou gets up.

He goes to the window. My window has enough glass for a conference-size glass Parson's table. He holds out his cup for a water refill, no new bag thank you.

"Her frame is giving me psychic pain. She's too good for me. Next to her, my frame feels wanton." Head back, draining the cup. "Do you think it's a sweet frame-up? No matter how hard I pound it in, she pounds back it's the City putting words in my mouth. I pound harder, in and out, in deeper, out briefer, in like I'm going to come out the other side, hammering the message home." Lou puts the cup down. He sees himself to the door. "I've been perfectly candid with you. I'm afraid of what will become of us. How long can a man continue to pound sense into a woman, how much pounding can a ninety-pound woman take?" He opens the door. He steps into the hall. "Be perfectly candid. Do I stand a chance against her frame?"

Besides provide information.

I can be as perfectly candid as the next person. Being asked to speak candidly is not an appeal to say something off the top of your head; it's a plea to dig deep down, to get your snout in there, root around, squeal on what's really on your mind.

"Pigs root around."

"Are you drawing an analogy?"

"The potbellied pig can't help himself. Taken in as a domestic pet, given all the privileges of a dog, still the pig will conduct himself like a piglet."

"So it's hopeless?"

"Pigs oink, they are born oinking, they die oinking."

"What you're saying is pigs will always be pigs."

I shake my head no. "On the other hand, in the blink of an eye, things can change. I'll do everything in my power to assist you, thereby averting anyone (namely you) from filing upon anyone (namely Susan). First."

The road kill smiles.

Road kill leaves.

✗

Besides . . . Susan would insist I help Lou.

It would be the City talking for me to ignore a road kill.

✗

Not long after Lou, I leave (for parts known).

✗

Alex is so preoccupied with his nose (preening, petting, everything but sword-swallowing) he doesn't see me. Which is just as well. There are times a tenant wants to feel like she can walk out of her building without being set upon.

✗

One foot puts me in the herd. The day the rabbit had me underfoot the herd scattered. Taking skittishness into account, herds of large populations are still strategically safer. You are just that much harder to see. Crowds, however, make it just as hard for you to see.
And blind spots absolve us from blame altogether.

✗

Both Barry the bereaved and his son land on my front porch like newspapers. Barry's older son is almost as tall as his father. A slender boy without facial hair. Ears like billowing sails. Barry is wearing a dark overcoat. It works. The movement of his bereaved dick is muffled.
"Dennis and I just came back from the cemetery."
"I'm so sorry."
"Wife number one was the great love of my life. The only woman for me. An impossible act to follow. I'm lost without wife number one." Barry reaches for my hand. My hand ends up in the dark inner folds of his coat. Dennis recovers my hand and returns it to me.
Dennis's ears are shamefaced.
"We've enrolled Dad in a program to help him channel his grief. He's beside himself."
Barry seconds that.
"Barely dead weeks. Married thirty-eight years, I've waited this long to bed another woman, I can wait a little longer. Wife number one was an all-consuming passion."
"Thank Marge for me . . . for the fruit salad."

155

"The mother of wife number one told me to get my filthy hands off her tits."

"Dad's going to get better. Soon as the program channels him."

Dennis and I shake hands. Barry and I do not. I watch them go. The herd swallows them up. Amen to that. I applaud Barry. He's being forthright. Now that I know he knows, I don't have to pretend he doesn't. Barry's mushroom has turned into a skirt-chaser. What I applaud most is his way of expressing numerical order.

Wife number one.

✗

Pure inquisitiveness. On the way to Hardware on Third, I visit Hardware on Second. Not a Harold in sight. It wouldn't inhibit me to think the Harolds circulated the hardware stores. It wouldn't inhibit me from carrying on a normal conversation. It wouldn't inhibit me from walking. It wouldn't inhibit me from dining out. But if they were to skip away, hardware store to hardware store, it would inhibit culmination.

It would leave me hanging.

Cliffhanger is the worst ending of all. Worse than no ending is being on the brink of one. I've tried to be unobtrusive, observation without active participation. The moment Harold threatened to have me barred—true, he was overwrought, his wife had just offered me her hand in marriage—my determination to do whatever it takes, be on hand no matter what, grew monumentally unusually stronger.

Over my dead body.

Come what may, regardless—the heavens could open up—Jane Samuels is unstoppable. Amen to that.

✗

Hardware on Third.

People are swarming the new wings. Last night there were no new wings. There's even a separate level. I escalator up. From the upper level, the lobby is a hive. Glass counters, sales assistants, samples distributed. Retail busy. It's a mixed crowd. Cross people, and people like me. People whose laps are at various inclines. Some sitting on air, some barely protruding. If you don't know how to look, you could miss it altogether. Next to a counter of bold Warhol-colored wrenches, a man with a ponytail calls out:

156

Ya, ya.

Laps all over the store sit up and take notice. "Ya, ya."

The ponytail guy jumps on top of a counter. "I'm here for the same reason you're here. To hear it from their own lips. They got this Cross bag. We got laps that won't quit. Ya, ya." A bebop strut. "And what was it we asked?"

Raised fists.

The lap crowd yells, "How are you?"

"And what keeps us coming back?"

The crowd chants. "Ya, ya, ya."

Even the Cross crowd picks it up. Owner too, snapping his fingers. Ya, ya, ya. Finally, I'm among my own kind. I actually feel tribal stirrings. Why there must be an entire population out there with collapsible laps.

And a keen sense of ya, ya.

Yet two of Hardware's most prominent people are missing. Upper level, restrooms, old wings, new wings. No use. Either the Harolds are lost in the herd or they've absconded with my finish line. Owner is easy to pick out. Six feet, bald, red rose in his lapel, and dollar signs in his eyes.

I descend.

"Lemme go," he says when I grab his arm.

"Tell me where the Harolds are."

No amount of shaking will shake me off. For a while he just carries me on his arm like a handbag. Somehow I manage to climb up to his shoulder, giving me a direct line into his ear. "I'll contact the Cross people, by the time I'm finished, you'll never realize a cent in hush money."

"They're seeing an eye specialist. That's all I know. I swear."

He puts me down.

He smoothes the hair he doesn't have.

We smooth each other's feelings.

"Sorry about—"

"Me too."

"Come what may, regardless, the heavens could open up, over my dead body, cliffhanger theater is not where it's going to end."

His answer, my national anthem.

"Ya, ya."

✗

I work my way home.

Checking trees as I go. Cats have nine lives. Why not nine afterlives? Last stop, the pocket park. I shake the branches out like you do with piggy banks, hoping for a jingle. Not a wooden nickel, not even a false sighting. I cross the street, entering my building through the service entrance. A time-honored route for deliveries and thieves. There's no door like a back door. Doormen do not have eyes between their shoulder blades. It's Marilyn who zaps me. This way, get moving. It's not up for discussion. Her eyes are bayonets.

Now what?

Do they want me to cast some sort of deciding vote?

✗

"We won't keep you." Marilyn wears hot-pink lipstick. The hips that once gave me the back of her hand are squeezed into a black leather skirt. She squeaks as she moves. If I wore what she wore, I wouldn't wear it in public. She gives me a box with a bow on top.

Tampax.

I thank her.

"We won't keep you," she says, keeping me.

Alex is obviously still having problems with depth perception. Bulky noses are like going from compact to wide-bodied cars. His nose reaches for a handkerchief and misses, Alex uses his hand instead. The sides of his nose look inflamed, too much sex, too little time off for good behavior. He sneezes, but not into his hankie. A heavy mist splatters me. My expression does not scream you sneezed on me as I have never been sneezed on, not by anyone the whole world over. My expression reads, I would like to humiliate you, there would be reprisals. Marilyn would rearrange my lap.

"Tell her what we talked about," Marilyn giving him a little nudge. I stand ready to jump out of the way in case the next jab throws him into a nose spin.

Alex complies.

"I'm not quite there but I'm close. Marilyn's days of searching for a man to make the repairs of which she is so sorely in need of are over. I care enough for her not to take her for what she is, but what she can be. No more winters of searching in subfreezing temperatures, summers she can relax in the shade, knowing she has finally found a man willing to itemize her in tedious detail." Marilyn wiping his nose of sneeze residue. "She need never hunger again. She need never experience the frustration of having lain

158

with hundreds, bringing men along by the thousands and being told they like what they see."

An opening. I take it.

I walk to the elevators. Marilyn bringing up the rear. I press the button. Nothing. She presses the button. Both elevators instantly open. There is magic. She holds the hold button. There goes the magic.

"Release the button, Marilyn."

"One thing I won't do is settle for second-rate change. Not after what I've been through. You don't know the half of it. Spreading my legs was the easy part. In my search for a man to do a woman's work—improve on her, not so she can put her feet up, so she prevent filing, filing, filing, him on her, her on him, both on each other—I actually had to date men who sent other men to break their dates."

She relinquishes control of the elevator.

I quickly press eight.

✗

Is it better to be file-obsessed early on, before anyone tells you meat begets dead meat, or to wait till file, file, file falls in your lap?

✗

Planning ahead. What to wear for my debut as vaginal coach? I go right to my closet. The door is open. Has someone gotten there ahead of me? Can three wraiths be three stooges? Helen hangs upside down like a closet bat. Sam's unopened umbrella is horizontal in midair. He sits on it like a man on a park bench. My closet, the park. Yvette parks herself on the other end of the umbrella, tipping her side. Sam is stuck on the high end of the see-saw. Monumentally outweighed. Helen's hands are cupped under her chin; will upside down sound the same as right side up?

She speaks.

"It's an issue I can identify with. You want to look presentable for the wife of a man whose mushroom you've tasted. Go in looking like a dog, you create an issue where there is none: Surely, my husband can do better than this. I didn't see him through his training so he could cheat with a zero in the looks department. Go in looking like a million bucks, more issues. How could he do this to me, am I zero in beauty too? Make no issues where there are none.

I'm issuing you an order. Wear this." Helen nods to Yvette, Yvette nods to Sam. Yvette rises. Reverse seesaw. Sam opens his black umbrella.

Out falls . . . the ideal little black dress.

Should I stand on principle?

Violation of privacy is a legitimate issue.

The phone rings. Stand on principle or pick up the phone? Might be Nora. Probably is Nora, undoubtedly is . . . forget it ever happened . . . moved too fast . . . if you won't tell, I won't tell.

"Answer the phone," all three wraiths, "Nora's calling."

How can three be so right on a dress?

And so wrong on phone?

Nate wet kisses me on the phone. "Four o'clock's available."

"From two on, I'll be at the beauty parlor."

"It won't take two hours, say yes."

Twelve forty-five, see Nora.

Four, see Nora's husband.

Tutor Nora's vaggie.

Play with Nora's husband's gerbil.

Am I so unprincipled?

"Four, your place." Nate hangs up.

The wraiths do a slow fade-out. I dive for the little black dress. It's a fit. Tight but not too tight. Figure hugging. My full round breasts look high, wide and available. I buzz Alex. "Let him up."

"Him who?"

"The next man who walks through the door."

"Ms. Samuels, I—"

"Do it."

"Gotcha."

Twelve forty-five, Nora.

Four, Nora's husband.

Read my paws: Gerald's on his way.

All in the course of an afternoon.

Sex, sex, sex . . . in a little black dress, dress, dress.

✗

Door ajar. Gerald will let himself in.

Ten minutes later, footsteps.

I cringe.

Holy Mother of God. His nose looks like hair after you've taken your hat off. It looks like when you've packed in a hurry. The mut-

160

ton, the samurai sword, the tail of Hercules, the slab with no flab, Holy Mother, his joint has tennis elbow.

He sits on the sofa. Head back.

"It only hurts when I breathe."

The nose needs a transfusion. If the damn thing bleeds all over my black and white sofa I'll wipe the floor with it.

Clipping his nose. A clothespin.

"My joint just couldn't take the heat," nasal voice.

I think about ways to make him disappear. Poor little black dress, dress, dress. No sex, sex, sex.

The blood clots.

"I'll make you a promise," undressing, shedding his clothes. His nose is incapacitated, does he have backups? "As long as I have one working joint left in my body, I will fuck you with it."

I've never had a man say that to me before.

He cracks his knuckles, bends his elbows, wiggles his toes. Which joint will have the most bite? I used to let the boys in high school put their hands up me, nearly up to their wrists, in the days when I wouldn't go all the way. He takes ten of his working joints and goes to work. Ten toes. Under the little black dress, foot sex. My keyboard all keyed up. Safer than marbles down there. Swallowing marbles in your vaggie may one day lodge them in your ears.

For good measure, digging in his heels.

x

Twenty minutes later, I send him on his way. I kiss his toes as I have kissed no man's feet.

x

Shoe mutiny.

First pair I try on pops a strap. Second pair is two left feet. Third pair, each shoe walks in different directions. There's bad blood between shoes and me. Shoes think I walk all over them. Give shoes the same preferential treatment as bras, socks, and bathing suits, or shoes will never put their best foot forward.

I search, I seize a pair of black flats. I am shod.

When dealing in matters of some delicacy—vaginal coach can expect awkward humps—paperwork helps. I carry a large yellow pad. Will I really be able to coax a great performance out of a

161

female who doesn't know the first thing about her dick? For all I know, I could be squeamish. Touching female genitals other than my own is a touchy subject. A pencil could be used as a pointer. I'll have to psych myself. Visualization. Her mound is a kiwi. There is still time (if I hurry) to take time out (if I hurry), to go across the street where it's restful (if I hurry), time enough to sit in a hurry.

Will I have to kiss her full on the mouth?

✗

Someone else is waiting for the elevator. That someone else presses the button. That someone else remarks how slow the elevators are. That someone else and I take the faster route. The steps. That someone else makes some offhanded remark to Alex about his nose. The last I see of that someone else he's pinned to the wall by a disgruntled nose.

✗

The park: Four trees, two benches, no Suki.

And no room on the benches. The look the women give me is Us and Them. They don't want to move over. They spread. A novice would not think premeditated shifting; I know a spread with malice when I see one. No moment in the sun. Maybe it's just as well. Sitting next to people you don't know is asking for an aside besides. Tangential talk coming your way. The overheard. Snatches of other people's conversation. Thoughts landing in your lap. I'm the first one to say a woman has to have other things going for her on the side besides. But who needs petty gossip? Sometimes it's plain junk mail. Sometimes it's gruesomes falling into your lap. For the sake of clarity, I call these kind of experiences chair experiences. For my own sake, the fewer the better. Had the ladies on the bench offered me a seat, I probably would have forfeited. The beauty of forfeiting a chair experience is knowing you've filed on it. First. The fallacy of that kind of filing. First. is what you're really saying: Can't cut it, I am a wimp. I don't want to hear of heads without torsos.

Or sexually transmittable anything.

Or who came to a bad . . . end.

✗

I take a cab. I have the cab drop me off a distance from Nora's building. In front doesn't give you a feel for the neighborhood. I walk. Nora's section of the city isn't as played out as Susan's. Fewer commercial stores. A vestige of horizon. The sun sightings in this part of town aren't UFOs. The buildings are short and stocky. Somewhat gawky. As if they were new to the city. The area looks law and order. Her residence even has a name. Sunflower Manor. The doorman wears white gloves. The doorman is a concierge. "Jane Samuels to see Ms. Fergenic."

Jarlsberg-colored marble vases in the lobby. An elevator there to fetch you when you want to be fetched. The door to her apartment is bigger than the door to my apartment. In my building, her door would hit its head on the ceiling. This is a door that could earn a buck on a movie set.

It does not sweep open.

When it opens, I do not sweep in, no fancy footwork. I try to approximate a lady of good breeding; failing that—I don't see how you can, little black dresses are the cornerstones of ladies with good breeding—I try not to walk like a guy. We spend the next few minutes seeing if our first impressions match our phone impressions. Women meeting each other for the first time, sniffing each other out. Civilized facing off. Crotches sizing one another up. The zero and I go through the ritual dance.

She's a doe.

Wiry and graceful. I don't see glamour, I see tousled. The curls atop her head are wildflowers. Not landscaped. Growing as if they were dropped by Johnny Appleseed. I see skin so white it looks like rice powder. I see a face that might have been on a cameo pin. A callow face. A face that looks like it could barely withstand scrubbing.

And I see sincerity, don't ask how.

We go on to an alcove off the kitchen. On the wall, wall pegs. Ribboned straw hats on the pegs. And visors with real grime. There's a school desk with an inkwell. Nora sits on a slatted bench, swinging from the ceiling. Her little black dress is the kissing cousin of my little black dress. The legal pad is on my lap. Both lap and I are seated on a chaise longue.

I can't speak first, don't ask me why.

"I meant every word I said," Nora says. "I've taken courses in calligraphy, bookbinding, weaving, repairing broken doll limbs. When you start out as a zero there's nowhere to go but up. Anything you show me would be greatly appreciated. It could be as

163

basic as a kiss. If you could just improve my technique."

Make her better than she is.

A humanitarian mission.

Bring her along.

She doesn't want a man to change her life, she wants a Marilyn Beats. Somebody who'll roll up her sleeves, make repairs, get the place fixed up for hubby so hubby won't file. In his lifetime. Nora is a woman in need of a woman's touch. Am I really equipped for this? Only one way to find out.

"Sit on my lap."

"Can I offer you a beverage?"

"Sit on my lap."

The zero walks over like she's got lead in her shoes.

"Go back, try again. Walk like it's not your last mile. Pretend I'm a giant Häagen-Dazs ice cream cone, sprinkles on top."

The first hurdle.

She dashes over. The woman really is a zero.

"This cone wants nothing more than to be licked, but the cone, much as it wants to coat a tongue, is selective about who it coats. Your walk will have to catch the cone's interest. Roll those hips. Fingertips on tits. Harden those nips."

She tries, she flunks.

"All right, sit." I pat my lap.

A sure sign of being stiff in the sack is stiff in the lap. I arrange her arms. One around my shoulders, the other under my little black dress. It's not subtle but if we get the broad strokes down, we can work backwards from there. The hand under my dress is a sweaty palm. I take the hand out from under my dress.

"Kiss me," I say.

We kiss. She is awful.

We kiss. She is awful.

I put my hand under her little black dress.

We kiss. She is not so bad.

✗

The thing I liked best about her: I said I was going to the beauty parlor. She said my hair could really use it.

✗

Hair.

Hair isn't the bane of my existence. My banes could be stacked end to end, hair would not be amongst them. But hair is a mettle-tester. Ever so slow to grow hair (and other maladies like war-torn rubble head) makes you feel it's never going to get there. And where else is there but the finish line. Dealing with the bureaucracy of a hair salon is the real bane in the neck.

I walk to Clip Art.

I get to Clip Art.

"Here for your hair?" the girl at the front desk asks.

✗

Clip Art was designed to look artsy. Work stations are sculptures on a stark stage. The chairs are Rubik Cubes. Black is the only color scheme. The lighting from the overhead lights is movie projector tubular.

An usher shows me to Alissa's consultation chamber, way off to one side, away from the mainland where all the styling is done, where James does his salvage work. She sits me in a black device, anything with straps and warning labels is not a chair built for comfort. She guards me till Alissa comes, as if it would never occur to me to break and run, throw money at James, offer him a yacht, or Alex's nose.

I've had words with Alissa before.

Alissa inspects hair. Hair will be processed or sent home for further ripening. Alissa is unapproachable. A hanging judge. No leniency, no circumstantial. The mere mention of a special occasion to her, a big one falling in your lap, turns her from stone cold to sadistic icicle.

It begins.

She puts on her rubber gloves. Snapping the rubber. The fighter pilot goggles are a new touch. She circles me. Her hair is what you can get away with if you have a perfect body. Ripped instead of shorn. The fingers on my scalp take soil samples. She pulls my hair, I sit there and take it.

It's a repeat of last time.

"No." A smug shake of her head. "Not a chance."

"Now."

"Not now. Soon." Her smile is a closed grin.

"How soon?"

"Too soon to tell."

Why do I put up with it? Suffice it to say, I've known James

165

at least as long as I've known some of my bathing suits, some seventeen-odd years. File on James? Start all over again with someone new . . . leave him in the dust?

Uh-uh.

On the way out of Clip Art it's my honor to catch a chair experience without even being seated. Tidbits of people's lives. The pulse of the City.

"He cut off one of her—"

Preempted by my forehead: "Read my paws. Your father's let himself into your place. Go home. Sometime later you will be contacted by a dead pet. Forgive me for hitting you over the head. But how it hits me is how it's gonna hit you. Beware Barry the bereaved. You read my paw?"

✗

For a ten-dollar tip the cab is an ambulance chaser. All attempts to interrogate my forehead are futile. What's Dad doing in my apartment? When will I see Suki? Why the warning about Barry? And by the way, are you now or have you ever been a school crossing guard, and if there's no magic, why are some people psychic?

From cab to stairs, Alex is a blur.

I get to my apartment. I maul the locks. I must look like I've come to the morgue to identify a body.

"What's wrong?" A simultaneous exchange.

Frank is leaning against a wall. The wall sags, a give that doesn't give much. He still looks like himself. White-haired fireman, year-round color that passes for year-round tan, a minimum of ravaged beauty, well-preserved. He looks exemplary of a life.

"Things have never been better." Words to reduce my anxiety, only they don't. "The world's a lot less constricted than it used to be. I met your friend Marty. Marty's the kind of guy I'd like to see you end up with. He's homeless only in the sense that he lives in walls. He's repulsive only in the sense that he's nothing to look at. But he's the least walled in person I've ever met."

Dad dips into the wall. Hands reach out for him.

I yank back.

The stench of unwash fills the room. I can't tell if it's him or the others.

"I know what you're going through. You don't want to be around when life files. First. Why wall yourself in any more than you have to? Knock down the walls of the past, dismantle existing

166

structures, abandon what was for what's yet to come. Have you thought of what you'd be giving up? Long-standing relationships replaced by a slew of acquaintances. People you hardly know. Some you get to know. But any way you stack them they don't go back years. Just try talking to someone you don't know for decades, it won't do a thing for you."

His look says save your breath.

"Whatever you say." He steps across the room, his feet in the floor. He climbs into my sink. And whoosh. Down the drain. I run the water. I throw lemon slices after my own flesh and blood.

✗

An unsuccessful bid.

It's an impasse.

Intellectually, I understand what he's doing and why he's doing it. Emotionally, I understand his desire to be a free spirit. Anyone can relate to leaving it all behind. Degree is where Dad and I differ, where Harold and I differ (the Harold of yesteryear prior to his conversion), where I differ even with myself. Stuck with socks and bras and bathing suits and fall with all its fallout, I know a prison wall when I see one. As the walls of Jericho fell, so too shall they . . . the day pigs stop being pigs . . . the day frames and lobes are multiple choice.

Some historians are born to it.

Along the way, some are born again.

✗

The baptism of my little black dress: Gerald's toes, Nora's kisses, and Nora's husband's gerbil at four. An auspicious beginning for a little black dress. Though it hasn't set a record. Before the little black dress there was (still is) a little black jumpsuit. It's true what they say about black. Black doesn't show wear and tear. Black hides filth. The things you do in black can be done in white.

But white can't carry it off.

Little black dresses will continue to outsell little white dresses. The consumer wants a dress that will see her through a hectic day. Today's consumer is active. The black dress will go down in history. You can never have too much black.

It's all very black and white.

Black hints of a past, it doesn't reveal the past.

167

"Nice dress," Nate says at the appointed hour. "Sit on my lap."
My walk tells the cone I want a lick and I want it now.
"Kiss me," Nate sticks his hand under my little black dress.
Nate's hand is not a wet palm. Nate is adequate with his hands.
Competent brushstrokes. Fair to good eye-hand coordination. Till
now, never so fully realized: Surgeon hands, hands with X-ray fingers, spiders crawling in my bush. "On the floor." Nate pushes my
little black dress above my knees, knickers below my knees. Nate
takes off his shoes and socks. Nate rams his toes up me, his fingers, both hands. Twenty digits. I scream for him to stop, he stops,
I scream don't stop. Twenty staunch men, a work crew. He-men
fingers working their fingers to the bone. Ditch-diggers. I deed
myself over, take me, help yourself. I lose boundaries. Under my
little black dress, I come on each one of those twenty. Sometime
later, I don't know when, Nate puts himself in me. I'm limp. Semi-
conscious. He has his way with me like he paid for it. He suits
himself. A one-way ride under my little black dress. He uses me,
slapping my face, I arch once, thrashing like a fish, he comes, he
comes out. His fingers and toes visit their old haunt. I won't give
in to it. Slap me, but ask me first.
Nate sticks his tongue in me.
He leaves me for dead.

It's all very black and white.
Black keeps them guessing, black is inscrutable, wave a little
black dress in a man's face, he can't smell where it's been.
The scent he picks up is yours.

I change my underwear.
Lipstick and makeup redone.
The little black dress, it goes on holiday.
Why did the little black dress go on holiday?
Burnout.

A distress call from Susan. Meet me. The steps of St. Patrick's Cathedral. Look for the lady in lemon. Hurry, hurry. I saddle up, jeans and standard T. Posse fast. It isn't easy pulling yourself together after you've been left for dead in a little black dress. It's brutal. I'll need at least a day's moratorium on sex. Or a very good reason to break the moratorium.

✗

Torn.

That's what I am when Suki my dearly departed cat (as foretold by my forehead) appears in the park just as I am on the way to administer aid to longevity Susan whose husband's frame is road kill. Whose husband is pounding it in. Whose husband is in psychic pain. Whose husband may be a mouthpiece for the City or just a mouthpiece for himself. How could I reconcile putting a dead cat before a live longevity?

I can't.

I'm torn.

✗

Suki, speak to me.

✗

Suki is curled in a tree, on a limb that has good forearm. She looks miffed. Death has brought her new life. When I knew her she didn't have all that much to say. Mostly she just slept. "A hepcat set me straight. You gave away my litter box and my bowl because you're not hep. You don't know the first thing about being hep. I saw how it was between you and that dog. The second I turn my back, you take up with somebody else. More than seventeen years, three we spent living together, one year of correspondence, how can a dog hold a candle to me?"

Disappearing without listening to my side of it. I stand falsely accused of filing. First. Of course I see the irony in it, but more important, I miss her. Pure and simple, the bond goes beyond till death do us part.

✗

169

I can't find a cab. The street corners are three and four deep.
Cab-competitive people. People lined up along the sidewalks look
like there's a parade going by. Others stand between cars looking
for cabs. Decent people bickering over cabs. People kill for cabs.
Looking for cabs is a marked danger zone. You do it knowing your
life is on the line. It's the unmarked danger zones that give me the
creeps. It's the creeps that give the city its unmarked danger
zones. Walk into a danger zone, your number may not be up but
you will feel your number is up. For years afterward you might go
around spooked: Hey, didja hear, my number was just this far
from being up, for a while there I was monumentally unusually
so-so in the head, but hey, some good came of it, I number myself
one of the lucky ones, all I have to show for it is this lousy lump on
the head. (And one more thing besides.) Suppose there's another
close call, hey, it could happen, I've got to get something going for
me on the side.

Hey.

Indulge me.

I tell ya, my number was nearly up.

No empty cabs in sight.

I give up.

Less cabs than people hailing them. The numbers speak for
themselves. Numbers don't lie . . . there's more to numbers besides
the figures . . . numbers count.

My body to St. Patrick's.

And straight from my research files . . .

My mind on . . . numerics.

Break a Code, Reveal a Secret

*Crytopographers responsible for government security choose numbers with ex-
cess of one hundred digits. These are the hardest to factor. It would be like sorting
through a jigsaw puzzle of fifty million pieces.*

*In June of 1990, researchers cracked a 155-digit number. The number: 13,407,
807,929,942,597,099,574,024,998,205,846,127,479,365,820,592,393,377,723,561,
443,721,764,030,073,546,976,801,874,298,166,903,427,690,031,858,186,486,050,
853,753,882,811,946,569,946,433,649,006,084,097.*

*Dr. Gus Simmons, adviser to the Defense Department on how to make coding
secure, said that security had been compromised. He proposed an immediate
change.*

"Do I advise the Government to use bigger numbers? You bet," he said.

Besides provide.

Besides provide a systematic way to stay on top of shortages of thought. Knowing you're never going to run out of thoughts is a beaut of a thought. Too little going for you on the side feels like too little spending money.

Aside from that, numbers are timely.

If the most formidable numbers in the world can be cracked, other formidables can be cracked. Prison walls, frozen lids, anything. If their number's up, the odds can be beat.

Besides can provide . . . for miracles.

✗

St. Patrick's Cathedral doesn't have many steps but there are lots of places along the steps that someone can get lost in. Everyone in the City isn't here. It only looks that way. Picnickers, sunbathers, lounge lizards, students, tourists, natives, refugees from Rockefeller Center, the oglers and the ogled.

Look for the lady in lemon, Susan said.

The first three ladies in lemon aren't Susan. The fourth one stands in a group of clergy. Fathers shaking her hand. Probably some visiting dignitary. I turn my attention toward another sherbert lemon lady. Not Susan either. I scan again. The yellow lady surrounded by the priests waves at me. I wave back. She skips down the steps.

"I will not copulate with men of the cloth. They haven't got the moral fiber I've got. The City was sitting right on their shoulders. I could hear the City telling them, Ask her to meet you in the laundry room. A peek at her titties, pretty please. The City gave them hard-ons, but the City didn't give me a hard-on." There are red marks all along her eyes to her ears. The eyeglass trail. "Confession is good for the soul. I confess a passing interest in all eight of their cocks, my pussy was smacking her lips. Away from the City, my pussy's lips would be sealed. These are troubled times. Our frame of mind is who we are."

Heading uptown.

Susan walks head down, holding on to her eyeglass frame lines like she's battling the wind for her hat. I wait till we're a block from her building before I confront her.

"Lou visited me. I've never seen him so distraught. He's concerned he might inadvertently hurt you. Has any part of his message penetrated? Every time you confess some near miss, it stimulates him. I got a definite sense the day's not far off when that will have to be cut from the script. What he wants now is

171

simply a better frame of mind. Quit telling him his character is no good. Don't put him down."

Tony gets the door.

We get the elevator.

"Speak to him on my behalf. Get him to back off before he breaks every bone in my body. Day in, day out, he's after me to stop reminding him of what the City's done to him. The moment he stops needing reminders will be the happiest moment of my life. I don't doubt he described my confessions as titillating, probably he alluded to some kind of frame-up, it's just an indication of how much headway the City's made. He's misguided. How could he want a wife on his level? Why would he want to drag her down with him?"

Just before her apartment . . .

"The men of cloth invited me into their confessionals. I told them I'd think it over."

X

Patches and Susan go into the bedroom. The door is closed. The living room is in semidarkness. At the far end of the couch, next to the window, Lou sits. Slumped. The lights from the office building across the street give the room a film noir cast. Shadows, partial disclosures. Like what under your bed looks like. I walk over. Lou doesn't look up. I get straight to the point. "As much as I sympathize, I can't stand by while you squash my friend. You're going at it all wrong. The City, with all the resources in the world at its disposal, can't dent her frame."

I sit down on the coffee table.

"Then how do I change her mind? All I want from her frame is for it to be more like mine." An exhausted voice. Extensive pounding drains a man's reserves. "Nothing I do or say makes an impact. I might as well not be there."

He and Harold both.

The hunt for keys to frames.

"I just can't crack her code."

He and I are on the same frame wave. "Upwards of hundred-digit codes can be cracked. Pigs will be pigs. It was thought codes will be codes. Fortunately that no longer holds true."

He doesn't get it.

I zip down my fly-front jeans. I zip down his fly-front jeans. I lower myself on him. I pound it in: Codes can be cracked. He

172

pounds back: Say what? I pound harder: Codes can be cracked. He pounds back: Her number will be up. We pound each other, gathering speed as we go. It would be immoral not to cross that finish line.

✗

I leave him in a better frame of mind.
I've been a dear, dear friend.
Numerically speaking, you can't always play by the numbers.

✗

Dusk.
The kick-back-your-feet hour. Dusk is placid. The City's percussionists have mellowed. Traffic, industry at the top of its lungs, everyone sings a softer key at dusk. Dusk has its own decibel. You need less of a good ear to pick out the yelp of car alarms at dusk. The thuds of bodies hitting pavement carry better at dusk. Hear a pin drop at dusk? Everybody's number would have to be up. A monumentally unusual drop of population. It would make for unfinished business.
Dusk.
I finish up at Hardware on Third.

✗

The Hardware Store has turned in early. The only lights are the glow of night-lights. The socket kind used by children. No ya-yas, the Cross crowd is gone. Not a straggler to be seen. Everything looks neat. Tools in size place. A city health inspector wouldn't be able to issue one citation for moldy wire. I don't have far to roam. Next to the escalator, Mrs. Harold is sitting on a pool float. She looks fatter, a canvas stretched to splitting, and puffier like air kernels. The diva roundness isn't smooth. I can tell under the maternity tent, nothing runs parallel. I sit on the first rung of the escalator. Mrs. Harold fans herself. Thermostat on the blink. Her lids may be frozen, but her temperature fluctuates. "I went to an eye specialist today. Someone with firsthand experience. He's a nonblinker, his wife's a blinker. Their only child has one blinking eye, the other eye never drops a lid. His wife the blinker doesn't get a charge out of anything, everything gives him a charge. The kid doesn't have a conflicted outlook." Her tent dress is girdle-tight across her chest. You wouldn't know it to look at her. Lizards have more expression. "It was his hypothesis that an eye with frozen lids doesn't have to be thawed to change the outlook. The secret is not to believe what your eyes tell you. Of course I don't believe everything my eyes see. I only believe that in the blink of an eye, things change."

She crawls over to the escalator.

Knee raised. One leg, the other.

Her bottom is spread to Chicago.

"He didn't tell me anything I don't know. They all say the same thing. To change how you see, put the lid on what you believe."

She has me follow her to the front door. With difficulty, she opens it. Water-retentive fingers. She's probably outgrown her shoes.

"The offer still stands. To anyone who flips my lid, my hand in marriage."

✗

Dusk.

The tail end of dusk is like a final coating of paint. Each coat darker than the one before, application after application, till at last dusk is dead.

Final thoughts at the demise of dusk?

Besides oxytocin and lobes, Mrs. Harold is between two besides. Under the best of circumstances, a potbellied pig doesn't change its spots. But her lobes may yet hit the winning number combo. How hep will Harold get? The king of the jungle never was and never will be a chimp.

Dusk is no more.

I people pass. The act of people passing is like hitting typewriter keys. The faster you go, the less notice you take of individual letters. On the eve of the fourth anniversary from the man who filed. First. I thought I was observing people at a safe speed, slow enough to spot any leg traps, fast enough not to look like a sitting duck. I was finger typing. Hitting a few keys at a time. Dwelling on individuals as individuals. I didn't claim then I wasn't looking where I was going and I don't now. I merely claim a reserved pace. I was able to key in on the rabbit. I watched him closely. I didn't hit the wrong key. Nor did I hit the keys at the wrong speed. In those days I didn't have the psychic warning system I have now.

174

In those days I didn't have a forehead telling me I was about to be slugged by a bunny.

Or to watch out for Barry the bereaved.

Evasive action. I see him before he sees me. I look away. But not before I get a good look at his escorts. Three elderly women. All in widow's black. (The black of mourning is as different from the black of little black dresses as black is from white.) These must be the helpers hired by Barry's family to guide him through his grieving period. As a child of two senior citizens who aren't exactly what they look like, I don't jump to conclusions. Maybe the choke collar they've got around whatever is protruding from the folds of Barry's coat is simply a neck brace. Whatever their kind is I don't want to tangle with them.

They give me the creeps.

✗

They give me a reason to hurry home.

✗

The night doorman is a young lad. I don't know his stats. He doesn't say, I don't ask. I don't want to know how he is except on the most perfunctory level. If he's fine, fine with me; not so fine, that's fine by me. Jane Goodall didn't spread herself thin. She had staff do that for her. The elevators hassle me, but less than usual. It could be mechanical exhaustion. The accumulation of weeks of running behind schedule. The mechanized can spread themselves thin too. My elevators are strung out from calling the shots. I press every button. It's childish. It's nonsensical. It's not hep to go for the jugular of your elevator while you're still in it. I disembark on eight. The hallway looks uninhabited. I let myself into 8G. I close the door. The door buzzer shoots its mouth off. Somebody's on the other side of the door. I don't answer. When you don't answer they're supposed to think you're not home. They're supposed to go away. Buzzing and knocks. A double dose. I still don't answer. When you don't answer they're not supposed to think you're in there pretending not to be home. Nonstop sniper fire. When they think you're in there, they go for the jugular.

They don't skip a floor.

"Who the fuck is it?"

"Alex, it's important, could I—?"

175

"This better be good," opening the door.

Alex looks buzzed. He's wearing an off-duty outfit it hurts to look at. Paisley that's caught poison ivy. The parted side of his hair has fork-in-the-road parts. His nose is grinding teeth.

He smacks his forehead.

"It hit me. I never went on a flaw hunt before. Every once in a while a flaw would surface naturally in a woman. She didn't advertise. It was always something I tried to overlook till it couldn't be overlooked anymore. Minor imperfections, small fry. But with Marilyn, now that I've really gotten pore close, you wouldn't know it to look at her from a distance, she's spoiled goods. Big bloopers. Couldn't be in worse shape. I was bad off when she found me, I couldn't have been that bad off. Now that I've seen what needs to be done, I don't know if I'm her man."

"How direct do you want me to be?"

"Be totally straight with me." His nose sweats, beads sliding off the tip like skiers off a high jump. "She's still doing a job on me, isn't she? Here I am thinking the woman is no bargain, panicking, she's worse off than I ever was, wringing my hands, what did I ever see in her, getting ready to call it quits, when I realize she's still doing a job on me. Give it to me straight. Is it a weakness in her character to put me through this just to build my character or is it a weakness in my character to think it's not a strength in hers?"

"There is no magic." My all-purpose answer for when I don't know the answer.

"So you don't think much of it?"

"There is mystery."

"There's that, yes."

"There is the burning question."

"Which is?" his nose resting on my shoulder.

"Is the end going to be a crowd-pleaser?"

"To find out—"

"Stay on top of it."

He toys with it. Repeating it to himself: stay on top, stay tuned, stay alert. I tune him out. I close the door. I tune in to my own burning question of the moment: Wear a nightie to bed or the bathing suit?

✗

Compromise: Top half of the bathing suit on me. Nightie bottom

176

for my bottom. The lower half of the suit on the pillow next to me. On top of the lower half of the suit, the top of the nightie. A new breed. Bathing suit with no history (new kid on the block) teamed with the nightie (a long rap sheet). Am I making a personal wardrobe statement or a personal wish list?

✗

Sleep well, my loves.
Swimmingly so.

✗

After a night's sleep, it is my habit to wake up.

✗

"Did I wake you?" Marty Nesterbaum is sitting on the bed, lower suit-top nightie side of the bed. "I could come back later when you're decent. Give you time to pull yourself together, coupla hours should be ample, need more for your hair, just say so. Wouldn't hurt to skimp on the lipstick either." (I don't take off my lipstick at night due in part to what I feel is a chin plot to overthrow my face.) "Your lips are not your most outstanding feature."
No guile in the voice.
He's not deliberately trying to drive me up the wall.
"Wait in the kitchen, I'll be with you shortly."
Holding up the bottom half of the bathing suit, "Water sports tone you, but you're way off on the suit. For the shape you're in, it's too high cut."
"I'll be with you shortly." Right about the suit. Dead wrong on the lips. Colored lips throw off the trail of chin.
At the doorway, turning . . .
"On second thought, stick with the lipstick, it'll detract from the chin."
"I'll be—"
"With me shortly."

✗

In short order: a pair of little black sweats, a rubber band for my hair, teeth brushed . . . bloodred lips, extra moist.

177

x

I am with him shortly.

x

My breakfast, his filling station.

We sit across from each other. The breakfast nook used to be part of a Brooklyn diner. Like Egypt, Brooklyn is possessive of its antiquities. Brooklyn made me an offer anyone would have refused. And when I didn't, Brooklyn bitched. In the end, I got the booth, Brooklyn got the bucks. On an empty stomach, Marty turns my stomach. I talk and chew at the same time, everything but eye contact. "All my father needed was some pointers. How to screen for violent off-the-wall women. I never meant for you to induct him. He has a wife and child. His roots are here."

A gas guzzler.

Every five minutes, a refill on the juice. "People weren't designed to live a lifetime off the wall. Look how they treat each other. Most off-the-wall people are stressed out. It's an environmental thing." His food comes up after he swallows it, cow regurgitations. "Your father is a lot safer where he is now than out there. Pass the margarine please."

I hand him the margarine.

Several sesame buns.

A fresh container of juice.

I pour the coffee.

I refill the cow creamer.

"Do any of the homeless ever go home again? Is there any reason why my father can't be the one to pin my mother to the ceiling?"

Marty takes my hand.

He gets up.

I get up.

Something tells me breakfast is over.

"Having your head in the wall doesn't mean burying your head in the sand. We know what's going on in the world. Don't fence your parents in. They've come this far. Through barriers more real than any wall you see."

Now that breakfast's over, I take a good look at him. In the sexual sense, if he were strictly off the wall, I wouldn't ride in the same elevator with him. Fondling ghouls is sick. But you take that

178

same hunchback with that same goiter head and foul breath and put him up against the wall until the wall gives and so do I. He folds me in his arms. His chest is dank. I've been in musty basements that have smelled better. His out-to-there is working its way into my in-to-here.

I pull away.

Mixed feelings always mix me up.

"Let me take you inside the wall. Not just over the top, but through the roof."

"Is that what it's like where you are?"

"Actually no." Burping in my face. "There's leeway in gravity, there's no getting away from gravity. Thanks for breakfast."

"That's it?"

In the wall and gone.

I guess it's the same the world over. Inside the wall and out. One minute you're in the mood, the next, the mood's . . . out the wall.

✗

Breakfast dishes are cleared, bed is made, the hair in the rubber band is pulled back tighter, a lion tamer's last-ditch efforts to cower the savage. The hair detonates the rubber. And shortly thereafter, the mother who is balling beasts of a higher quality than what Sotheby's is auctioning paper beasts for phones. We haggle. I don't want to visit her in her den of iniquity. She doesn't want to visit me in mine.

It's settled. Häagen-Dazs.

✗

Just as a neighbor steps out of the elevator, I step in. The elevator shuts off life-support. No lights, no power. Plenty of elevator music, loud enough to wake the dead. Retaliation for pressing all its buttons. "Kindly leave the elevator at once or the elevator will drop you eight floors. No skin off my nose."

"Who said that? Identify yourself."

Is nobody answering because nobody is there or is nobody answering because whoever's there wants me to think nobody's there? Or is it me, projecting through some kind of thought transference what I'd say to me if all my buttons had been pressed out of spite, or is there a creep in the wall which would explain

179

everything, the elevator's rotten attitude, the elevator's poor work habits, the elevator's deviant history?

"Creep," I hiss it out.

The elevator door closes, the music lowers, it's a pleasant ride all the way down.

✗

"Not now," rushing by Alex.

"Your lipstick."

Retracing my steps. "Too red?"

"Understand, I don't go out of my way looking for flaws, I'm a laid back kind of guy. You've been straight with me, somebody should be straight with you."

"Dammit Alex, is the lipstick too red?"

"It's not your only flaw, take it from me, you are a monumentally flawed person. Not without your redeeming qualities, which by the way, are flawed too. But for your sake as well as mine—"

My hand is an attack dog.

Rubbing his cheek, the red isn't a lipstick kiss. "That was uncalled for. Slapping another person to make a point is a big blooper. Is there anything about you that doesn't need work?"

I answer appropriately.

"Creep."

✗

Let's hope it's not a permanent change of frame.

✗

She said we'd meet at Häagen-Dazs. She didn't say we'd stay. The forearms are treadles, the forearms are pistons, blue-collar forearms, forearms that work with their hands under little black dresses, and my mom, braided down her back like a schoolmarm, orders her kid to stop staring.

"Move it."

"Where to?"

"To meet Dad. He's going to try to pop out of the sidewalk."

I put my arm through hers to give her some support. But I'm the one doing the clutching. Mom is examining the sidewalk, a search for an earring she hasn't dropped. "It wasn't urogenital after all.

180

Last night he was in and out of every drain in the house. At bed-time he hid in the wall. I was sitting in bed reading. The book was propped on my knees. He turned the pages with his—"

Dad springs from the sidewalk.

Mom squealing, the same pig-in-the-mud squeals she gave when she bared her breasts to the beasties.

"Frank, it's chilly. Go home and get a scarf."

"What's for dinner?"

"Chicken."

"Roasted or broiled?"

"Roasted."

My father is popping like toast out of the sidewalk, his prick is porno, my mother can't take her eyes off it and they're talking chicken. It feels monumentally anticlimatic.

✗

We stroll. Her walk is slower than usual. Slower than a window shopping walk. Slower than walking with bundles. Slower than a pebble in your shoe.

"You haven't injured yourself climbing walls?"

"Never felt better."

"Do your shoes hurt? The shoemaker up the block has a leather stretcher."

"Shoes never felt better."

"Then we can speed up a bit."

"That would make me a moving target, I'd rather not play hard to get."

"You're hoping someone else will pop out."

"It's not inconceivable that I could be swept off my feet."

"Dad's not enough for you?"

"He's all I've got. Try to forget I'm your mother. Just for argument's sake, I'm a woman. Don't I need a little something going on the side? One doesn't depend on one outfit or one pair of panties. You can't. What with one thing or another, a person could be caught short. It sounds mean-spirited, you probably don't relate to it at all."

Alex was right on the money.

I am flawed.

I lie with ease.

"I'm with you on the panties. Dad is not underwear. A system like the one you've described doesn't apply here. It's a perversion

181

of the system to take a system designed for underwear and use it in ways it was never intended to be used. What if the system goes haywire? Ever hear of women being victims of the system? For every besides on the side, you could end up wanting another. Besides for the besides. Sound innocuous? Think again. Do you want to spend the rest of your life living by implication?"

The side of a bank building we pass is doing a little business on the side.

A hideous homely (of the male sex), long hair down his back, beer belly, ink stains on his fingers, and a rod you could walk from Manhattan to Brooklyn on, makes kissy-kissy with his mouth. Irma tells me to run along.

I am flawed.

Yes mommie, I say.

✗

Would I be so two-faced as to have a besides right after what I just carried on?

Try me.

✗

My body to Hardware . . .

My mind on rabbit stew. With or without mushrooms?

My Besides on Mushrooms
The Larousse dictionary is the French Webster's. More than one million are sold annually. A high volume are bought each September at the start of the school year.
In the 1991 edition there was a mushroom error.
Next to the Aminta Phalloides, the deadliest mushroom in all of France, was a black dot.
Red dots mean poison.
Black dots mean no harm will come to you if you ingest this mushroom.
The French are a nation of fleshy fungi lovers. They roam the woods for mushroom. One hundred and seventy-five varieties.
The venerable Larousse publishing house (established 1806) called the dot error the worst mistake the company has ever made.

It is impossible to think of mushrooms and not think of my ex mother-in-law (now common wraith). Her interest in mushrooms includes the kind not dug up. When I think of all the besides I've

182

ever thought, mushrooms don't seem at all beside the point. I am a flesh fungi lover of the opposite sex. In the larger sense, mushrooms dig deeper. Events can mushroom before your very eyes: Disasters. Mushroom clouds. Cravings. Attractions. Hostilities. Coups. You name it, it can mushroom without warning . . . Mrs. Harold standing at the crossroads. Any moment. Mr. Mushroom could cross her path. Harold, one wink away from being blinked away. Harold and Mr. Mushroom crossing swords. Harold is crossed out. Mr. Mushroom and Mrs. Harold crosshatch. And Jane Samuels crosses the finish line.

✗

My kingdom for Mr. Mushroom.

✗

Owner, whose first and last name are irrelevant, is sitting behind the counter. He sees me, he pulls me aside, now it's Owner and I who sit behind the counter. His usual apparel is no tie, no suit, no vest.

"You look like you're going somewhere."

"Mark Cross is sending a rep. You'll hear the announcement over the loudspeaker. Everybody report to the second floor."

"Payday for you, you'll be able to retire."

"My hush money."

"Cross bought your silence."

"I'm entitled to some compensation. Coming in every day, never knowing what I'm going to find. A lesser man would think less of himself. It would never occur to a lesser man that he has money coming to him."

"It's fall."

"What difference does that make?"

"The Big One falls into your lap. For you, it's a windfall."

"And you?"

"Any day now."

✗

The store is congested. A blend of irregular shoppers, locals strictly there for hardware, and the irregulars. The Crosses, the ya-yas (there for other things besides). Laps in all states of stance.

Some balcony out, some so subtle, it's a toss between fatigue and poor posture. The leading clue isn't a clue, it's a dead giveaway.

"How are you?" echoed from lap to lap.

Harold has a room to himself. Floor to ceiling books. Shelves of aged wood, a ladder on wheels to reach the books at the top. Leather chair for him. Ladies leather for me. His Cross must be the crowning glory of Crosses. Top of the line. A Cross of unlimited power.

"How are you?" Unusually, monumentally urgent.

A delayed reaction. Suppose the man from Cross isn't just coming to give everyone a preview of the new spring line? Anything could mushroom. He could use his influence with Owner to shut down the store. The chimp study would be kaput. The finish line postponed years.

Incomplete findings.

Cliffhanger theater.

I hate cliffhangers.

"Ashes to ashes, dust to dust. She'll bite the dust before I let her make me history," Harold rubbing the arms of his chair, making them apple shiny.

The bookcase oscillates, the chairs too, the room gets fuzzy around the edges. As if we were under plastic. A sci-fi here now, gone tomorrow. The attaché case puffs away like it's doing steps. It falls to one side. The hum of machinery winding down.

"The upper hand's hers. But the winning hand's going to be mine."

He picks up the attaché case. He extracts the owner's manual. He flips through the pages. He makes adjustments. Both hands in the case. The Cross takes deep breaths. The room comes into focus. The Cross is humming.

The voice of Owner . . .

"Attention." The loudspeaker is megaphone loud. "Proceed to the second floor. The man from Cross is here."

✗

I've made my mind up.

No ifs, ands, or buts . . . Cross is going to hear from me. Don't rain on my finish line. I hurry on ahead. Gridlock at the escalator. Trooper that I am, I take the stairs. No ifs, ands, or anythings . . . Cross crosses me, Cross is history.

✗

The feel of outdoors, indoors.

The second level is an atrium. Glass sunroof. Look up, see sooty sky. The smell of fresh paint. Perfumed chemicals. The speaker's platform in the center is a theater in the round. It doesn't fool anyone. We cluster in front, not around. On the platform, the ya-ya man. His ponytail keeping its own ya-ya beat like a foot keeping time to music. His hair is an alien life form. The mike he steps up to is a plain pole, the kind found in school auditoriums. "Whatever's goin down we're gonna finish what we came here to do. We're gonna get us some answers." I feel like I'm at a student rally. The ya-ya man leads us in a rah-rah cheer.

Owner adjusts the mike.

A good two inches trimmed off.

"Welcome to the man from Cross," Owner urging the audience to clap, lets-hear-it hand motions.

Cross steps stage center.

The man from Cross is no bigger than I. Under five seven. Little nose, little hands. Late thirties, early forties. Neat. The type that spreads his butter evenly, tucks his tie before eating. Hair every other week trimmed. Glasses that aren't aviators or oval. They look like the first pair he ever owned. Soon as his bills come in, he pays. No outstanding anythings.

He'd be lost in a crowd of four.

Make it two.

"Mark Cross has an unblemished record. Cross stands for excellence. This is a factory recall." (No ifs, ands, or buts, I feel something.) "The defects are not safety defects. There is no risk." (What is it I feel?) "Cross has authorized me to offer triple your money back. It's to your advantage. The circuitry needs recircuiting." (I don't want to believe him, yet I do.) "There was a shipping error. These models were never meant for distribution." (A vague thought crosses my lap, but goes over my head.) "Mark Cross leaves you with this promise. Cross works hard. Cross wants your repeat business."

Working the crowd . . .

Shaking hands, chatting, patting shoulders. He glances my way. I glance away. My lap awash in feelings? My lap lurching? My lap in the lap of the gods? Lord not now. Of all the besides that should have fallen on deaf ears . . . my kingdom for Mr. Mushroom was strictly off the record. Finally I can put a name to what

185

I couldn't give a name to.

MUSHROOM LOVE.

The updated version: Mr. Mushroom crosses Jane's path. Mr. Mushroom comes across. Mr. Mushroom and Jane crosshatch. But does Jane cross the finish line? Will Cross double-cross Jane? Already the man from Cross and I are at cross-purposes. He's proposing a buyout. I want the Harolds right where I found them. Is mushroom love a cross to bear? Will there be cross fire? In a crossway, you have to look both ways.

Shit.

It's fall.

I fell for a mushroom.

I fell hard.

✗

The crowd swells, the man from Cross is carried away, crosscurrents carry me the other way. Are we star-crossed lovers? I fight my way to Owner, the man from Cross, where is he? Owner says that-a-way. No man from Cross. No Cross inside or outside Hardware. No Cross in the Greek diner. No Cross buying a marzipan cow. Five blocks away, still looking. People watching in the fast lane. Hitting those keys.

Hitting a time.

Hitting a place.

Hitting déjà vu.

Hippity hop down the block. Looking not a day older than the day he bopped me. Freshly shampooed, his fur is pure fluff. He's a bruiser, ten steps for every five of mine, swinging his arms, walking like he owned the block. Ears sticking straight up like corn husks.

Hitting my top speed.

Hitting a snag.

The man from Cross across the street.

What to do, what to do? When things mushroom, they come at you from all sides. Hard hit. Go for one, lose the other.

Hit on my blind side . . .

Jowls that need jock straps. I evaded him last night.

Today he flies low under my radar. The widower with his three escorts. Like tugs with a tanker in tow. Where oh where is hunch when you're caught in the crunch?

I try to shake Barry.

"Some other time."

Circling for the kill. They're right on my tail. Four of them to one of me. Hitting them with everything I've got. "Get out of my way. Don't make me use deadly force."

Laughter.

I've hit their funny bone.

"Meet the widows. Ardeth, Gert, Hilda."

It's no use. Rabbit and Cross, I've lost them both. The circle becomes a tight-knit circle. Me in the noose. Any closer, my air supply would be cut off.

Hands shaking mine.

The ladies clear their throats like mortuary staff. My mom has pots and pans like these women. Passed down through generations. Built to last. Pursed lips, crow's-feet. Collagen would die in those trenches.

"I miss Betty more than words can say. Not a moment goes by when I don't think of her. I've suffered an enormous loss. I owe Betty. I want to help build a better world for our sons. In her honor, a heritage of decency. A cleaner New York."

I play dumb.

"Are these Betty's friends?"

"They're going to help me through the grieving process."

"How?" These are not merry widows. I'm smiling into scowls.

"By teaching me how to express my sorrow. If I have to whack off I do it in a mayo jar. It's more honorable to fuck a mayo jar than support people who corrupt young minds."

Nicely put.

"Tell your female friend good-bye." The widow with dentures that look hand-me-down makes Alissa look like a welcome mat.

"Good-bye to you too, Barry." I take the initiative.

They break rank. I'm free to go.

✗

History will vouch: Where there are groups and interests, there are special interest groups. People with agendas, ways to make their views known. In our country, just to take an example, many groups would like to ban *Catcher in the Rye*, *Huckleberry Finn*, and anal sex. And many groups would like to ban the groups that would like to ban *Catcher*, *Huck*, and anal.

✗

Wraiths coming at me . . .

Bringing with them a mushroom cloud. Fog, smog, smokeless smoke, take your pick.

"When you've gone to as many mushroom conferences as I have, you learn a thing or two about mushrooms. The good ones don't come to you, you've got to go to them. Make no issues where there are none." Helen has the voice of a drill sergeant. "Never retreat from the issues. Issue your name to the mushroom. Your phone number. Issue an invitation."

Black umbrella fanning the smokeless smoke, fog, smog. Sam succeeds. I can see him. He's in a safari suit. Umbrella case slung over his shoulder. "Give a mushroom room," Sam says. "These things have to mushroom on their own."

They gave me my little black dress.

Maybe they do have my best interests at heart.

"She doesn't know the first thing about his mushroom. Safe to consume or lethal?" Yvette is thinking ahead. "Where's his mushroom been lately? Where have all the sterile mushrooms gone?"

The fog, smog, smokeless haze, take your pick, evaporates. So do the ex in-laws. If I speak now, I'd be talking to thin air.

(It wouldn't be the first time.)

From me to air: "Mushroom love on my part. On his, I'm not sure he knows I exist."

It's out of my hands. The oldest system in the world: When things are up in the air, go on the air. Anything spoken aloud immediately becomes public domain. The airways carry our words near and far. It's not only a shot that can be heard around the world. We are all somebody's chair experience. Seconds after I confide to thin air, I get back the following: "Leave off the pepperoni."

So-so in the head.

Monumentally, unusually so.

So I say leave off the pepperoni is a coded message. So I furthermore say codes can be decoded. So I say, so help me God, what they didn't say was leave off the mushrooms. So I in closing say, by not saying leave off the mushrooms what they were really saying: call the man from Cross.

So I proceed to do so . . .

✗

. . . in three steps. Beginning with looking up the number in the

188

directory at the first telephone. The second phone, I call and hang up. The third, cross my heart, I cross into the promised land.

"Good afternoon, Mark Cross, how may we help you?"

"I'd like to speak to one of your staff. About five foot six. Dick Clark hair. Glasses that date back to the fifties."

"One moment please."

"Good afternoon. Chuck Bellview speaking. How may I help you?"

"I heard your pitch at the Hardware Store."

"I'd be happy to pick up the case right now. Payment the moment the bag exchanges hands."

"If I had a Mark Cross, I would. I've got a Claiborne."

"Oh."

"But I'm a great admirer of Mark Cross bags, wallets, key holders, credit card cases, appointment books, photo albums, diaries, travel journals, overnight bags, small change purses, shopping bags, weekend cases, luggage—"

"Are you calling to place an order?"

"I saw you at the Hardware Store. I liked what I saw. I'd like for you to have my number. My name is Jane Samuels, 788-3016."

"Again, slowly."

"I'm a great admirer of Mark Cross bags, wallets, key—"

"I can't reach you if I don't have your number."

"Jane Samuels, 788-3016."

"It was good of you to call. Mark Cross will get back to you."

He hangs up. Second.

✗

Mushroom love.

I'll always remember this day. To bring it to a swift close, I hurry home. I kiss Alex on the cheek where I slapped him prior to mushroom love. I ride the elevator. The elevator creep and I have not come to an understanding. But this time we're civil to each other. Hello to my next door neighbor as we pass in the hall. I unlock. I lock. I undress my face, I undress myself. I get under the quilt. I kiss my bathing suit good night.

Day to a perfect close.

The end.

✗

Three A.M.
Day reconvenes.

✗

Awakened by the howl of a cat, I Mace up. One three-ouncer strapped around my ankle, one economy size in hand, one travel size in my bra. I follow the howl so plaintive, so familiar. The park across the street from my street. By the light of a tarnished moon, a cat calls my name. Suki, my dearly departed. What is it that couldn't wait till morning? Sitting on a moonbeam, sparkle in her eyes. A wedge of moonbeam cheese hanging from her neck. She extends her paw to me. I stand on the bench. Her touch lighter than air. By the light of the golden moon she tells me not to wait up. "I'm going to Africa. Where animals talk before they're dead. Where animals are born talking. Where the heppest cats in the world are said to be. No more just getting by. You gave me a terrible scare. It scares me to death to think I could spend what's left of my life-after-death trying to get over you and a dog. It could be you're hepper than I thought. Or just like me, you chase your own tail. I'm not hep enough to know. Sad to say, I'm looking forward to getting on with my life."

Suki come back.

Suki take me with you.

I should be beating my chin. Screeching. Doing something soap opery. Claw air. Beg Suki to reconsider. Climb the tree, howl at the moon. Beat the ground with my fists. Rent my clothes.

Instead I wave.

She'll never pull it off.

Suki break clean?

Suki start from scratch?

Suki get over me?

Now that would be magic.

✗

Later in bed . . . I remember what it was I forgot but didn't know I forgot till I remembered I forgot it.

A question:

Stack the man from Cross against my life with the Harolds, what would stay and what would go?

Still later . . .

The clock on my night table says go back to bed. I stuff the clock in a drawer. The question I forgot but didn't know I forgot till I remembered is not my only question.

Second question:

I once said of Jane Samuels, come what may, over her dead body, the heavens could open and she wouldn't let anything come between her and Hardware. What if the man from Cross—Chuck Bellview—asked her to choose between mushroom love (the new kid on the block) and the Harolds (the nightie with the rap sheet)?

✗

Within the same hour . . .

Follow-up question:

Did the second question expand on the first question I asked when I remembered what it was I forgot but didn't know I forgot till I remembered I forgot or was it a repetition of the question I asked when I remembered what it was I forgot but didn't know I forgot till I remembered I forgot it?

✗

The clock in the drawer is ticking let me out, let me out.

✗

Considerably later . . .

Call the man from Cross, don't call the man from Cross, give the man from Cross all the space he needs, don't give him a moment's peace, give him time, ration his time, make him take his turn, take his turn for him, replace his turn with your turn. That would leave him two turns behind.

✗

The clock in the drawer is ticking Don't-you-have-an-y-thing-bet-ter-to-do-with-your-time?

✗

Around the time Lou Gold phones, I am grappling with the issue of making issues. Am I making issues where there are none? Am I making more out of the issues than I should? When to force an issue? When to let it slide? When to kill it off altogether? When to put it to rest? When to put it aside . . .

Lou's comment on my phone manner:

"You sound disappointed, were you expecting someone else?"

"Maybe never."

"Want to talk about it?"

"When to force an issue, when to let it slide, when to kill it off altogether, when to put it to rest, when to put it aside . . . no I don't want to talk about it."

"Look, if you think I'm making too big an issue out of the amount of physical damage my wife incurs during rough fucking, just say so."

"The pounding I administered to you on the couch should have alleviated the pounding you're inflicting on Susan."

"Her number's not up yet."

"Numbers of 155 digits have cracked, I made it clear that pigs will always be pigs but anybody's number can be up."

"I need to see you before—"

"Filing. First." Soon as I say it I wish I could take it back.

"Five o'clock. My place. Susan will be at St. Patty's confessing to eight clergy with hard-ons."

Road kill ends with a thank you.

I sign off with you are welcome.

✗

Erratic ticks from the clock in the drawer. Arrhythmic heartbeat. Gradual cessation. Expiration. The clock in the drawer's number just came up.

✗

He hasn't called. He hasn't called. He hasn't called.

✗

He said he'd get back. He said he'd touch base. He said he would, he didn't say when.

✗

The instrument of my torture rings. A first ring pickup tips your hand. Same with the second ring. It's like answering your door on the first knock. Three rings lets the world know this is a woman on her way up in the world.

It must be him.
It must be him.
It must be him.

✗

Not him . . .

✗

The preliminary hellos have been said.

"You sound disappointed, were you expecting Nate . . . none of my business, what you do in private with my husband, your lover, is between you and your lover, my husband."

"You are too kind."

"No, you are too kind."

"Kind of you to say so."

"I mean it, only a kind and thoughtful and nurturing person like yourself would do the noble things you do for Nate."

"I wouldn't call—"

"I meant his Castle Milieu, in acreage alone, ten. Every room full of jokes, riddles, dreams, minutiae he's stored for years."

Silence.

"You do let him talk to you?"

Silence.

"You don't let him talk to you?"

Silence.

"Me either. Ten minutes in the castle, I'm looking for an ice pick. My husband is an addict for substance. A substance substance abuser. His idea of a relationship is when people really get to know each other."

"How are the kisses coming?"

"I've kissed one orange and four apples. My elbows, my knees, various parts of the feet. That's why I'm calling. Could you do a two o'clock today?"

"Three works better. At two I'm going to the beauty parlor."

"Didn't you go yesterday?"

"I'm going again today at two."

"Twice in two days?"

"I'll see you at three."

We close without good-byes, the way I like it.

✗

The little black dress or the little black jumper or the little black sweats? According to the law of any occasion deemed in the slightest way special, looking like you're ready for it, in my case, running into the man from Cross, can result in penalties. One Fate saying to another Fate, the ruling for today is all females dolled up for some fateful encounter in hardware stores do not stand a chance in hell.

I'll wear sweats.

The black jumper goes into my Liz.

For something else besides.

✗

Phone lore also subscribes to its own set of rules.

Take a shower, phone rings.

Bathe, phone rings.

Empty garbage, phone rings.

Make love, phone rings.

Inconvenience and unavailability are said to influence phones. Personally, I believe no stone should be unturned.

I shower.

No ring.

I tub it.

No ring.

Garbage, two trips.

Double yes.

✗

First trip back from emptying the garbage, a message from Nate. Next trip back (impromptu garbage created out of four unused tissues) Nate's second message. Both saying the same thing. Call me.

This is the tricky part. Don't return Nate's calls, it may come

194

back to haunt me . . . Chuck Bellview, man from Cross misplaces my number. Return his call . . . use his body to make love (cross-reference back to phone lore—make love, phone rings), I am making an all-out effort to achieve my goal.

Do I want to make love to Nate?

Or should I save myself for Chuck?

Is it an issue?

✗

I dial Nate's private office number.

"Any cancellations?"

"Barry tells me you ran into him yesterday."

"I want your sex."

"Trade you, castle for sex."

"Outside the castle, not in it."

"Doorstep."

"Agreed."

"One o'clock."

"I'll let Alex know you're coming."

✗

Working backwards: Lou Gold at five, Nora at three, beauty parlor (surprise assault) at two. Hardware, a given. And in no particular order: See what parents are up to, put the squeeze on the school crossing guard, don't step on her toes, stop at Saks, the belt department . . . belt it out, loud and clear . . . it's fall, I fell. I got it bad.

✗

A full day's activities should make the phone ring off the hook. If there's magic.

✗

The creep in the elevator wall shuts the door in my face. Despite a temporary cease-fire, the elevator wars are resumed. I wait for the other elevator on the floor below mine. It's not yet clear if the elevator creep is two creeps or one with a monopoly over both elevators. The other elevator skips my floor, I try the floor two floors below mine.

At six floors below, the door to the other elevator opens.

I press lobby, the elevator goes up.

"Why don't you creeps go back on the street where you belong?"

"My, aren't we sunny."

"Can it."

"I will not be spoken to like I'm a garden variety creep, maybe the creep in the other elevator will let you get away with gutter language but I am a lady creep. Save it for the creeps under the bed, the creeps who come through windows, the creeps who rent videos and don't rewind."

"Then act like the lady you say you are. Down please."

"Down please, lady creep."

"Please lady creep, I'd like to go down."

"It'll cost you."

"What is this, a toll bridge?"

"What is this a toll bridge, lady creep."

"How much . . . lady creep?"

"Put your money away. Don't look at me like that. I'm not going to molest you. A favor, that's all . . . speak to the creep in the other elevator. Don't make it sound like I put you up to it. He's a smooth operator, the moment I expressed any interest in him, he started playing elevator tag, the few times we're on the same floor together, he swears he'll get back to me. That was months ago. I've tried ignoring him, but let's face it, when they hit your buttons . . . forget it, inside joke."

"I'll put in a good word, lady creep."

"Ups and downs are my bread and butter but elevator tag's a real downer. Creepy how a thing like this can suddenly creep up on you out of nowhere."

The lobby floor. Ten minutes to do what could have been done in three. How could I fail to be touched by her plight? He's got her climbing the . . . floors.

✗

Nose in the air. I whiz past Alex. I'm outwhizzed.

"Just hear me out," Alex throwing himself against the door.

"Make it fast," looking at my watch.

"That slap in the face yesterday, I had it coming. It takes an exceptional person to accept constructive criticism, the fault was mine. With unexceptional people like yourself, the language of

196

criticism must be couched. Or you get a backlash. You did me a great service."

"Good, now out of my way."

"Don't you want to know what that service is?"

"In making your presentation to Marilyn, you're going to couch your language as you would with any unexceptional person. Move aside."

"Your lipstick's—"

"Don't."

"Couched language, I promise."

"Get out of my way or I'll knee you in the nose."

Alex jumps clear.

"Mr. Nate Fergenic will be by at one, just let him through." I don't wait for an answer.

A knee in the nose is not the same as a good swift kick in the pants. A knee in the nose is a knee in the groin.

✗

After Hardware comes belts.

The purchase of new belts and new shoes (unlike bathing suits, socks, and bras) does not bother me in the least. The inconsistency doesn't either. I can discard belts and shoes (unlike bathing suits, bras, and socks) at the drop of a hat. There is no one explanation, no overall unifying theory. Just a grab bag of reasons. Belts encircle the waist. Metaphorically suggesting to me it's a waste to keep going around in circles. Belts are straps, do I want to be strapped in? Sashbelts tie, an obvious double side of the coin, historians tie people to events, people to people, events to the big picture, but must I be bound hand and foot? Belts have loops, loopholes allow for flexibility, loopholes are easy outs. Loops are for sizing, historians like to size things up, but sometimes it's excessive. A belt (when looped) has no beginning, middle, or end, nice when you want it not to end, nasty when there's no end in sight. By buying belts I am buying into more than a belt, by filing on them, I'm filing from the lap.

✗

Shoes.
Likewise.
I can give them the boot.

Shoes walk with you every step of the way, a comforting thought. Walking away from your shoes can be a step in the right direction. Shoes have soles, a metaphorical Grand Canyon. Who needs too much soul? And beware the shoe that fits like an old shoe . . . it's then that things start to fall apart. Heels are a pain, can't live with them, can't live without them. Boiled down: Shoes stand for more than I'm willing to stand. Boil that down: I can't stand what shoes stand for. Don't boil it down: It may just be, when it comes to shoes and belts . . . I'm fickle.

✗

Something's up.

Hardware is down to its bare essentials.

The store is decapitated. Second level cut off at the neck. Waist pinched. The full figure has regained its former figure. All this I see from the entrance. No sign of glass counters. I'll wager the annex is gone too. The rooms that comprised the Harolds' living quarters, are they still here? Are the Harolds present? What's happened to the Cross crowd and the ya-yas? Owner is so busy counting his hush money he doesn't even look up. I invade the aisles. Nuts and bolts. No Harold, no number two. Screwdrivers, hammers, nails. No Harold, no number two. Around the corner to insulation, wiring, drills, and power hand tools.

The Harolds.

She's wearing a flannel nightgown I wouldn't empty the garbage in. He's pulling on the nightgown. She pulls away. The flannel nightgown rips. Gashes right down the side. His grip slips momentarily. She gives her Cross a push with her foot. The Cross and Mrs. Harold are gone.

But not her voice.

"Do not look upon this as a trial separation. Mrs. Harold has taken up permanent residence in wood paneling, do-it-yourself paints, and wallpaper. If you'll excuse me now, I have pressing engagements."

She doesn't waste any time filing.

A line of men in single file file into the store. One irate man taps me: "If you think you're going to win Mrs. Harold's hand in marriage, think again. I've got an idea that will flip her lid. The end of the line is that way."

Harold's eyes are the eyes of a bull charging the matador. He races to the head of the line, I race with him. As we go Harold shouts to be let through, family emergency.

Wood paneling, paints, wallpaper is two over.

Reclining in her Mark Cross, Mrs. Harold's feet stick up. The Cross is an overgrown cradle. Satin lining on the inside. A nice coffin touch.

"Wife number one, kindly tell husband number one not to interfere. Either he bows out gracefully or I will have him forcibly removed."

Harold turns to me.

"Explain to her wives come and go. The seed of the loins is forever. The husband was present at conception. Explain Harold the man to her. Cutting the child off from the father without the father's consent makes it impossible for him to ever walk away. It would never be finished for him. The rest of his life would be after the fact."

He grabs my arm.

An odor grabs the rest of me.

His socks need Right Guard. Armpit smells. On the pants, by the knees, sweat stains. His entire life, dry till now. He must feel like he's bed-wetting.

That other Jane, Jane Goodall, was a pro. Chimp babies falling out of trees, chimp warfare, chimp fatalities. Through it all she remained the impartial observer. I am not about to break radio silence except to say . . .

"How are you?"

"There's got to be a loophole." (Echo of belts from Harold.) "Anybody walks, it's me." (Echo of shoes.) "The days of running around in circles are over, if there's a step in the right direction I'll find it." (Echoes of belts and shoes.) "I've got a bag of tricks too." (The Cross of course.)

Harold's bag is back in insulation, wiring, drills, and hand tools. To which we return forthwith. Owner (when you've got a label for a name, who needs a name?) is standing in insulation, wiring, drills, and hand tools.

"Mark Cross is paying good money for these babies. Some unscrupulous person could have taken the bag and run. I'll give you five grand, no questions asked."

"Put the bag down," Harold in a street fighter's voice.

"Cut me in," Owner clasping the bag to his massive chest.

"Get lost."

"Look around you, everybody's sold out. You and wifey are the only ones left. Unload the bags while they're still worth something. Wait too long, all you'll have left is an empty hull."

"The bag." Harold reaching for it. Harold kneeing Owner (not in the nose), the bag dropping, Harold and bag reunited.

"The both of you go." Harold to both Owner and me, wife number one.

✗

Just when I wanted to stay.

✗

Involuntarily transported once by Harold, I don't want to try for excommunication. Leave now, I can always come back. Refuse to leave, I end up exiled. To have it end like that would be a loose end. An unusually monumentally so-so end. A strong end is what makes a final curtain feel final. It's what there is no sequel for.

It's the Big Scene.

✗

To that end, I rush to Saks.

✗

Getting out of the cab in front of Saks, I tell the cab driver, Wait here. The cab driver tells me something that could not be printed in a family newspaper.

✗

Belts.

Big black ones for little black dresses. They must have moved the colored ones to another department. No matter. I grab a handful of blacks, by force of habit, putting my face to them in the mirror, seeing what the color does for me. Drained. Beyond the pale. The face of someone who looks in the mirror and flinches.

The belts are the least of it.

The most of it is Barry the bereaved.

And widows three. Widows Ardeth, Gert, and widow somebody-or-other. In basic black. Their fashion statement is simple: Vagina deceased. Barry hugs me. Overnight he looks fifteen pounds lighter, none of it off his jowls—those tender little succulents are the shape of pine cones. He's lost his abdominal paunch, information I come by visually. The hug was the least amount of body parts. A chaste embrace. (Barry's horn rocketing to its feet is not the same as a gent rising for a lady.) Maybe these widows are just the thing.

"Got a minute?" Opening his bag. "Let me know what you think. All this weight loss, my sports jackets are hanging on me." Pulling out a navy blazer with brass buttons. "In memory of Betty, I no longer dishonor the living. Those who don't live by a code of honor are saying sin isn't sinful." Trying on the blue blazer, brass buttons buttoned. "In memory of Betty I've examined my values. Am I making a wholesome contribution to society? As an individual, what can I—"

Jailbreak.

A ripping sound like when you bend in too tight pants.

Narrowly missing me . . .

The eel who lives behind Barry's zipper. Wicked Willie himself, baton out, a thread (tire thick) looking for the eye of the needle, a fuzzy-haired reptile, stalker of flesh, risen and rising like a full throated cry of surf's up. The head down to the hefty stem, pudgy genitalia. Barry's weight loss, its gain. The chin on the head of the penis is scraping floor.

Penis patrol swings into action.

Whipping out jars. Watercooler size. They tip them like rain barrels. Barry fills the tank. Three jars full. Barry's spurt is monsoon.

Barry is radiant.

"I held out, the longest yet. No dishonor on Betty's memory. I acted impulsively but I didn't pillage the community. I'd sooner fuck a dozen watercoolers than purchase printed matter defiling women. Betty, in her time, was female. The sons and daughters of Satan throw females at men. Females test a man's character. The honorable thing to do is fuck jars."

All turn to me.

Am I about to have my rights read?

Widows speaking as one: "Swear by everything holy you'll make a daily effort to live honorably."

A rigged request.

"My word. Every effort to live honorably."

I evacuate.

I speculate.

It's people like the widows three who won't let people like me approve of people unlike myself who change sex to match the season. Watchdog people. People who beat you over the head with their sense of honor.

And I defend their right to do it.

But let them do it to somebody else.

✗

To that end, I rush out the same way I came . . .

✗

. . . at the last fraction of a second, seeing my mistake, trying to correct my error, failing that, I sing the multiplication tables. The little warmongering children who were about to clamp the leg irons on me see their mistake, try to correct their error, failing that they are stuck with me, fumbling the key until I snatch if from them, all the while singing my times tables, cruel and unusually just punishment. I am in danger. If I let them, the foes of fur coats would fry me.

And I defend their right to speak.

Just lay off the heavy metal.

✗

If only special interest groups had more interests in common.

✗

The common turf of the moment: The corner. Barry, widows three, fur fiends, and me. Commonsensibly waiting for the light. In the commons (the crosswalk) stands a crossing guard most uncommonly devoted to the common good. She does the common courtesy, escorting us from corner to corner. I double back.

Bringing the commonplace to a close.

"You didn't accept the desk job after all."

"I tried it for a day, see how I'd do with the walls."

"Didn't agree with you?"

"Your warning about the walls was a false alarm. They didn't start to close in on me, in fact it was the opposite. I felt them give way. But this is where I belong, spokesperson for system awareness."

202

"And easy street for a hopping good time."

"You are misinformed."

"That's what you'd like me to think. Your secret's safe with me. Closed in by four corners, I'd take to the streets too, just the way you did. Bunny crossing guards. Am I right?"

"No system is foolproof."

"Am I right?"

"Every system—"

"Am I right?"

"It's a harebrained scheme."

"AM...I...RIGHT?"

"Must pedestrians always have the right of way?" Her braces are the old-fashioned metal kind, glinty when she smiles in the light. "Yes, you're right. Now are you satisfied?"

Saved by a cab charging through the light.

I board, bound for glory.

Satisfied, never. Not till I nab Big Ears himself.

✗

Arriving at my destination: Hardware.

"Some kind of grand opening?" the cabbie asks.

"They're waiting to see a woman."

"That's a lot of guys, what gives?"

"She wants somebody to flick her lids."

"I did a walk-on in a Pacino movie."

"Forget it, it's not what you think."

"Level with me. I did a Pacino."

"I told you—"

"No charge, ride's on the house."

Giving up, "Everybody's been cast."

He hands me his card, gets out of the car, comes around to my side, and holds the door. Acting's a hard business to break in to. The perseverance, the single-mindedness. Year after year, waiting for the Big Break to fall into your lap.

No way could I subject myself to that.

✗

Sniffling men.

Owner is distributing free boxes of condoms to the blubberers. He looks a little teary-eyed himself. His shoulders are slumped, so

203

are theirs. With Mrs. Harold, everybody's a loser. It's a private moment. One in which I have no place.

"Jane, could you give me a hand here?" Owner leaving the group, cutting off my avenue of escape. Pull my Liz, you pull me along. "Their egos are crushed. See what you can do." Owner not letting go of the reins.

The men doughnut me.

"One at a time," Owner doing crowd control. "Get the woman's angle from a different angle. Flick her lid, restore your manhood."

Trying to extradite myself, "I don't flick easy, give me a little credit, what you need is somebody—"

Clamping a hand on my mouth. "OK fellers, the same way you told it to Mrs. Harold. Step right up."

Eye level with a man in a navy business suit:

"I would give you an unlimited expense account."

Flick.

Eye level with a man in a pin-striped business suit:

"I'd tattoo your name on my cock."

Flick.

Eye level with a guy's guy:

"I could get you on the next space shuttle."

No flick. The guy lunges. I bite Owner's hand. I do something to the lunger that puts him on the blink. All the men sympathy flick. I am asked to leave.

I won't be gone long. Long enough to check my phone messages. Has he called? Has he called? Has he called? And make love to Nora's husband (see index, Phone Lore, having sex). Preceding all that, bed-check the trees in the pocket park for Suki who told me not to wait up because she's not hep to herself.

Filing first is strictly for cool cats.

X

Tranquillity. The pocket park isn't that far off the beaten path. It's not a secret hideaway. But like a jewel it does have facets. The few leaves left on the trees are teardrop earrings. I can hear strains of violin from an open window. Cloudless sky overhead. A thick scent of fresh-baked carrot cake piggybacks the wind. I follow the trail. Which leads under the benches, to the base of a tree, to down the block, around the corner, up the next block, stopping at the source.

A bucktoothed babe.

White paste-up tail.

"School crossing guard, right?"

"I'm not supposed to say. Let me pass."

"A chore, educating the public. Systems fail, backups break your heart. Corners start to inch up on you."

"Are you a crossing guard too?"

"Know of any rabbit who wants his paws read?"

Whiskers curling, nose twitching, ears rubbing like they were trying to keep warm. Her teeth are carrot-juice orange. "Sorry, no." Offering me a nibble of carrot cake.

I decline.

"Thanks, I'm cutting down. One more thing, do you believe in magic?"

"Lots of systems make you wonder. I've never run into a magic system."

Hopping off.

A real bunny who hopped like that would be laughed out of the brier patch. Mr. Read My Paw wore his costume like he was born to it. You find this with some Macy's Santas too. Some just belong in red suit and beard.

Unreal how authentic they are.

✗

The lobby of my building.

I hold my own door. Alex is busy writing. His list, I suppose. Am I feeling contrite enough to ask how he's coming?

"Coming along?"

"Can I run a couple by you? See how they play for content as well as polish. Pick your category of flaws: Marilyn's body, her hair, taste in clothes, the way she eats, her breath, the—"

"Breath and body. One from each."

"Tact and text, got it?"

It's twelve forty, the Fling's due at one. I assure Alex I get it. History's a weave too.

Alex scans his list.

"With every sweet breath, your chest rises and falls, sweeter still with the right breath protection."

He flips to the second page.

"The mole on your neck is equivalent to a meatball."

His nose is a question mark. Well?

He needs the benefit of my maturity if he wants to live to a ripe

205

old age. "More couching, you want to bring her along, you don't want to blast her out of the world."

I skip the elevators entirely.

No time to play matchmaker for two creeps.

✗

All for naught.

My only phone message is from Lou, be prompt.

I slip out of my sweats into a tight white T and panties. I look like somebody trying to be somebody I'm not. Nate's always punctual. Forget my face, forget my hair (a mop top that would eat its young).

Two minutes after one . . .

Nate knocks, I open, Nate walks ahead of me into the bedroom. The man who says women are too body-conscious looks like a gift box. Toga-loose clothing. Somebody you have to unwrap to get to. Undoing layers and layers to reach the contents. Today's box is a gag gift. So much to unravel, so little there. A dick the size of an infant fist. I lift infant fist dick out of his crib. (Phone is not ringing.) I give him his night feeding. Suckle my flasks. (I glance at the phone, phone's not ringing.) Burp for me. Or pay the price. He doesn't burp. I sit infant fist dick straight up on my veranda. (One hand on the phone, no ring.) Twist infant fist dick, not like I'm wringing a neck, closer to how I'd wiggle a ring off my finger. Infant fist dick squalls. (Phone to my ear, just to see if I get a dial tone.) We play worm on the hook. The hat pin the size of a hypodermic barely makes contact when infant fist dick explodes out of his infancy . . . into toddler dick. The crawler. Can't pass a thing without touching it. My cabinets, crannies. Across my lap into my rear. Toddler dick bursts out of his diapers. Teen machine. (I wouldn't answer the phone now for my own mother, for Cross I'd put Nate on hold.) Teen superstud. He puts his .38 into me. He fires off a round. I return fire. He immediately sits me up in bed, propping a pillow behind my head. A combo of two orgasms and single woman phone syndrome, I immediately slide down under the covers. He goes to the bathroom and returns with a cold compress for my head.

"Time to make good on the trade. Sex for the doorstep of the castle."

Specifically in accordance with phone lore, I donated my body. This is my reward. If ever a girl needed something else going for her on the side, besides what was right in front of her face . . .

206

Marine Life: The Swordfish's Tail
  How did the male swordfish get his tail?
  Studies by Dr. Alexandra L Basolo suggest that before the appearance of the tail of male swordfish, the female swordfish already had a preference for it. A pre-existing taste. Like a wish list.
  When the tail finally appeared the female swordfish naturally wanted to chase tail.

Nature cooperated with the female swordfish. Nature tailor-made the male swordfish by tacking on a tail based on female wishes and desires. Nature looked favorably upon the female swordfish. The female swordfish had nature on its side. Mother Nature took the female swordfish to heart. As of this day, I, Jane Samuels, swear never again to order swordfish, male or female, in a restaurant. And furthermore, Ms. Samuels will support any leg-islation to insure the survival of swordfish. She will adopt a swordfish and keep it in the bathtub. Any swordfish passing through town is welcomed to stay.

If nature will only do for me what she did for the fish.

". . . growing up in a town of ten thousand people, you are privy to everyone's life story." All his training and Nate still can't make his milieu psychologically compelling. "I remember our next-door neighbor, Mrs. Nagle. At the time her piano playing became obses-sive, I was four years old. All night and—"

I take the wet compress from my head and put it on his.

"I've got an appointment," throwing the covers off.

"Just this one other part."

"I have more than fulfilled my half of the bargain."

He swings his legs around, slipping one under my rib cage, the other above. Nutcracker with a walnut. The walnut tells him to quit acting so nutty.

"You and Nora both. The fear of letting me open my mind to you borders on the pathological." Pressure on my ribs increasing. "So nuts about me you've convinced yourselves once you enter my mind, I'd take you for granted. Your love for me manifests itself by doing everything in your power to avoid setting foot in my castle." Pressure leveling off. "On top of that you're so convinced my mind is irresistible, you're afraid you'll lose all will to leave." He lets go of the walnut before her rib cage cracks. "I'm pent up in-side. Festering from what you've done to me. It builds. There's no need for you to apologize. I'm a psychiatrist. Your motives are self-explanatory. If you let me, I can treat you. Together, we can lick this."

I have a comeback.

"Get this through your head. Any woman with an ounce of feeling for her plants does not venture into the badlands. She knows there are regions where she could be entrapped, held against her will. Hot air areas. Places that are full of themselves."

Nate dresses.

Nate kisses me.

Nate leaves a happy man.

Probably he's put it together: You can squeeze her ribs. She won't file. First.

Except: Seeds of a revolution, new bathing suit.

Except: Dawn of a new age as the old age ends in a Hardware Store.

It's fall.

I'm determined.

On the lips of every leaf: Let's go out in style.

✗

True to my word.

I elect to take the elevator on the left, habitat of the lady creep's elusive creep. Within five minutes of his summons, he pulls up to my floor with a tire screech. I press lobby. The doors close. The elevator shakes. A saltshaker shake is a vigorous shake. This is a shoulder shake. More forceful than a shrug. Not anything like a jump for joy. Bounce without bounciness. Glum. Tremors of tears. I put my ear to the wall. Bleating. Someone in distress.

"Mr. Creep, what you need is a shoulder to cry on."

"You've got the wrong creep." Voice thick from crying, unmistakably lady creep.

"What brings you over here?" Silly question, the answer is here is Mr. Creep's pad.

"Haven't you ever been in the neighborhood and just dropped in on someone without calling ahead?"

Main floor.

"The creep made up some lame excuse, said he'd be in touch, oh he was polite all right, but by throwing myself at him I may have missed my floor entirely. You'll talk to him for me, won't you? He's hiding out in my elevator."

I assure her, first chance I get.

"A bit of advice till then, give the creep some space. Trust me on this."

Doors open.

The lesson has not been lost on me. Give Chuck Bellview a few more days, the creep may yet call.

Alex salutes me with his nose. I am an asset to my community. I counsel elevators and doormen on matters of the heart. I mentor vaginas that are zeros in bed.

✗

Next stop, Hardware.

✗

Just in time to see the line disperse.

Are the men leaving because they've given up or has someone successfully waggled Mrs. Harold's lids? Owner and I did not part on the best of terms; what if he denies me entry? I step forward, over the threshold. Owner tells me freeze. I am just about to make a run for it, into the bowels of the store, when he holds up a paper. Is this a trap? What would I want with a piece of paper?

"It's a note," Owner waving it back and forth.

"Who from?"

"The man from Cross, you just missed him," barely containing his excitement. "Why didn't you tell me you're affiliated with Cross? Any friend of Cross is a friend of mine."

He wants confirmation.

I neither confirm or deny. Nor do I clutch the note to my bosom. I break the seal: "Dear Jane, I've made inquiries. We've tried to prevail on the Harolds. Because of your association with them, perhaps you might make some headway. I'll get back to you. Coffee sometime?" Now I clutch. Bosom and note, back to back. He called. He called. He called . . . in writing. He didn't actually commit to a day or time, his place or mine. The warmth was of a distant kind, negligible amounts of intimacy, but my oxytocins are flowing, my lobes are sunny-side up. The curse of mushroom love. On top of being so monumentally so-so in the head, I'm monumentally so-so in the heart.

Where romance falleth, logic ploppeth.

Persuade the Harolds to fork over, I get a hero's welcome. Instant heroine. Chuck Bellview gazing into my eyes over coffee cups. Struck dumb by my desirability. No, strike struck dumb. Replace with cross-examination. Chuck saying the three most

209

wonderful words in the English language.

How are you?

I can't see the Harolds, not in my condition. Ready to throw it all away. Climbing on the Cross team might be a means to an end, but would it put an end to an era? I'd be changing the natural course of events. A question of methodology: Am I a purist from the Goodall school or is it going to be the school of Sap?

Note to bosom . . . unclutching.

Fleeing the store, walking it off, taking deep breaths. Not ready to reenter. Standing at the entrance, asking Owner for an update.

"Status quo on her lids," Owner says. "Only odd thing is how much fatter she is. In her twelfth month, if she's a day. A Super-bowl blimp. Any friend of Cross is a friend of mine. Why don't you stay?"

"I have to attend to my hair."

Owner doesn't miss a beat. "Glad to hear it."

✗

I hit the ground running.

✗

Clip Art.

The waiting room is full. Standing room only. It takes a while to reach the front desk. The receptionist refuses admittance. She won't look at my hair. The snap of her gum is a starting gun. I appeal for clemency. I tell her my hair has no tress. My hair looks like behind my refrigerator. Ends like a choir that can't hit the notes at the same time. The mane is a blob. Spreading like a pestilence upon the land. Hungering for human flesh.

The bitch says nay.

I say over my dead body nay.

The bouncer says hold it right there, buddy.

I surcease. Hair is for the living. Coming to an end over split ends is a sorry end. I badly wanted to die trying. I didn't want to die. My hasty retreat isn't fast enough. All of two feet from the door when I'm swatted. A chair experience. Raw unfiltered verbal sewage. Snatches of conversation. With or without a chair, with or without eavesdropping. A wild card. The refuse of the airways. It is proximity that determines eligibility for a chair experience.

That and having two ears.

"He climbed on top of her. She tried to fight him off."

"My cousin too. Now she's got a missing—"

For the recipient of such information—me—it's never too late in the day to regret that the recipient—me—isn't wearing earplugs, earmuffs to keep the earplugs warm, scarf around the earmuffs for extra warmth, my collar turned up, a ghetto-blaster turned on high, my forehead quicker on the draw.

Some things you're better for knowing.

Some go without saying.

✗

I want my mommie and daddy.

Some things never change.

✗

Then again, second childhood is marked by dramatic changes.

✗

Do my mommie and daddy want me?

✗

They must have changed the locks. My key bends in the key-hole. Full weight of the Liz on the doorbell. Frank, Irma, open the damn door. The voice of a woman ready to hack off her own hair.

Mom to the rescue.

Or some facsimile.

She stands in the doorway. Her little black dress above her knees. All these years she's worn machine washables. She's had an undefined waist. Now I've got more grey than she does. Her braid doesn't have a split to its name. She's got definition. Her teeth are uniform. The overhang from her nose is missing. I know how hard she's worked to earn this. If it were my friends' mothers, and not mine, I'd tell them with pleasure, go fuck a wall.

"The place is a mess. If I don't do it, it doesn't get done." The voice of someone who's been up several nights running. Doing God knows what.

The last thing I want to do is put up walls between Mom and me. I disapprove of her conduct, I don't disapprove of her. Her

211

problem is really no different than the working woman's. How to strike a balance. Ball beasts, clean house. Too little time, too much to do.

"Prioritize. Schedule yourself. Learn what works for you, compromise, no shouldn't mean maybe, you shouldn't be rigid, be a listener, don't impose on others, let no one take advantage, invite feedback, speak your mind, never let your personal feelings interfere with your judgment, always be sensitive to the needs of others, be open-minded, be assertive, curb your testosterone, allow yourself to be spontaneous, exercise restraint, follow through, know when to cut your losses. Above all, remember you and you alone make the final determination."

I ask myself in.

She says now would not be a good time.

I push past her.

The crowd in the walls invites me to join them. The walls are crammed with shapes. Wall plasticity. Everything but meltdown. What they're doing in there is what people do under sheets. A tangle of arms and legs and moans. Oh baby, baby.

I don't give my parents the go-ahead.

They go anyway.

Marty sticks his head out of the wall. Peeking at the world. He's done something to his hair. It used to be every which way like he put it in a socket. Now it's matted down like somebody sat on it. "What's keeping you?" His way of telling me the water's fine, come on in. "Irma's got a waiting list." Marty bragging about Mom. "Some off-the-wall women take months to get a following." He puts his hand out. "Life out there is so square. Don't box yourself in." Floating on his back, his cock perpendicular.

"I can't watch my mommie and daddy do it."

A female inside the wall passes the word along.

"Irma, your daughter's a throwback. Next thing you know, she'll tell you her parents doing it inside the wall with multiple sex partners gives her the creeps. Now that's just around the bend to calling us creeps."

Father is the voice of reason.

"Value calls are always going to be found on both sides of the wall."

I call out good-bye. Me to everybody. My party good-bye for when I don't want to go around individually. Not long ago, my parents were like me. Decent. Leaving the bed-hopping to rabbits. Anyhow, the homeless aren't out of the danger zone yet. This is an election year. The politicians may pipeline creeps in. The walls could end up looking like the streets.

Walls.

I sit on every side of the fence. Walls between people give people some idea where they stand. Walls offer privacy. Walls challenge you to climb over them. But the wall hasn't been made that can lure my parents into it to engage in deviant sexual practices and earn my unequivocal blessing.

I need my mommie and daddy.

✗

Sad tidings . . .

The flasher in front of my mother's building is obsolete. An open fly under open sky is a piece of memorabilia. Quaint. Out of step with the times. I don't want to be the one responsible for cutting his ties to the past. So I fake it. Astonishment, horror, look how you've scandalized me. You dirty man. Not only have I honored tradition, I've discouraged him from inventing new traditions. Dangling it in front of my face, asking me to shake hands with it. That would be less obsolete (but not for long). I've made him happy so he doesn't do something to make me unhappy.

The embodiment of the advice I gave mom.

Sad tidings.

✗

At the all-important juncture.

I've made a pact with myself. Continue to monitor the Harolds, continue to proctor myself. The first hint of intrusion on my part—this is a stickup, hand over your cases—I will exit. Jane Samuels is Jane Goodall's apostle. No interference. This is the homestretch. Come what may (the heavens can open up) Jane Samuels is unstoppable. The Big One will fall into her lap. Harold will be a footnote to history. The End.

✗

And if Owner knows what's good for him he will refrain from pointing out the obvious. A trip to the beauty parlor, what's with the fright wig?

213

✗

The cab driver who takes me to Hardware wants to know who does my hair.

✗

Catching himself in time. Owner looks directly at my hair, looks down at his fingers, looks up at my hair, down at my fingers, back to his. I leave him studying his hands. I walk directly to wood paneling, paints, and wallpaper. Harold is stationed on the border. His shirt is opened. Chest hairs curled with sweat. He looks like a desk that's been riffled. He looks like he's looking for a life jacket. He looks monumentally unusually filed. First upon.

Mrs. Harold is a beach ball.

The curve of her belly, as she lies on her back, is a hike to Mount Olympus. Her nightgown's ripped. Plenty of ventilation. Room to grow. Instead it looks like a kid's dress after a growth spurt.

"Baby's due any day now. I plan on home birth. Right here in the Cross. Deliver it au natural. Be my own midwife." Pointing to her chest. "Nurse the whelp, mother's milk for strong bones and teeth. I'm an equal opportunity employer. Either the kid makes a difference in my life, changes my outlook, or gets the hell out. Down the chute." Her arm zipping around like a plane, then crash landing.

She studies my face.

"Upsets you, doesn't it? Don't bother denying it, your eyes give you away."

Harold runs at her.

Collapsing at the foot of the Cross.

His head lowered. Panting like a wounded animal. He has a Cross case too, why doesn't he use it? Suffering so. What has the poor man done to her but try and give her what she wants, every word, every deed done with her in mind, never mind the rigors. Save the child. The child cannot perish. A loss of that magnitude would make him so monumentally unusually irretrievably so-so.

So why is my lap down around my ankles?

✗

"Hot tea for Mr. Harold," my fist down hard on Owner's counter.

214

I rush the door.

Fall draws to a close. Resolution is imminent. What ever happened to Hollywood endings?

✗

Women who go to four-hankie movies say it's cathartic, nothing like a good cry to make you feel better, after the outpour you're a new woman. For me it's the opposite. I always feel worse off than I started. The situation in Hardware is grave. If something weren't bringing me back time and time again, I wouldn't go back time and time again. One thing I will have to watch for, it hasn't cropped up till now. Not just taking part, but taking Harold's part. What a twist that would be. What a fool I would be. In playing catch-up, getting too caught up is a real tearjerker. Exactly the end I don't want. It would be the end of me.

Love for Harold is a dead end.

✗

In a diner.
Doesn't matter where . . .
I order tea.
Six cups into it, it leaks out my eyes.
Not teardrops.
Tea drops.

✗

On to Nora . . .

✗

I am not Nora's sex object. Nor her sexual partner. This is not a sexual relationship. It is sisterhood. Also I am doing myself a favor. Teach Nora all I know, maybe Nate will tell me don't wait up.

Life without Nate . . .
A Hollywood ending.

✗

Whiteout.

Nora's concierge's gloves are standouts. Whiter than my summer whites will ever bleach. Dazzle white. Bone white under the Sahara sun. White the likes of which hasn't been seen by any white on white linen. Whiter than hospital whites. Paler than chalk white. Were I to commend myself into the hands of someone who wore nothing but concierge white gloves, throughout the commending I would be as anxious about where he put his hands as I am when I dine at a table where the cloth shows every scuff mark.

A little early yet.

The gloves I dare not touch because of accidental spills at the tables may deport me. The gloves may flick me off. The gloves may wave me through.

They do.

✗

Unless Nora vetoes, today's topic will be nipples. How to make a nipple do your bidding. Even women with a healthy respect for nips may disavow a partner's too soon. Spending an inordinate time on nipples, however, is time well spent. Attention to detail is what makes haute couture better than ready-to-wear.

Fawning elevator.

Nora's elevator is not a creep.

I knock on her door.

Door opens.

Lesson of the day trashed.

Nora's not the only woman who's ever answered the door in the buff. But she's the only one I've ever known who can do it with an outstanding body and still score zero. Nora is petite to my medium, my medium petite to Nate's steeple. As beads on a strand each of us would show the other off to his advantage. Nora is a bead in the rough. She dispels the light, she casts shadows, she's the bead you want to toss.

I strip.

Black sweats, Liz bag, undies. A bundle on the floor.

Folding clothes is inappropriate. It tells the person you are with you're already thinking about leaving. Mess with my body, don't mess with my clothes. It sets sex apart. It doesn't make the sex partner feel there's nothing that can't be done to you. Dishevelment is a calculated risk. A vital part of sexual play is to run risks.

I don't want to offend her.

She looks so naked. A naked female person instead of a naked nymph. But let her get away with opening the door like there's nothing behind it, Nate (and castle) may never file. On me. I give her a warning look. This will hurt, hold on. I don't want tears. "Naked females opening doors would do well to think of themselves as refrigerators." Good, she's nodding. "You want to open the door in such a way that the person being opened on will realize how hungry he is."

I don't get tears.

Nora pivots.

She shows me to the bathroom. She gets on one side of the door, I on the other. I open on me. I show her pelvic tilt, hip swerve, ankle turned thus. She opens on she. She shows me zero. I open on me. I show her leg spread, torso thrust, eyeball zing. She opens on she. No progress. Progressively worse.

We take a break.

Kiss me, I say. Get in position. Hug me. Part your lips. Ease the tongue out of neutral. Don't gag me with it. Court me with your mouth. Keep it moist, splashing gets you thrown out of the pool. Narrow the opening. You are not saying ahh for the dentist. Bend my neck back any further, I'll break your arm. A little less gnawing action. The tongue is a muscle, work it. Don't work it to death.

Little bird cries from her throat.

She sucks my mouth like she's sucking out the juice from a sun-dried tomato. Her withdrawal is salivary. Her kiss sounds are hacking coughs.

Door rehearsal again.

This time, if I were filming it, I'd yell take.

Like most women, she's a woman. Get a few kisses down her gullet, she opens the door like she's been popping out of cakes all her life. Why I didn't kiss her sooner is because a crutch is worse when it's a false crutch. Kisses kick it in. But sensitivity to kissing, like pain, fluctuates. The thresholds aren't fixed. At some point, for whatever reason, kisses can leave you cold. What are you going to do then—throw away an opportunity for sex because you're not in the mood?

Door closed for another take.

Just as I thought, she requests a kiss.

I feel for her, I really do. If piano teachers kissed their pupils to make them play better, I'd be the first one to say pucker up. But that's not how it's done. You don't leave it to chance. You plug away. You put in hours. Perspiration is inspiration. Musicians make pieces work. Professionals don't save themselves for

mushroom love. Amateurs treat sex as optional. They don't intercourse with people they don't care for. They don't always have sex
with people they do care for. The professionals sheet music sex. A
repertoire is kept on hand. Instant recall material. It's the difference between never missing a note and forgetting your lines. Only
when rehearsed can you carry off being spontaneous. The most
fluid ballerinas are the ones who've put in hours at the barre.

Nora wanted a vaginal mentor.

Nora's got a maestro.

And the maestro's gone and got herself sudden insight.

(Teach a lesson, you get taught one in return.)

I jump the bundle on the floor. Breakaway speed. The last time I
saw anyone dress this fast was the Fling. I leave Nora behind the
door. I let myself out. I haven't given notice. I haven't filed. I leave
a two-line note to my student. It more or less doesn't sum it up.
But if I had left a tell-all it would have read as follows:

Girl.

Do not think for one minute this is what it looks like. True,
you're a zero. A klutz. Teaching you is a drag. And next to your
crotch, my crotch's summer whites look like smoke-stained teeth.
But I'm not leaving because the lady is a tramp. I'm leaving because like most women, I'm a woman. My proficiency at the piano
far exceeds my proficiency at mushroom love.

I too am a zero.

✗

More tea, same diner.

More tea drops, same eyes.

The waitress leans over the counter.

"Honey, life is short, it's full of heartache, it hurts, nobody gives
a damn, you're a speck, it doesn't add up to a smudge, just when
you think, yeah, you get knocked, stomped, hit real bad by the
love bug. No mosquito netting, no insect repellent, no flyswatter,
no flypaper can keep out the bug of love. It takes a chunk out of
you a piece of time, till there ain't nothing left. Zero, the end."

I defend her right to say it.

I defend the love bug's right to bite.

I defend my right to bite back.

✗

Hardware is self-defense.

✗

. . . and if Owner knows what's good for him, he will not remark on the obvious, a tea-streaked face, the skin under my eyes, tea bags. That's not grey you see in my hair, that's Earl Grey.

✗

Upon my arrival . . .
Owner offers me a soothing cup of tea.
I decline.
Borrowing a line from lady creep, "Owner, I was just in the neighborhood . . . at the time I left, Mr. Harold was down on the floor imploring Mrs. Harold for exemption, not for himself, but for the newborn, due any day. For some time now I have been faithfully visiting the Harolds, and I will continue to do so on a regular basis, but sometimes secondhand information is more informative than firsthand—especially for people who at one time had personal ties, the information (firsthand) ties you in knots."
He says say no more.
"Mr. Harold has since crawled into his Cross. I just looked in on him a moment ago. He's got a DO NOT DISTURB sign hung on the outside. From what I could see he's turning and twisting knobs, lots of gadgetry. No results yet. Too late now to take the money and run. If you ask me, his bag's seen better days."
A cry.
Owner goes, I stay.
The cry subsides.
Owner returns.
"Whatever he was working on, no success. He's groveling again, all fours. His wife is doing her toenails. He asked if he might do them for her. He's awaiting a reply. Shall I go back and check?"
It won't be necessary.
"Sometime soon, I'll be in the neighborhood again."

✗

Walking toward Eighth Avenue. My appointment with Lou isn't for half an hour. I do not lack for things to do. I could go to

219

the library and brush up on the *Titanic*. Or I could do trees in Central Park; it wouldn't be for botanical reasons. Tea is out. Diet Pepsi is in. Or I could pursue my newest pastime: rabbit-hunting. Scorching the earth for Mr. Read My Paw. If dogcatchers can do it, so can vigilantes.

People rhapsodize over sunrises and sunsets.
Fishermen over the size of the catch.
G-men fuss over their most-wanted list.
Mobsters over their hits.
I am in good company.
It's like that for me. I want a rabbit trophy.

✗

All I get is a bunch of kids in rabbit ears playing leapfrog.

✗

A sandlot pocket park. Under the watchful eyes of nannies munching lettuce, the offspring of school crossing guards are doing the bunny hop. At my approach, the nannies pack up the lettuce in tin foil, clapping for the children's attention. Hop, skip, and jump. The bunny kids, the nannies . . . gone. There was a hole (not a rabbit hole), more like a pothole.

✗

Almost five.
The elevators in Lou's building are schooners. They fly. So anxious to please I feel a tip is in order. Lou doesn't have Nora's problem. When he opens the door, even if you aren't hungry, you can't help but notice the slab in the middle. I pounded him once. In the name of friendship, I saw my longevity friend's husband was road kill and I pulled over to help. A smidgen of your longevity friend's husband is not a betrayal of longevity. I've dieted, I've cheated on diets. More than a smidgen, you feel guilt. Smidgen or less, no guilt. Lou offers me the best seat in the house. The sofa seat next to the largest cactus, dwarfing the others by several feet. He sits on the sofa too. Dead on, Lou's a looker. The angles from the sides too, born for the lens. Instead of the throes I expected, road kill appears to have a little life left in him. He graciously offers me tea, I graciously refuse refreshments. "Susan's relationship with the

City has been one of the most rewarding in my life. I owe every one of my erections to her. The cocktease. The sweetest frame-up ever. I've got no gripe with being big. There's just no pleasure in living with someone who's your moral superior."

Covering old ground.

I play with the threads of my sweat pants. I stand ready to cover old ground too: Her number will be up. Pigs will be pigs. But all codes have a key. Be patient, if you insist I will sit on your yard-stick (a smidgen) and pound this message home.

"She's my first mate. Tonight I'm going to test the waters." (What is it with these guys, are they all Sindbads under the skin?) "I'm going to make my move. I think I've got her number. If all goes as planned, her desire to do no wrong, her sense of right and wrong, her willpower, her self-righteousness will be shattered."

Is he planning an unspeakable?

Something so dreadful it will snap her frame?

"Tell me," the voice of authority. I've been saving it up all my life for when the physician won't give me the bad news.

Lou stands.

He strokes his cactus, a king-size penis plant.

"I'm going to put the fix to her."

"Fix?"

"Fix her good," two hands on the cactus, running up and down the shaft, I swear it's getting bigger in the head. "Pit her frame against something she can't ignore." The cactus is a rocket trying to launch.

A scene like this, there's more than one way it can go.

The cactus comes.

Lou comes.

I come.

Nobody comes.

He squeezes the cactus, the cactus looses control of its bodily functions, cactus juice drenches Lou, I climb on his back yelling Stop, you are killing a household plant, Patches growls at me, Lou begs the cactus to understand, its number is up, the cactus swoons, the cactus croaks, Patches goes back to sleep, Lou turns to me, eyes full.

"Susan has it coming."

Enter Susan.

Through the front door, white lace shawl, white communion dress. She rushes over, puts her ear to the cactus. Nods as if she were listening. Holds her hand up for us to shush. After a few minutes she picks the cactus up, carries it to the trash compactor in the hall. Lou and I observe a moment of silence for the corpse.

Susan returns.

"Confession is good for the soul. A deathbed confession from a cactus should be accorded the same respect given to any confession. The cactus said it was the best sex ever. Which one of you had sex with a plant?"

I turn myself in. Maybe Susan will file on me. Finally.

She asks for details.

"I put my hands on it."

"Not your mouth?"

"Mouth too."

"You gave the cactus a blow job?"

"With my own two hands."

Her eyes are carbonated. "You're worse off than I believed humanly possible. This City is sin city. And you are one of its disciples." Turning to Lou, "You watched didn't you, your dick in your hand, you'd do anything for an erection, exploit any occasion. I made my confession to the fathers at St. Patrick's, the pack of them, City boys, the smell of semen and lilac atomizer filling the confessional. I told them you'd use that too. Right now you're thinking of picking up my skirt, pounding me, banging me, giving me the ride of my life. You are the scum of the earth, both of you are. It doesn't make me love you any less, whatever your frames of mind, you are as dear to me as life itself."

Lou moves swiftly.

He lifts her to the sofa. Rips her hose. She kicks off her panties. He pounds his message home. "Your frame's giving my frame psychic pain."

More old ground.

I pet Patches. I leave.

✗

Will he file. First. by killing her? What is the fix? What's my frame of mind? Susan and I went to grade school together . . . she was best longevity man at my wedding. Should I call the authorities or wait to see what happens? Cliff-hangers. How I loathe them. Confession is good for the soul. I confess ahead of time I may be an accessory to a murder.

✗

Being called dreck . . . really rubs.

✗

Traffic is a crawl.

It would be faster to phone Hardware than to go. My overnight bag is packed. I am on a twenty-four-hour alert. Baby on the way, a baby who may or may not be around for long. If it ends the way it looks like it's going to end, then I end up haunted. A never-ending story. Just the opposite of what I wanted to get out of fall.

The fall of nostalgia.

✗

An absentee doorman.

Alex is rarely absent from his post. Having just witnessed a homicide (of a cactus) by strangulation, a violent coupling of a husband and wife, maybe Alex has been . . . fixed. I'm in a fix of my own. Do I change the course of history at Hardware by defending the child, thereby making tomorrow's headlines WOMAN ENDS LIFE IN A BAD FALL—or do I let nature take its course? In the distribution of things falling into laps, my lap is up to its neck.

✗

By and by, the elevator on the left touches down. Doors swing open like palace doors for the king. I enter. Doors shut like bank vaults. It seems to know where it's going, still I am a creature of habit. I press eight. Buttons pop. If the cables break, heaven help me, I will rise from my hospital bed to go to Hardware. The buttons are rolling all over the place, I scramble to pick them up.

"I never figured you for the one," the creep calls out, unmistakably not lady creep.

"It wasn't my doing. Your buttons weren't fastened."

Clinking sounds.

Is a clinking elevator a thinking elevator?

"Button your lip, I'm trying to sort this out in my mind. Back in '66 I popped a button, a single button, I was alone at the time, and let me tell you, popping a button is not like losing baby teeth. Anyone who's man enough to pop all forty of my buttons and live to tell about it has essentially popped the all-important question in

223

the only way that holds any true meaning. I can't tell you how many lady creeps pop the question without popping the buttons. Not that they haven't tried. My forty buttons have never spun off for anyone."

This I kill before it flies.

"Recently I've met a man. It's mushroom love. I won't even look at another guy."

A dip of the elevator. Like I do with my lap. Only these are with cables. My life may be hanging by a thread.

"Believe me, it's not a reflection of you. Someone got there first. Someone I care deeply about."

"What's he got that I haven't?"

"Look, let me sleep on it, OK? And you sleep on it too."

Tinny sounds, his parts need oiling.

"I know what you're thinking. Once a creep, always a creep. Sure, I play elevator tag, those days are over. The question's been popped, whether you meant to or not, you've spun and asked. Tomorrow you'll have my answer. Or do you want it now?"

No ifs.

No ands.

No buts.

"Tomorrow."

The elevator rights itself. I fasten the forty buttons. The eighth floor. Till tomorrow, he says. I alight, I break into a run. Unlock, lock. Bolt. Twist the knob to test the bolt. The bolt holds. What kind of fall is this? Does an elevator falling for me fall under magic or mystic? They are not interchangeable. If magic is for real, then what isn't for real? Ends would be unending. Present, past, future, the whole system would have to be revamped. Ending the world as we know it, leaving it all open-ended, one big question mark.

An end unbefitting a historian.

There better not be magic.

"I need your opinion." Marilyn Beats walking out from the kitchen. Anticipating the words out of my mouth. "Door was open." She sits down on my sofa. Her head in her hands. Bobbing shoulders. Sobs cinch it: Man trouble.

I slip out the door.

As if by magic . . .

She slips out after me.

As if by magic . . .

I slip in fast.

As if by magic . . .

224

She apprehends me.
There is no magic.

✗

There is a resumption of sobs. There is opportunity. She sobs, I consult my answering machine. The total number of messages on my machine is no messages at all. He hasn't called. He wrote. What he wrote didn't pin down the when, the where, the soon, the how soon can you be here? I quickly dial Owner. A misdial. A woman picks up on the first ring. For her, there will never be magic.

"Owner, it's Jane."

He picked up on the first ring too. Is it epidemic? These people are spoiling it for the rest of us. "Give me the latest developments."

"Mr. Harold presented a proposal to wife number two. Hand the kid over, he will devote the rest of his life to finding a man and/or woman to flick her. Mrs. Harold countered with a proposal of her own. Give her his Cross bag, she'll consider it. The outcome is pending."

We wrap it up.

Leaving it with me calling him, if I don't for some reason, he calls me. What would I do in Harold's place? The Cross bag is high-to-the-sky technology. The closest thing to magic he's got. Surrender that . . . he's history.

Marilyn owns the couch.

Stretched out like a Southern belle on a divan. Her hand beckoning, hold me. Her tears are tributaries. I get her a plastic placemat, laying it across her chest. The adult bib. Her face is framed by majestic curls, a natural redhead. She has a waist that could pass for a neck. Alabaster skin. Until your chin looks like gizzard you can't know the meaning of loss.

"I'm so happy." A gush of tears.

"Marilyn, you're not happy."

"Happier at this moment than I've ever been in my life."

"I wasn't born yesterday."

A crying jag, it takes a good five minutes for her voice to find its footing.

"Alex came through, it took some real last minute repair work to rectify his latest flaw. Hiding under couched language is a mousehole. Mousiness has to go, mousiness is more than weakness, it's an acid eating away—"

"So he dispensed with mousey."

"Broke the ice, ripped into me, let me have it right on the jaw, item for item, nothing got by him. He picked up on things I didn't even know were there. It just goes to show you, when you put your mind to repairing somebody . . ." The bib is getting a work-out. Happiness levels are climbing.

"He was brutally honest." I capsule it.

"And I'm going to make him as happy as he's made me." She reaches down her blouse, taking out her lists, pages and pages.

"You don't think telling him his cock-nose is not ridged enough is too couched, do you?"

She takes the bib off.

She sits up.

"I'm so content." She makes a face that could send a wall running for cover.

She lets herself out.

I predict a long and happy future for Alex and Marilyn. If they weren't made for each other before, they are now. The mating of killing machines.

Some women have all the luck.

✗

Hardware's line is busy. I get through on the third try.

"Owner, it's—"

"I was just trying to call you. Your line was busy."

"Did Harold yield his case?"

"A whole delegation of Cross execs came in. They're in conference. Looks like an international summit. Can't get anywhere near them, you'd be wasting your time to even try. Give it, oh I'd say at least a half hour."

He promises to keep me posted.

✗

Hmm.

Hmm.

First hmm, what have the Cross people come up with?

Second hmm, a psychic flash. Read my paw: Open the door, Jane. You have a visitor.

Too vague for me. A visitor could mean anybody from Alex to

226

Mr. Read My Paw to Chuck Belleview. I peek. I debate. Do I save myself for Chuck and pass on Gerald or do I have a little nightcap?

Hmm.

✗

The nose is a double-jointed tail.

Untying the knot of my sweatpants. His nose traces the outline of my lips. Blowing moist equatorial air into my ear. The nose slips behind me and lifts me into a bicep curl. Gerald and I slow dance, me on the seat of his nose. He whirls me into the bedroom. Tenderly lowering me to the bed. I finish undressing. I loosen his belt, open his shirt. I even unzip him. Although his tool is already out (a penis nose is never zipped under a fly), I like to make love to the whole man, give his other parts some recognition; not being the filing type, I try not to leave anything in the dead letter file. His nose, for all its weight, has a light touch. Someone's been practicing kissing with his nose. His nose in my mouth is a mouthful. His tongue-in-nose is worth patenting. Gerald and I hug and rub. His hands between my legs are doing some exploratory work, scouts sent on ahead to see if the way is clear. Down there, I am water balloon heavy. My vaggie filled to capacity with enlarged blood vessels. Chunky. It could be a desk paperweight. His nose trembles at my touch, deep sighs. It curls away from me, I grasp it with both hands and pull, guiding it down, it rears up. The nose-cock is hard, I'm a waterfall.

Why the delay?

Suddenly . . .

Something smaller than a nose noses around my hothouse. It feels like an intruder. I start to sit up. Gerald tells me to lay back, enjoy it.

Wrong.

I've been duped.

He's brought in another joint to play the lead. An understudy. Here I expected the head honcho, a nose that in a street would be an avenue, and I've gotten a penis that in a street would be a line on a map. Is a so-so meal a memorable meal? Is a so-so dick a to-die-for trip? It's a delicate moment. If I don't phrase it just so, I get tears.

Meanwhile.

I've gone from being treated like a lotus blossom to pinball machine. His resurrected penis (the joint between his legs) is heavy-handed. Coke bottles have more nerve endings. Now I know what it feels like to return to where you've parked your car and watch some idiot impound it. Three quick needle jabs. He spurts. As in nothing left over for me. I get to be pinned under him, he gets to fall asleep on top. I lick his nose. My tongue swishing inside each nostril like I'm scrubbing the bathroom bowl. Snoring nostrils. Sleeping beauties.

And it's not over yet.

His dick (not cockface) wakes after the briefest naps. On the second time of showing me a good time, he shows me such a swell time I take his nose into my mouth like a pacifier the whole time he shows me a good time. My vagina is a lobster in a pot with a riveter gun. I've seen kneaders do more for bread. At dance class, this would be the one that stepped on your toes, the one that failed to pass factory inspection, the bird that never learned to wing it, the flame that couldn't light a match, the chipped dish, the seconds store's last mark-down, the arm in a sling.

And now that it's over . . .

He dresses. He walks to the door.

"Remission," Gerald explains. "The guys in group tell me joint disease is chronic. I'll never be cured."

Good.

I'd end it in a minute if I thought for a second he wouldn't have a total relapse. I was never one of those female swordfish fixated exclusively on tail. Joint cooperation between man and woman should be a joint venture. No one should be subjected to a joint not of her own choosing. It's boys who never get past tail. Real men capitalize on disjointedness. Real men learn to think with their knuckles, toes, nose.

Go. I push him out the door.

Ten minutes later, overnight bag in hand, I leave for Hardware.

✗

I take the stairs.

Alex is still missing.

I am near the end . . . the end of my rope.

✗

Just like the first time.

The door to Hardware is locked. The sign in front says closed,

228

reopen at nine. I let myself in. Lights are low. I can see just ahead of me, like headlights on a dark night. I follow my ears; the sound is nothing like the outbursts of earlier. This isn't noise, it's a symphony concert. Classical music, someone humming along. Do I hear the baton of a conductor?

I put down my overnight bag.

Harold dusts off a seat. The baton in his lap, not quite laid to rest.

I sit forward on the rattan.

His smoking jacket is a fine black cotton. The white silk scarf is very forties. His hair is slicked back. He's clean-shaven. He smells like a lemon grove.

"How are you?"

No magic.

Only mystery.

It's fall. I fell for the oldest trick in the book. Expect one thing, get another. Suddenly I find myself snug in bed. Assuming Harold would answer my question, I did not give enough weight to his eyes: Something else, besides.

The end when it comes . . . will it be surprise, surprise?

✗

Just me.

Cream on my face. Hair off the face. Face off the pillow for minimal sleep marks. Room temperature moderate, humidifier on. Bathing suit asleep on the pillow next to me. Night-light in the bathroom on. A pitcher of water on my table. Phone within firing range. Locks secure.

The closet begins to rumble.

Mayhem in my bedroom closet. Shoes hitting the door. Shadows streaking to my closet. The walls in my room are a light show. A clamor of voices. Then one voice. "Don't you dare, unhand me. I demand to speak to the lady of the house." Marty comes out of the closet with a couple of his homelies. All of them in sleep shirts that stop at the knees. Patched together from pillowcases. The creature in the middle gives me the creeps. Yellow eyes, flowing chiffon gown, fleshy purple lips, her waist-length breasts hang over the front of her dress, parts of them flatter than others, breasts with slow air leaks.

I hide under the covers.

Marty taps me.

I uncover to my nose.

"Phantoms of the closet are the ones kids see at night. The traditional role of phantoms of the closet is to terrorize young children at bedtime, swing open the door, rustle clothes, call the child by name, make spooky wind sounds, reach out with spindly fingers and touch. We got word from your phantom in residence there was a creep in the closet."

She tries to break free.

They restrain her.

"Lady creep to you. As I tried to tell that monstrosity you call a phantom, closets make me claustrophobic. All those walls pressing in on me, I'd go mad. I'll have you know I am the aristocracy of creeps. A lady creep who inhabits elevators in an elegant way. I didn't come to muscle in on anybody's territory. Only to strangle that man thief in her sleep."

Marty looks from her to me, me to her. "It's late, I've got a big day ahead of me."

"You'd leave me here to be strangled?"

Lady creep's smile is a freak show. Double rows of teeth, bloody stumps on her flicking tongue.

"I make it a point never to get involved in cock fighting."

It's all in my lap now.

I wrap the blanket around me, Greek goddess style. I stand on top of the bed. From that height, everybody still looks grisly.

Lady creep screaming, "Homewrecker."

My screams matching hers. "I did everything in my power to discourage him. I told him I was in love with somebody else."

Her bite couldn't be worse than her laugh.

"You call that everything. It wouldn't discourage me, not after someone spun my forty buttons."

Throwing it right back at her.

"Any ideas. Tell me, I'll do it."

Marty yawns.

His homely buddies yawn louder. The room smells like a zoo. He and his pals scratch themselves in places you shouldn't touch in mixed company. They rub their eyes, take out baby bottles from under their nightshirts. One by one they walk sleepily into the wall.

It's Beauty and the Woman from Hell.

I yell Wait for me. I run to the wall behind the bed. Where my arm meets wall, it's hard and cold. When I bang the wall, it hurts.

Beauty using her noodle.

"Kill me, he'll never be yours anyway." Pressing the right button.

She retracts her claws. "There is one thing."

"Long as it doesn't involve body contact."

"Elevators are triggered. Once an alarm is set off, all bets are off. Alarms are bigger than the spin of buttons."

Do I look as dumb as I feel?

"Not the alarm button, alarms in the mind." She picks up her breasts and points them at me. "These are lethal weapons. You have till tomorrow to set off his alarm or I'm coming after you. There's no hiding from a lady creep, no safe refuge, no homely can stop me. Nobody comes between me and my man." Exiting through the closet.

Love bug bites again.

Killing for love, an honorable end.

For a chance to see how the Harolds end, I will fight to the end.

✗

There is no need for me to ever sleep under the stars.

Night air, under the stars, does not come in through a crack in the window. Air is everywhere. Hidden by darkness, living creatures whimper, nuzzle, roughhouse, titter, climb, chew, spit, and mutter to themselves. Wind rustles through the trees. Branches bump and grind one another. Water trickles. Brooks bubble. Streams burn shoe leather. Shadows throw their weight around. Leaves crunch and cackle and hitch rides. Spiders scheme. Night under the stars is the city that never sleeps.

Like my room.

Home was never like this.

People who can sleep through phantoms, homelies, and creeps are people who can sleep in any kind of racket.

✗

Last night: Who slept?

Today: Ex in-laws who are wraiths.

My three former in-laws look three dimensional. Hovering in the air around my bed (am I lying in state?), they seem substantial, so themselves. (Is this a deathbed scene?) Sam is East Coast gentry. A button-down cardigan, wool riding breaches, a switch—correction—umbrella pointed at me. "She doesn't know." All three stare.

231

The way you do at newborns knowing there are trials ahead. Helen is resplendent. Purple pants I-would-not-go-so-far-as-to-say were slacks meant for the daily grind. "On your feet, soldier, this is a direct order. Report to the Hardware Store." Bless Yvette. It can wait, she tells me. Do something with your hair. Unfit to be seen in public was how she put it.

I will say this for them.

Of all the scenes we've played, this is axial. I sprint into action. Brushing teeth with one hand, makeup with the other, moving like I'm dodging bullets, pleading with the wraiths to stay, how I hate cliff-hangers, the in-laws meshing into each other like colors bleeding in the wash. Gone without another word. Into the vacuum speeds my forehead. The space above my brows is the last word in strange little men in the head. (Or big bunnies.) A flash of things to come. What is to be. Forced feedings of READ MY PAW.

Now is special:

> Special Occasion . . . coming your way.
> Wear the lamé.
> Special Occasion by five today.

Hairpin turn into my bedroom, opening my closet expansively, in rich musical tones like organ music, I speak aloud the words I've wanted to say forever and a day since the very first eve of the anniversary of my deliverance from the man who filed. Me flat.

"Haven't got a thing to wear!"

✗

My finish line.

No time for elevator creeps now.

I take the stairs.

Sliding down banisters. The lobby. Watch out Alex. Alex jumps aside. Anyone in my way, I pancake first, ask questions later. Last act. Fall finally falling to the archives. The archives are a nice place to visit, but who'd want to live there? I swipe a cab from a man on crutches. A lady opening the door from the other side tries to pirate the cab. I fend her off with the man's crutches. Without his crutches, the man folds over the open door. I return his crutches. Remove your fingers from the door to my cab—I warn him there will be no repeat warning—or you won't have fingers. Susan would say urban decay, the City is morally responsible for my inhumanity. I'd say my head is off the wall.

Jane Goodall, forgive me.

I don't enter the Hardware Store. I make an entrance that belongs more to an emergency room than to the world of commerce. The turbulence frightens shoppers. I hear the buzz behind me—she on speed?—Owner overtaking me, making sure I get the right of way. My walk, when I see Harold, screams tell-me-now-this-instant what's going on.

In lieu of telling me, he demonstrates.

Marching over to Mrs. Harold encased in the Cross. Her case the size of a large copper bucket, same coffin satin lining. Mrs. Harold stares straight ahead. If she recognizes him, she gives no sign of recognition. He tips the case. Mrs. Harold adheres. He and Owner lift the case, turn it upside down. Mrs. Harold adheres. He extracts handfuls of spiders from his bag and dumps them in hers. Mrs. Harold adheres.

What gives? Owner asks.

How are you? From you know who.

"Last night the team from Cross told us to name our terms. They've agreed to put the best minds on her hand in marriage. Flick her or get the hell out of her life. Put her on the blink, they get the case and the woman in it. At precisely five o'clock tonight, Cross is reassembling here. At five, my wife could be betrothed to all the best minds in Cross. What will become of my child?" Bending over, loud in her ear. "At least listen to reason, the child could be in jeopardy."

Five o'clock. Dot of. Not a moment sooner.

The numbers are winning numbers. Five o'clock is numero uno. Five is quitting time, the end of most working days. No better hour for zero hour. Five is the sum of four and one. On this, the fourth anniversary of, the one to follow will be the first without the man who filed. Me flat.

I have my forehead's word on it.

Bewitching hour.

Goodall would stay to see the chimp sweat it out. Goodall would record each scene, each posture, one more memorable than the last. Goodall would postpone all but her most pressing needs. The most pressing of which would never be heels.

Goodall or Samuels?

Tough choice . . stay and join the historical ranks of those who looked out of place in their big scene, or go dressed to the nines (as is germane to extravaganzas)? Pumps are not trumpery. Pumps are trumps. Pumps compliment the celebratory spirit. Pumps rise to the occasion. Pumps boost. Pumps are a step up in life. But heels are a pain.

Does pain heal?

Now there's an inspirational tie-in.

✗

Bottom line: You want it, you hoof to it.

✗

Heel hunts. My last heel hunt (cross-reference to mammogram morning) didn't kill me, it only felt that way. And that was only after hitting every store within a fifteen-block radius. This heel hunt, it's every store in the hive (with promise). Heel hunts, like hiking trails, can be graded by degree of difficulty. Lots of shoe stores are on level ground. But some sites are more accessible than others. I need strategy. Heels give me blisters. Heels leave burn marks. Heels are hard-core. What if the scrunch is too much? If the style's not my style? New York City is the shoe mecca of the western hemisphere. Surely there must be something. (Surely . . . no one can be sure of anything.) I may or may not be able to pull heels out of a hat.

Heels do not just fall out of the sky.

The rules of heel hunts are simple: Don't see what you want, ask the experts for help. They know what they've got, they know your feet better than you do. When you do see what you want, ask for your size in your size, in a half size smaller, in a half size larger. If your feet run the way mine do, size alone will not make a fit, fit will rarely fit the size. The shoes I have the ownership papers to did not wash up on the beach. I didn't pick the cutest ones out of a litter of six-week-old shoes. The time it takes for me to find shoes, continents shift.

In fiction, I buy it when heels fall out of the sky.

In real life, heels falling out of the sky is fictional.

In my life, heels don't fall in my lap.

✗

Plan of attack:

Like a mapmaker, VISUALIZE the City's topology—angles, boundaries, directions, elevations, distances, latitudes, longitudes—TAKE those angles, boundaries, directions, elevations, distances, latitudes, longitudes, CORRELATE WITH THE NETWORK—tips from inside traders, affidavits from family and friends, depositions taken during debriefing (under the guise of lunches), information culled from those who have been in the field (under the guise of small talk), undercover work, years of being an operative, cruising shoe stores, finding out when new shipments arrive, surreptitiously getting on the preferred customer lists, cultivation, ingratiation, insinuation—INCORPORATE into a TIME MANAGEMENT PROGRAM the correlation of angles, boundaries, directions, elevations, distances, latitudes, longitudes, and affidavits, depositions, debriefings, culled information, undercover sleuthing, cultivating, ingratiating, insinuating, KEEPING IN MIND the gauntlet of untimely interruptions, extraneous internal thoughts (counterproductive to your goals), each of which takes time to recover from and external interruptions, your fellow man asking you for the time, forcing upon you opinions of weather, ALWAYS BLOCKING TIME TO SAVE TIME, blocks based on ANALYSIS AND EXTRAPOLATION of correlations between VISUALIZED angles, boundaries, directions, elevations, distances, latitudes, longitudes, and NETWORK tips, affidavits, depositions, debriefings, culled info, sleuthing, cultivating, ingratiating, insinuating, THEREBY DETERMINING at the onset (before setting forth) what looks promising (most to least) for the accessibility and feasibility part of the criteria, SO HAVING DONE YOUR HOMEWORK, CONSTRUCTING THE MEGASTRUCTURE (merged the visualization of boundaries, angles, directions, elevations, distances, latitudes, longitudes with affidavits, depositions, debriefing, culled info, sleuthing, cultivating, ingratiating, insinuating) and APPLIED THE PRINCIPLES OF TIME MANAGEMENT, blocking, and rating—you have saved yourself massive legwork.

✗

Max's Shoe Palace.

Max's slogan: If Max doesn't have it, Max will get it; if Max can't get it, it's not gettable.

Max has met my tootsies a total of seven times. The moment I enter, Max hails the staff, announcing a code red, jargon for hard fit. Just as they do in teaching hospitals, he asks everyone to take a close look at the patient, see what they come up with.

"Her shoe size runs anywhere from seven and a half to nine medium triple A," Max reciting from memory.

"Aren't you the least bit curious what I want?" The question is not meant to be rhetorical.

"Remove her shoes." Max asks for volunteers. Finally he appoints someone. What's usually a two-second procedure becomes a four-minute ordeal. On my feet, shoes are not just for walking. Forever, the terrible twos.

I take a head count of my toes.

"What do you see?" Max putting his pupils on the spot.

"Five toes on each foot?" Someone other than the girl who wrestled my shoes off.

"Flat feet, no arches?" Same one who removed my shoes.

"Funky looking?" A girl with spiky hair.

"Could you be more specific?" Max examining my feet with a stethoscope.

The group is stymied.

"Educated guesses, anyone?" Such a kindly way of asking, he's like the professor whose class you don't take cuts in.

"Her toes are uneven?" Spike again.

"Big toe's too big?" A guy with baggy pants.

"Heels squarish?" Twin to the boy in baggy pants.

"Her feet look all right to me." Thigh boots up to her ass—how can she bend her knees?

"Shapely feet." Max waiting for the thigh-high to stop doing trampoline jumps, the excitement of having said my feet were all right and having the professor agree, yes her feet are the right shape. I'm flattered, who wouldn't be? But my time management program would call this a waste of time. "How can someone have feet size seven and a half to nine medium triple A and still every shoe, every single one, will be off?" Max snapping his fingers. "Bring me size seven and a half to nine triple A medium."

Pumps, I say, not too high in the heel, gold.

They all disperse. Max, in the interim, has his hand out, waiting for someone to put a shoe in it. Within seconds, boxes piled at my feet. He slips the first one on. Speckled gold, bow in front, buttery. I test-drive. Not a foot out of the driveway, jellyfish stings. Next shoe, tan, gold trim. Puncture wounds. Next, navy. A radical shoe, two tiers. They have to shoehorn me out. Followed by black and gold checkers. Squeaks and peeps. A snazzy golden grey. Fine till I get them on. Sandpaper seams.

Max snaps again.

236

"Shelve the heels." He glares at me like it's my fault. In his shoes, I'd feel the same. The kids return, taking up the glare. (It's not like it hasn't happened before.) More often than not, shoe people eventually develop the same misgivings about me shoes do. Typically, I don't elaborate. But on this, the afternoon of my Special Occasion, I do.

"Here's how it stands. Shoes and belts are the only two standouts in my outstanding record of standing by my belongings: Socks and bras and bathing suits. For metaphorical reasons, too time-consuming to go into, shoes and belts stand with consumables. Shoes are singling me out because I single them out. I know I haven't got a leg to stand on. But here and now, I'd like to put aside our differences. Just this once: any heels that aren't a pain?"

Obvious from the way they look at me:
On the lips of every leaf: Blow me.

✗

To fortify myself, I go for a Häagen-Dazs high.

It isn't my neighborhood ice cream rink. But it bears the Häagen-Dazs stamp. Slick white counter, generous glass windows. Streaming through, what passes for light under a darkening sky. I crave forearm. Is there a child who does not have fond memories of straddling and mounting? Playing horsey on the backs of adults, perching on shoulders. Forearms are the right shape for frolic. The forearm standing behind the counter is not a good specimen. The blue of the veins bloodshot. A gouty look. Bloated. Sluggish. The day I can't distinguish between a forearm that's wearing a G-string from one that's not putting it out, that's the day I begin to doubt everything I see.

Heel safari resumes . . .
On a Häagen-Dazs low.

✗

The shoes in Fancy Footwear are not priced by the pair. The proprietor's philosophy is that of an art gallery. Her shoes are displayed in ornate frames, given titles, sold separately, and come with certificates of authenticity. I've yet to buy, but I've been in to look. A shoe voyeur. Her shoe erotica is museum quality. Fancy Footwear is on my official long shot list, but Max was listed under most promising and look where that got me. Fancy Footwear's door opens with a chime. It's never done anything but chime. I try to open the door, the door won't budge.

"This is your door speaking. No one enters without first passing through door security. To expedite matters, you will place both feet in the designated shoe slots."

Am I desperate enough?

Do I want heels or don't I want heels?

I step on the carpeted panel slid through a slot in the door. Beneath my feet, vibrations, a warmth I feel from the ground up. I'm there for all of two minutes when the door turns me away at the door.

"I'd sooner let in an art critic. Shame on you, madam. How can you be aware of shoes in and out of the context of walking gear, and still treat them like doormats? Opening and shutting the doors in their faces till they don't know whether they're coming or going. Shaky ground is what you offer. Even if they toe the line, the rug gets pulled out from under them. Take a hike."

Twice now.

✗

One hundred and eighty-four stores left on my master list. Of the long shots, Fancy Footwear was the best shot. One hundred and eighty-three stores rank below Fancy Footwear. In a separate ranking altogether is the store called What Have You Got Besides? Located near Susan and Lou, it's the place I go when I've been turned away everywhere else. The selection isn't grand, the shoes have a life span of about two days, after which they have to be incinerated for their own good. Even the local shoe repair shops will not try to resuscitate. The woman who owns the shop wishes all her customers were like me. Buying without trying. So easy to please. The least fussy person she's ever had the pleasure to serve. To Flora, my credentials are impeccable.

✗

In my time management plan I did not schedule myself so tightly there was no time to devote to my would-be assassin, lady creep. My stay of execution is temporary. Guaranteed, I will wake up dead of unnatural causes if I don't invent a way to set off Mr. Creep's alarm.

Elevator thoughts.

Unless I run into a reason to steal time away from that time, to pass the time in some other way . . .

Like settling an old score.

✗

How fitting that on the afternoon of my Special Occasion I finally get to meet my archenemy, Mr. Read My Paw. His pace is leisurely, a child could cut it. The distance between us, less than four paw lengths. I must say he looks dapper. Seeing him in street clothes detracts from the wild animal quality. But more than any other bunny I've yet to encounter, he is a creature of the wilderness, an area I have some expertise in. (Lady creep may run elevators, but she's no operator.) When the four corners closed in on him, they must have thrown away the key. It's hard to believe this jackrabbit mammoth was or is a crossing guard (or in any area of traffic control). Perhaps, like the bunny kids playing leapfrog, he is kin to a crossing guard. Easy street, of course, is not a crossing guard invention. In the Gold Rush days, people who panned had a different conception of the good life. But it was easy street all the same. I've never stood on a corner year after year. Just from what I know of walking on a daily basis, the heat is on. And really turned up if you have the unpleasant duty of spreading a message no one wants to hear. Namely, all systems are warped. How law-abiding Mr. Read My Paw is today. Arms by his sides, swinging only slightly as he hop-walks. Still, he might spring, he did once. Read, read, read. Read what? When he planted his filthy paws on me, did he have any inkling of the effect it would have? Or is the psychic part just a side effect? In the system of things, not everything is cause and effect. As a conscious practitioner of besides, I can't very well deny that my subconscious may also have a little something going for it on the side. It may have been coincidental. What is not up for debate is presentation. The emergence of the psychic episodes may be more a product of my mind, but the way it's been presented from the start—read my paw—borrows heavily from the bunny. He struck me once, there's no reason to suppose he won't do it again. Walk right up to him and introduce myself? Can I get away with that? Unless he remembers my face he'd have a hard time placing me. There's hardly a trace of print left. Whatever's there, invisible under makeup. I must proceed calmly. Exercise every precaution. No sudden moves. My voice tempered. Good manners. He must not perceive that he is being threatened.

239

Fuck that.

I land the first punch. I land the second punch. Third punch, I land on my back. I grab him by the ankle. Hold on, you're not going anywhere, not till I'm through calmly interrogating you, an interrogation that will begin soon as I calmly regain my feet, lift you calmly in the air above my head, twirl you calmly around by your bunny ears, calmly rearrange your teeth, calmly tie a tin can to your tail, calmly pluck your whiskers, calmly bloody your nose, rabbit punches any old place, and calmest of all, wring your neck.

"You and who else?" he asks.

A point well taken.

Using my wits, my resourcefulness, my skill as a keen researcher, my clarity of thought, my charm, my breathtaking ability to take any situation and turn it around, my innate sex appeal, my monumentally unusually efficient time management techniques . . .

"How are you?"

"How am I?"

"How are you?"

"How am I?"

"How are you?"

"Fine, thanks."

And away he sprints.

In retrospect, I have to hand it to him. He was cordial. Would I do it the same way if I could do it over again?

All but the last part.

The last part was so-so.

Uptown by cab: The driver is willing to wait, five minutes max I tell him, all I have to do is buy a pair of heels. He challenges the veracity of my statement—some sly comment—women can't buy toothpaste in five minutes, you're telling me you can go in there, on the spot pick out heels, pay and be out in five? With time to spare, I say. This I gotta see, says he.

✗

What Have You Got Besides? is the size of my bathroom.

I rattle off what I want.

"Gold or black pumps, medium heel, seven and a half, throw in a nine medium triple A, and an eight just in case. Come on, get going."

"Heels are a pain." Something tells me Flora isn't sitting because her enormous weight is anchoring her to the chair. "Heels are a pain," as if I didn't hear her the first time.

I kneel in front of her.

"You stopped carrying heels?"

This brings Flora to her feet. "One pair left. Size nine."

"I'll take it."

"Heels are a pain. I wouldn't feel right selling it to you without you trying it on first. It never mattered before, it matters now. Heels are a pain."

She doesn't know.

No idea.

I can't risk alienating her too. Try them on in her presence, right away she'll put two and two together. Jane has a shapely foot. A shoe acts up, it's sending out a cry for help.

"I have a cab waiting."

She looks out the window.

She waves the cab off.

No more cab waiting, no more excuses.

Flora goes to the back room, I go with her. I help her look. Size nines, no sign of heels. We look for upside-down nines in the sixes. I find them before she does. The color's a perfect match for the gold lamé Marlene Deitrich number. But I don't give these heels more than a day before they expire, the flecks are already coming off, the leather is stiff, with Flora's merchandise, stiff could mean rigor mortis. For all I know the heels could be dead already. I throw some money at her. She makes a grab for the box. I try more money. She takes the money, she doesn't take her hands off the box.

"It's for a Special Occasion. Falling as it does in fall, I have a pretty good idea what to expect. An ending. I'm hoping for a strong finish. Flourishes are optional. The big appeal for me is an end that isn't open-ended, one that doesn't keep you coming back

241

for more, no cutesy ambiguities, basically a no-frills end, once in a while you look back, it's not a lingering look. Sooner or later, the last leaf falls. I want to be there when it does."

She lets go of the box.

Flora walks ahead of me. The doorway is big enough for two, but so is she. She sits in a chair. The chair sags under her. I open the door. I step out.

✗

No warning.

✗

Collision.

Susan doesn't know it's me till she hears my voice. People move around us. Her building is around the corner. I ask her if she needs help making it back. My longevity friend looks bleary-eyed. Her bowl haircut is full of static electricity. The face is strained, partially because her eyes are having trouble focusing. The tights she's wearing are wrinkled, as if she dressed in such a hurry she forgot to pull up.

"Eyedrops," wiping the corners where it's leaking. "Drops alone can't make me turn a blind eye to what Lou's done. I've been provoked beyond human endurance. Another moment at home, I would have done the City's bidding. Sucked myself sore on cocks I haven't properly introduced to. Anything to get even with him. He put me in this fix, it was up to me to get out. I must have switched my frame of mind thousands of times, but the fix was in. All I could think about was killing Lou, chopping his body into little pieces, feeding him to the cactus, and then jerking off on the cactus."

I can hardly wait.

"Fix, what kind of fix?"

"A rub-my-nerves-raw fix. A fix to break me down fix. A fix to unfix me in all my entirety."

I try again.

"Fix, what kind of fix?"

"Leaving the toilet seat up, crumbs all over the house, cupboards open, unwrapping wrappers without rewrapping. The bread is stale. Empty containers of Tropicana in the fridge."

Too choked up to go on. A strangled voice. "Hair in the sink."

Clutching me.

Pulling me down to look into her bleary eyes. The significance of this is lost on me until one of her lenses pops. Then we're both down looking. Susan has never needed corrective lenses before.

She finds the lens.

Sidewalk to eye socket, no detour for cleaning.

"In the fix I'm in I had to think fast. What frame is self-correcting, requires the least bother, no adjustment necessary, timing is built in, automatic pilot, works without my having to lift a finger?"

Her number is up.

She's doing a number on herself.

I could play devil's advocate. She'd say the City said to say it. A no-win situation. My money's on Lou. But by fixing Susan, he's stacking the numbers against himself.

Kill a man over a toilet seat left up?

What women hasn't been tempted?

✗

I've got my traveling shoes.

Traveling distance to my home is twelve minutes.

✗

I do it in eight.

✗

My homecoming is marred by a special interest group grouped in front of my building. This is a pluralistic society. Everyone has the right to be hostile. To be against whatever anyone else is for. The cluster of half a dozen youngsters doesn't look like a random clustering. No sign of leg irons, no leaflets. Still, people are being stopped. Maybe it's just Boy Scout cookies, school raffles, donations to a worthy cause. They don't get me, I crash right through the blockade. But they do get the person behind me. They're loud enough for me to hear. It's a new one on me. Not fur, not pro-life, not a cause with a big following, I don't think. "Down with angel food cake, down with angelfish, down with angel hair pasta."

I defend their right to free speech.

Lay off the angels.

Alex is concentrating so hard, I startle him. Don't quit on my account. Go on writing. Marilyn told me how you went from mousey to relentless.

"She's one in a million," he says.

"One in a million," agreeing.

"Say anything to her, she takes it like a man. The tears she cries, pure bliss."

My elevator is here. It may be they find my body floating inside the wall. If so, I really need to set the record straight with Alex.

"Marilyn's a lot softer than you think."

Alex rubs the side of his nose.

"How does this sound: Marilyn, you snore."

A hand slips round my waist, lifts me off my feet, and pulls me into the elevator. The doors close. All forty of Mr. Creep's buttons are spinning. Mushroom love. Creeps are romantic in a creepy sort of way. The arm around me is all forearm. Great cords of veins. The nails on his fingers are painted green. A closer look. Green bugs. Those veins slither in a way that sets off my alarm.

"I've done nothing but think of you, all night, all day, you, you, you, you, you, you." Alarming how well I think under pressure. "You, you, you, you, you, you and me. The years we'll have together, a lifetime, till death do us part, everywhere you go, I go. Up and down, down and up, as one." A spinning button stops dead in its tracks. "You, you, you, you, you, you and me. Us, us, us, us, us, us." Buttons one to six a standstill. Thirty-four spinning. "The days of elevator tag a fading memory. Eventually you won't even think of our life together as confined to quarters. Not you. You can't get enough of me, I'm your woman, you're my creep, locked up in this elevator for all eternity." The sound of his alarm going off, volume on low. "You, me, us, growing old as husband and wife. My body is yours, it belongs to no other. Just as your body belongs only to me. Exclusively mine, mine, mine, all mine. What's yours is mine, what's mine is yours. Our, ours. But honey, I want you to know all there is to know about me beforehand, so later on you can't say I wasn't totally up front." Buttons in cardiac arrest. "Try filing on me, and I will give you a case of the heebie-jeebies that will put you ten feet under."

Alarm.

Sirens going off like it's an air raid.

The doors open.

I am shoved out.
Doors close, the clash of cymbals.

✗

Under every male creep is a man.

✗

My answering machine doesn't cough up a thing, not even a wrong number. Cross execs will be at the Hardware Store at five, my mushroom love might be part of the delegation making an assault on wife number two's eyes. One more reason I have to look my absolute best. Can't a Special Occasion be special in more ways than one? Always room for one more. One special after another. Keep 'em coming. Open the heavens and pour. I run the tub, Heaven Scent bath oil. The steam rises like a mist of purification. I sink down on a heavenly cloud. The heat, the water, it feels like a ritual bath. This is not the soak of a slug, this is the ceremonial cleansing preceding the Big One (or Ones) falling into my lap. Finally I arise, the very essence of grace. I sanctify myself, sweet basil oils. Gliding across the floor, feet hardly touching ground, walking into the bedroom. For this all-important milestone moment, the bottom half of my bathing suit. When you are about to break with the past, it's only right you carry the banner of your revolution crotch-close. Scissors in hand, head bowed respectfully, I enter the closet domain. Virgin dress all a-shimmer, holding out its arms to me. With one incision I neatly circumcise the tags. Unzipping the dress, it feathers into my arms. I carry it out, into the light of the world, come meet your worshippers, your admiring public, welcome to the event of a lifetime: The Fall of Days Gone By. Dress and I merge. The feel against my skin is silk, even in the back where the dress plunges, the kiss of silk. Panty hose on, the sheerest black. And heels. Such as I have never worn. Heels shaping themselves to me, a blanket swaddling the newborn. My feet are in good hands. The rhinestone latch of my small black clutch bag picks up the golden hues of the dress. Benedictions from the mirror. My skin is dewy. Miracle of miracles, though there is no magic someone has waved a wand over my hair. A velvet of royal red. I am regal. I am a vision. I am about to receive the answer to my prayers. Petals in the hallway, my path is sweet. The elevators wait like royal carriages. Coachmen silently doing my bidding. No bickering from the creeps as I choose the elevator on the right. The ride to the lobby is more than swift, it is walking on air. Alex bows from the waist, his nose holding the door for the apparition in gold. The children, the little angel killers, let me pass, uttering no sound, gentle cherubs. Sidewalks glimmer, gold dust, air as it was in Eden. I alight to the park across the street, flower petals at my feet, what better time than now, my Special Occasion, for Suki to return, lovesick for the sight of her mistress. The park, all to myself, harps playing songs of welcome, welcome to the chosen one. I sit, the bench is downy soft. Royal treatment. Hear ye, hear ye. You see before you the blessed.

Fireworks from my feet.

Where am I going to find heels at this hour?

Heels do not just fall out of the sky.

Heels are a pain.

The toes of the shoes, which but a moment ago were seen and not heard, are now making spectacles of themselves. Curling and uncurling like living tissue. The tear of stitches. Surface mold, primeval ooze, slime. Demon shoes. Backs split right down the sides. A sharp odor of the undead. The shoes don't walk away, they crawl. A family tree of maggots. The heels stand alone, undecided. Stay here with me or go with the clan? One heel Pogo sticks away, the other turns, daggers into my foot, withdraws, swaggers away.

Where am I going to find heels at this hour?

Heels do not just fall out of the sky.

Heels are a pain.

For pilots, it's a wing and a prayer. For me it's the beating of wings overhead. A whirring helicopter sound. Special is the occasion when you get a special delivery. Special is the occasion when you are lavished with special effects. The delivery boy has the wings of an angel. Even more special, they are leaf-shaped. Look there how the lines duplicate a leaf and the colors, all the colors of fall, his wings a stained glass of reds and yellows, and rusts and gold, lots and lots of gold. Special is the day when your very own angel boy makes you the special of the day. Falling upon me, his fall-stained wings pinning me to the bench, his hands falling to the task at hand, rolling up my dress. How special to feel the rush of air between my legs. To be felled in fall, how special. His fall branch raking me, his leaf stalk is a thorn. Hoeing, prodding, branch beating me. How special to do everything to knee a groin and miss. His tongue falling with its full weight on mine, kissed by an angel with leaves for wings, an angel with devil's breath, relieving himself on me, fallen angel, leaf wings falling and rising, wings of fall, never touching down.

Angel boy, what tree did you drop out of?

Special are the days when into your lap, from out of nowhere, falls a heel.

Heels are a pain.

Why me?

Heels are a pain.

Why not me?

There is no magic.

✗

There are angels of mercy. Crossing guards, caretakers of corners. Lean on us, Jane, look around for her shoes, take your time, whenever you're ready, her goddamn shoes, search by the trees, you say he took your shoes, left your purse, we'll begin there— anywhere—then begin where you want to begin, yes we believe you, we have no reason not to believe you, an angel it is, from out of nowhere, heels falling out of the sky, wings the color of autumn leaves, beating you about the face and arms, back up a minute, Jane, now these heels, what size were they, you just take your time, he violated you with the heels, while the leaves fell from the trees, lean on us, Jane, are you saying his leafy wings didn't touch ground, falling up instead of down, no need to raise your voice, if you say it isn't a minor point, it isn't, but now that you raised the point, a point of clarification, Jane, these leaves you say didn't fall—wouldn't that be contrary to the laws of nature?

✗

Come back, Jane, we'll show you the way to easy street. Hop along, Jane, hop along with us, away from the four corners.

✗

I make admirable time.

The important thing is, in real life, here I am.

The man who chiseled me. First. comes out of Hardware. He approaches. What I must look like. My dress ripped, lips swollen, hair not there, purple bruises, barefoot. What he must think. He'll want to know. Are you all right? Did they get the guy? Here, take my arm, take both arms. The man, who chiseled me out of feeling number one, flags a cab. He gets in. He rolls down the window. "Wife number two didn't blink. Not even in childbirth. Not even in the face of death, she didn't bat an eye. As of five o'clock Eastern Standard Time, a son was born to me. The son's mother, deceased. Wife number two off everybody's hands. The End." The cab creeps into traffic. I can walk faster than it's going. Harold sticks out his head. The cab starts to take off. Harold calls out.

"And you, how've you been?"